# WORLDWEAVERS

## CYBERMAGE

+ BOOK 3 +

## ALMA ALEXANDER

*An Imprint of* HarperCollins*Publishers*

Eos is an imprint of HarperCollins Publishers.

Library of Congress Cataloging-in-Publication Data
Alexander, Alma.
    Cybermage / Alma Alexander. — 1st ed.
        p.    cm. — (Worldweavers ; bk. 3)
    Summary: Thea and her friends at the Wandless Academy must use
their abilities to keep the elemental magic of Nikola Tesla—imprisoned
within a magic cube—away from those who want it for their own gain.
    Includes bibliographical references (p.  )
    ISBN 978-0-06-083961-1 (trade bdg.)
    [1. Magic—Fiction.  2. Schools—Fiction.  3. Tesla, Nikola,
1856–1943—Fiction.  4. Fantasy.]  I. Title.
PZ7.A3762Cy  2009                                    2008014619
[Fic]—dc22                                                  CIP
                                                            AC

1  2  3  4  5  6  7  8  9  10
❖
First Edition

For Sara, the youngest—
child of the new millennium,
who has never known a world without cybermagic

## 1.

THEA HAD STARTED THE new school year at the Wandless Academy with enthusiasm and a sense of purpose—but then things began to unravel with unnerving speed.

The first unpleasant surprise was her roommate. Thea actually did a double take when Magpie all but fell into their room, a large and apparently heavy backpack on her back and a smaller duffel bag in each hand.

"Hey!" she said, dumping the bags on the floor in an untidy heap. "Back at the salt mines, eh?"

Magpie's right ear had been pierced at least a dozen times along its edge, and it was lined with tiny silver rings, giving it the appearance of being sheathed in chain mail. From each earlobe dangled long earrings wrought from copper wire and some sparkly crystal.

But something else was different. Something far more disquieting.

"Your hair," Thea said, startled.

Magpie flicked back from her face a long braid that had been dyed an improbable shade of platinum blond. A purple bandanna sewn with sequins held back the rest of her hair, which had been hacked into uneven layers as though attacked by a straight-edge razor. A couple of rats'-tails, left long on purpose, were hanging from the back of her head.

"You like it?" Magpie said, craning her neck a little to catch a glimpse of herself in the dresser mirror. "I just got bored—I've worn my hair the same way since I was in the cradle. My cousin Clarice did it. She trained as a hairdresser before they kicked her out of beauty school for, I don't know, being too weird for the clients or something." She turned to give Thea an appraising look.

Thea covered her own hair with both hands. "Don't even think about it."

Magpie laughed. "You might actually, you know, *like* it."

"But you were so *proud* of your hair last year," Thea said plaintively.

"It's a change." Magpie shrugged. The platinum

strand persisted in hanging over her face like some strange visiting-alien tentacle, and Thea couldn't quite tear her fascinated gaze from it.

"You usually travel lighter than that," she said, eyeing the pile of baggage on the floor.

"You wouldn't believe how much room makeup bags take up," Magpie said airily. She rooted around in the smaller of the duffels and came up with about seven different lipsticks, which she spilled on top of the dresser.

"Since when do you wear so much stuff on your face?" Thea asked with a sinking feeling in the pit of her stomach. "And what on earth do you use *this* one for? It's black!"

Magpie shot her a coy look from under lashes spiked with mascara. "It's fun," she said. "You're welcome to try them, if you like. Even the black one."

She was still bubbly, full of her usual brand of charm and high spirits, but it was different, somehow. Magpie was focused on different things now, and Thea was finding it unexpectedly difficult to reconcile the new Magpie with the friend whom she had come to know and even depend on. This was not the same Magpie who would cuddle close a wild creature wrapped in a ratty blanket. It wasn't as though they had suddenly found each other to be complete strangers—they were still friends, on the surface—but there was something missing, something that Thea couldn't quite put a finger on until she woke abruptly one night from a choppy and unsettling dream, nearly two weeks after their return to the Academy.

"Shhh," Magpie whispered from the shadows, "it's just me. Go back to sleep."

"What have you got now?" Thea said sleepily, propping herself up on one elbow.

"Got?" Magpie echoed, sounding surprised. "What have I got?"

"What sort of critter have you picked up now?" Thea asked. Then she caught her first real glimpse of Magpie, who was standing in a patch of moonlight that had slipped through the half-closed curtains. The dim light caught a hint of gelled glitter and dark eyeliner, and her mouth was a dark slash on her pale face. She was dressed in something tight and black, with the ensemble completed by a short flouncy skirt that barely came past the tops of her thighs; on her feet were a pair of lace-up sneakers with platform heels.

"No critters," Magpie said, even as Thea completed her astonished inspection.

"Where are you *going*?"

Magpie's sudden grin was a disconcerting flash of white teeth in the moonlit shadows; she looked like a cat suddenly yawning to bare its fangs. "I'm meeting Gary over by the pond," she said. "Be a sweetie, and if Mrs. Chen asks . . ."

"I'm not going to lie to Mrs. Chen!"

"You would have if I were out with a sick raccoon!"

"It's not the same thing at all!"

"Whatever," Magpie said, after a beat of awkward silence. "I gotta go, he'll be expecting me. I should be back in a couple of hours. Don't worry; I already know all the tricks of keeping myself out of harm's way."

"Wait a sec, I don't . . ." Thea called, but Magpie didn't wait for an answer. By the time Thea got to the door of their room, opening it a crack to peer into the corridor, Magpie was already gone.

They didn't share lunch the next day, with Magpie defecting to a new crowd of friends in the cafeteria who apparently found life a lot more amusing than Thea did. As Thea stood with her tray, Magpie did look up, but neither she nor any of her companions seemed inclined to invite Thea to join them. Feeling oddly hurt, Thea looked around and saw Ben sitting at one end of a long table, picking at his food without much enthusiasm. Across the table from him, Tess, her own half-finished lunch on the tray in front of her, had her nose buried firmly in a textbook. She was taking several college-level classes that year, and had been entirely wrapped up in the workload ever since they had all come back to school. Now that a rift had opened between Thea and Magpie, Thea was suddenly aware how little she had seen of her other friends since the beginning of the semester.

"Hey," she said to Tess, pausing beside the table.

Tess looked up. "Hey yourself," she said.

"Mind if I join you guys?"

Tess threw a quick glance at the large wall clock that hung above the cafeteria double doors. "I'm almost done—I've got class in ten minutes," she said apologetically.

"You're always rushing to class these days," Thea said, slipping into a seat beside Ben.

"With a bit of luck, I'll be able to graduate early, too," Tess said. "Terry already has enough credits to graduate at the end of the year if he wants to."

"You plan on graduating this year too?" Ben said, sounding a little astonished. "Why is everyone in such a hurry? What about you, Thea? That summer thing that you and Terry were on . . ."

"It wasn't for academic credit," Thea said. "I don't think it counts, really."

"Besides, it all seemed to end rather prematurely," Tess said. "With the FBM descending on everything and taking over. I was half expecting banner headlines in the *Daily Magic Times*, but they must have kept a pretty tight lid on the whole thing. Mom told me a little about it, after, and Terry filled in the rest."

"He could *talk* to you about it?" Ben said sharply. "How? He can't utter a word about magic without choking on it, that allergy of his—"

"Not in our *house*," Tess said, rolling her eyes a little. "Good grief, my parents took care of that when he was really little, as soon as they figured it out. Otherwise he wouldn't have lived long past his first attempts to talk—not in our household. With Mom and Uncle Kevin involved with the Federal Bureau of Magic on a daily basis, they had to clear the house for Terry or else. It's just that it had to be drilled into him that he couldn't breach that topic anywhere *else*—anywhere that he wasn't directly supervised or didn't have access to the antidote—same way that it was hammered into *me* that I could not eat anything outside our home unless I was absolutely one hundred percent certain of where it came from and that magic wasn't one of the ingredients. Hence the Academy—here magic is pretty much absent, and it was considered to be a safe environment."

"Yeah, until the whole spellspam thing descended last year and he started to turn blue when he so much as tried to open his mouth about it," said Ben. His nose wrinkled as though he was expecting to sneeze, but it was a reflexive action since there was no real magic present to trigger his own allergic response—only a vivid memory of it.

"Can we talk about something else?" Thea said, a little sharply. Every time she thought she had dealt with the whole experience of the spellspam epidemic at school that led to her summer encounter with Diego de los Reyes, something about it made her heart beat a little faster. She could not seem to quite shake the guilt of it, the sense of having been personally *responsible* for what had finally happened to Diego.

"Spellspam?" said an unexpected voice from the

far end of the table. "What did you have to do with that?"

In some way they were all misfits, every single one of them who wound up at the Wandless Academy, removed from their usual social and magic-rich environment by their inability to function within that world. But even at the Academy there were circles within circles, cliques within cliques, and students who invariably wound up on the lower rungs of the totem pole. It was one of these unfortunates who had had the temerity to interrupt the conversation: Kristin Wallers, a pudgy girl who wore her dishwater-blond hair down around her face in an attempt to hide the two prominent front teeth that stuck out like small tusks. Her large blue eyes had a self-conscious gaze that was half hope and half resignation.

Kristin wasn't part of Thea's circle. One of Thea's first instincts, in fact, had been to pretend that she had not even heard Kristin speak, lest she, Thea, be observed in actual conversation with a social outcast. But there had been a twinge of . . . sympathy. Something. The way Kristin had responded with such instinctive and overpowering curiosity, even concern.

Even that might not have quite been enough had Thea not happened to glance over at where Magpie was just getting up to leave, giggling over some shared joke with her new friends. There was a new and jagged hole in Thea's life—the place that Magpie used to fill.

"Sorry," Kristin said into the silence that followed her interruption. "I couldn't help overhearing. That three wishes thing . . . that got me pretty good."

"Oh yeah? What did you wish for?" Ben said, curious in spite of himself.

Kristin gestured at her mouth, a tiny, helpless motion that suddenly made Thea give her a sympathetic smile.

"I'm sorry. What happened? Didn't it work?"

"Of course it *worked*," Kristin said. "In the way it usually works. My first wish was something along the lines of, 'I wish my teeth would go away!'—and of course they did. *All* of them. Then I rushed to repair the damage and wished for 'them' to be back, and of course the only ones that came back were the ones I wanted gone. I'm pretty sure there must have been a way of putting things right, even then, but I panicked and just used my third wish to put things back the way they were.

And there I was, back on square one."

"Ben saved us," Thea said. "He figured it out, long before we got into any real trouble."

Ben squirmed at that. "Just by being in the right place at the right time," he muttered.

Kristin smiled a lopsided grin, made into a thing of horrid fascination by the protruding teeth.

Tess glanced up at the wall clock again, but she, too, was curious now. This was the Academy, and questions were not asked—but Kristin herself had opened the door.

"What . . . happened?" Tess said, with a small, diplomatic nod in the direction of Kristin's mouth.

"Beware of Faele bearing gifts," Kristin said morosely.

"A Faele did that to you by *accident*?"

"Nuh-uh. But the one who was supposed to be the last in line to bestow the Faele gifts when I was born wasn't there. Somehow my mother had managed to insult one of the Maledicent tribe, while she was carrying me, and they sent a representative along to the gift-giving and made sure she was last and wished . . . *this* on me. It isn't fixable, you know— not by mundane medicine, not by reversospells, not even by a veiling spell or masking spell. It's a

Faele gift, and it shines through *everything*. That's why they sent me here—in an ordinary school there would be constant badgering and teasing about it, and constant, *constant* questions about why I don't do the simple things to deal with it. Believe me, I've tried."

That was the longest speech Kristin had ever given in Thea's hearing, and she suddenly seemed to realize that, dropping her gaze and flushing a bright pink underneath her curtain of hair.

"Anyhow," she said, "I'm sure you've other things to do."

By now Thea was genuinely interested. But Tess was already stuffing her books into her bag, and Ben was gathering up the remains of everyone's shattered lunches to take back to the disposal units. Thea slipped out of her seat, hoisting up her book bag, and then hesitated, just for a brief moment, as she glanced back at Kristin, the only one who had not moved. Out in the "real" world, Thea had been an outcast, the one held back in Ars Magica classes in order to make repeated attempts at doing the impossible, and all of a sudden she felt a rush of sympathetic understanding for Kristin.

"See you later," she said, and then turned and

scurried away in a self-conscious manner—missing a thoroughly astonished look from Kristin.

Thea's next class happened to be biology, which ordinarily interested her, but that day she found herself staring outside at a handful of deciduous trees that still clung to the gold of their fall foliage and glowed among the dark cedars. She had to drag her attention back to the class by main force and at least look as though she was paying attention—because this was one of the teachers who taught through sarcasm and mockery, and any daydreaming, if the culprit was caught, was punishable by being publicly humiliated as the butt of some cutting joke. She escaped notice, but at least one other poor sap in the front row felt the lash. Thea, wincing on his behalf, noticed Magpie openly giggling with every appearance of enjoying her classmate's humiliation. She was not the only one, to be sure, but it just seemed another alienating thing to add to the list.

The class seemed to last forever. The day had darkened into late-autumn afternoon when the final bell went and everyone scrambled for their books and the door. Thea remained at her desk for a moment, scribbling down a few halfhearted notes about the homework. She was the last person out of the door, stepping into a corridor crowded with people scurrying frantically to get to their next class, dodging and weaving between stationary knots. She glimpsed Tess through the throng, lingering before her open locker and smiling up at someone Thea could not quite see. The crowd thinned for a moment, and Thea got a glimpse of the back of a male head as it bent to obscure Tess's face with a kiss. Then the crowds closed in again and Thea, whose own locker wasn't too far from Tess's, found herself hesitating, unsure of her reception if she turned up just at that moment, uncertain if she ought to have known that Tess had a boyfriend. They were, after all, supposed to be friends.

Thea suddenly felt very lonely. For a year she had tasted the comfort and security of being part of a group of friends who hung out together, who had shared something. But now, things were regressing to the bad old days, the days when Thea was alone and miserable, the family failure.

"Hey," said a familiar voice right beside her, making her jump.

"Missed you at lunch," she said, turning slowly to face Magpie.

"Just catching up with some friends," Magpie said

chirpily, tucking her blond tentacle behind an ear. "I saw you were making some new friends."

"Who? Kristin? She overheard us talking about spellspam. First time I heard how she came by those teeth."

"Fascinating," Magpie said, and now she was laughing openly. "You heard the *other* news?"

"What's up?"

"Humphrey's here," Magpie said. "I think there's trouble."

"What else is new," Thea muttered. "I bet it's the cube."

"What cube?"

Thea blinked at her friend. "Oh yeah, you never did see it. Terry and Tess were there when we retrieved it last summer, when we took Corey the Trickster back to the First World to be smacked down for interfering too much with our own world. That's when we found Beltran de los Reyes, the professor's missing younger son—remember? I wrote you all about it. Beltran had this bag full of weird stuff with him, ancient computer tapes and that cube. Humphrey called it an Elemental cube. Whatever that is."

"Back in your Element, are you?" Magpie said.

She was teasing, but her curiosity was only surface

gloss—she sounded glib, almost dismissive. Thea remembered the expression on Magpie's face when she had called the sacrificial Whale in the ancient way of her people and helped vanquish the doom of the Nothing that had threatened the future of their world. Thea felt a stab of loss; it was as though she and Magpie were sundered into two separate worlds with a glass wall between them—as though Magpie herself had forgotten, had *chosen* to forget, the incredible thing that she had been a part of.

"We might *all* . . ." Thea began, but Magpie shook her head, her earrings clinking like tiny wind chimes.

"Tell me all the news later," she said, lifting her arm to wave at someone farther down the corridor. "Gotta go. I'll see you back at the room after you and Humphrey have had a chance to talk."

"What makes you think he's here for me?"

"Oh, please, of course he is," Magpie said. "You yourself said it. And *you* are squarely in the middle of every single thing that seems to bring Humphrey May out of the FBM cocoon. Well, gotta run. See you later!"

"Wait—don't you want to know what's going on?"

"Of course I do. But you'll fill me in after you've talked to Humphrey. Later!"

She gave an airy wave and turned away, hair bouncing on her back.

Thea stared after Magpie for a moment, chewing on her nail and scowling. Then she spun on her heel to hurry to her next class—and all but ran down Terry as he reached out a hand to tap her on the shoulder. It turned into a more defensive gesture even as Thea stepped back, lifting her head a fraction to stare at him.

"Where have *you* been? Haven't run into you a lot lately," she said.

"You just did," Terry retorted with a grin, and then glanced over Thea's shoulder at Magpie's retreating back. "What's up with you two? You having a row?"

"That obvious, is it?"

"Let's put it this way," Terry said. "I sincerely hope that expression you're wearing isn't meant for me."

Thea couldn't help a quick grin at that, and then shrugged her shoulders. "Don't mind me. I'm having a bad day. Or maybe a bad week. Or *month*. I don't know."

"You should come by, later," Terry said, dropping his voice a little. He did not specify a destination, but with him these days, it could only be the Nexus room. "I've got something to show you."

"Is everything all right?" Thea asked, not knowing whether she was afraid or irrationally excited at the prospect of something bad, like more spellspam, crawling out of cyberspace.

"More than all right," Terry said, grinning. He glanced around, and lowered his voice another notch. "I fixed the hologram," he said.

"Holy *cow*," Thea said. "You fixed Twitterpat? Really? Is that why Humphrey is here?"

"Humphrey May is here? News to me—who told you?"

"Magpie just said . . ." She glanced at her wrist, straightened up with a wince. "I'm late. Gotta get to class, Terry."

"Come see later. It's pretty awesome, actually."

"I can't just . . ." Thea began, but Terry had nodded at her in a conspiratorial fashion and slipped away into the now rapidly thinning crowd.

Thea sighed and dragged her feet in less-than-enthusiastic fashion to her next class.

It happened to be English, and the current area of study was poetry, a subject Thea had been exposed to from her earliest childhood because her grandfather—Ysabeau's father—had published seven volumes of the stuff. Thea had always loved poetry, even when most of her brothers, with the possible exception of her bookish second-oldest brother, Ben, declared it to be boring. But perhaps because of the very familiarity of it, she found herself tuning the class out completely, instead mulling over the new developments since the beginning of the new school year.

Kristin Wallers, the buck-toothed pariah often referred to as Kristin Walrus by her classmates behind her back, turned out to have an interesting past.

Magpie had transformed into an alien thing with an active social life that didn't seem to include Thea.

Tess was caught up in her studies, and in some boy.

Ben seemed introspective and moody.

Terry, when not working on early graduation, was apparently bent on resurrecting Twitterpat, their late computer science teacher who had been one of the casualties of the battle with the Nothing last year. Or at the very least, he was trying to resurrect the hologram program that Twitterpat had left embedded in the Nexus computer.

And now Humphrey May was back.

## 2.

IT DIDN'T TAKE LONG for Humphrey May to show himself. Thea slowed as she approached the library on her way across the Academy's main quad, and then came to a complete halt as she saw a familiar lanky figure leaning against one of the pillars of the library portico.

Magpie's parting words echoed in her mind: *You are squarely in the middle of every single thing that seems to bring Humphrey May out of his FBM cocoon.*

"Hi," he said conversationally, as though there was nothing at all out of the ordinary about a high-powered Washington mage from the FBM being at the Academy.

"What are you doing here?" Thea asked warily.

Humphrey pulled one hand out of his pocket, and from his long fingers dangled something that looked like a large wristwatch, or more accurately, a wrist calculator, as it appeared to have a sort of tiny keypad on its face. "I'm here bearing gifts. This is for you."

Thea stepped closer, curiosity getting the better of her. "What is it?"

"It's a prototype," said Humphrey, "a sort of remote computer station. You can key in something on this keyboard and access a *real* computer somewhere else entirely. Like, for instance, the Nexus."

"To do what?" Thea asked.

Humphrey laughed. "Oh, don't be disingenuous. You of all people know how useful this can be."

"But my parents won't even let me lug around a *laptop* of my own," Thea said. "Does my dad know about this? Really?"

"Actually, there's only two of them in existence. *This* one, and one locked away in the safe back at headquarters. Nobody knows about them except the guy who developed it, the head of the FBM, and me. And now you. Thea, it's a bribe." The smile left his face, and he was suddenly very serious, even grave. "We need you. Again. Want to go for a walk?"

He sounded as though he stood in a springtime meadow in bright sunshine, not in the throes of a damp Pacific Northwest nightfall. But the invitation made perfect sense. Nobody *else* would be wandering about at this time, so there would be no danger of being overheard.

"Sure," Thea said, falling into step beside him as they walked away from the library and out under the trees of the central green. They walked for a few minutes in silence, with Humphrey apparently deep in thought. She finally reached up to tug her hood tighter around her face, and took a deep breath. "So, what's up?" she said. "Is it the cube?"

Humphrey turned his head slightly to give her a smile. "I guess we should have let you know what happened," he said. "Or at least I should have. When you brought *that* little puzzle back to us last summer, from wherever it had been all those years, things changed. I have a confession to make."

Thea waited, with a patience which would have made Cheveyo, her Anasazi teacher, proud of her.

"Remember when I told you that you were not the only . . . one out there like yourself?" Humphrey said.

"That I was just the first of those who will come. Yes, I remember."

"That wasn't *quite* true. Well, it depends on the

way you look at things. You see, there was more than one reason I made the arrangements for you to go to Professor de los Reyes last summer. The professor was one of the few people who could figure out—" Humphrey broke off. "Let me put it this way: As far as the Bureau of Magic knows, there are four certified poly-Element mages living on the North American continent today. Three and a half, if you consider that one of them is extremely old, and is more of a liability than an asset because he has to be restrained from having embarrassing and often dangerous outbursts of Elemental magic. One of the others, as I am sure you must have already put together, is the professor. He has mastery of two Elements, Earth and Water, with the occasional lucky stab at Air, and yet he's the best Elemental we have. And I . . . had a hunch about you."

"If you're trying to tell me that I'm an Elemental, wouldn't it have come up before?" Thea said, astonished. "I was tested for *everything* when I was a kid."

"Not necessarily. These are the most temperamental of our gifts. Elemental magic can manifest at any age—at least one infant Fire mage in history was lucky that he didn't immolate himself before he was two years old. And it sometimes doesn't kick in for those who wield it until they are well into puberty. It would not be unheard of, anyway. Elemental magic is so *rare*, so vanishingly rare, that it would not have been the first thing they thought of. Not even in a Double Seventh."

"So I'm an Elemental?"

"I suspected," Humphrey said. "And the professor's house, the Elemental house, confirmed it for me, once I heard how you interacted with it."

"What do you mean?"

"It unpacked for you, didn't it?"

"It does that for everyone, it's supposed to tidy up after people."

"Tidy up, yes. If Terry had kicked off his shoes in the middle of the room, the house would have tidied them away for him. But that's just part of the House-tidy spell; he had to unpack his own suitcase."

Thea blinked. "So the Gardentidy spell . . ."

"Yes, that was part of the professor's gift. He used the Earth Elemental magic to create that."

"So what am I?" Thea said, suddenly feeling a little breathless.

"I'd say Fire . . . and Air," Humphrey said slowly, coming to a sudden halt. "For certain. I am not sure . . . there isn't more."

"I'm a *poly*?"

"It seems that way. That's what I said in my report, anyway. The FBM people will have to confirm things to their own satisfaction, though—and perhaps we can help each other there."

"The cube," said Thea.

"The cube," Humphrey confirmed. "That pretty little white thing, with its Elemental symbols that come and go if someone with the right ability to trigger them so much as breathes on it, and remain stubbornly out of reach to everyone else. So far, we're not even sure what it's *made* of, let alone what's really inside it. Luana's tried everything short of a crowbar, but that thing isn't cooperating at all. We know it's Elemental, but we don't know anything more about it. I've questioned Beltran, the professor's younger son, closely, because the cube came back when he did, in a bag apparently associated with him, but he doesn't know any more than we do, or doesn't remember. And he shows no Elemental gift. None. I am not even sure how he and the cube came to show up together in the first place; the only connection I can think of is the connivance of the Faele, and perhaps your Trickster avatar. But

I can't prove any of that, not while the cube is still keeping its secrets."

"But I don't know either," Thea said. "The first I saw of it was when it tumbled onto the professor's desk."

"I know, but if I'm right and you're a poly-Elemental, then it's possible that you can figure out how to unlock it."

Thea hesitated for a long moment. "But you said there were four other poly-Elementals . . . and there must be even more uni-Element mages."

"If this thing was made by a poly-Elemental, then no single Element will be enough to crack it. As for the four mages that I mentioned earlier, as I said, one of them is feebleminded with age. Two of the others have been approached, and have both failed."

"And the fourth?"

"We can't ask the fourth," Humphrey said. "The professor is in the hospital. He's been in a sort of half coma for over a month now."

Thea had flinched just a little when Humphrey had named Beltran de los Reyes. Now the guilt she had carried around since the previous summer surfaced once more. Diego de los Reyes, Beltran's shadow-twin, *had* inherited the professor's Elemental gifts . . . and had used them to unleash the spellspam storm. Thea had walled Diego up in a mirrored world of his own illusions, from which he could never escape.

"Is it . . . because . . . of Diego . . . because of me?" Thea whispered, stricken.

"If it *was* because of Diego, it certainly wasn't your doing," Humphrey said gently. "Don't take *that* guilt on yourself. That isn't why I came here."

"What about the tapes?" Thea asked after a moment. "The tapes that came with the cube? Is there anything there that might help?"

Humphrey shook his head. "That's the *other* reason I'm here," he said. "Terry. The tapes are badly damaged. We haven't been able to read much from them, and what remains legible is fragmented and confusing. It's like trying to put together a jigsaw puzzle without knowing what the picture is and without any edge pieces at all. But there's a strong hint at something . . . that shouldn't be possible."

"I haven't seen much of Terry lately. He's been either studying or locked away in the N-room," Thea said. It was not likely they were being spied on, but she was still reluctant to utter the word *Nexus* out loud in public.

Humphrey pulled out the wrist-gadget that he

had shown Thea on the library steps. "That's why I brought this," he said. "You can weave us into the N-room. Using the N itself, remotely. Watch."

He toggled something on the side of the keyboard panel, and the panel slid down with a click, revealing a tiny screen behind it. He pressed three keys apparently at random, and the screen lit with a dull green radiance, a tiny cursor blinking in the upper left-hand corner. Humphrey typed in something, the screen blipped, and a new line of text appeared, demanding a password. Humphrey typed one in, and the screen changed color, becoming a deep blue.

He passed the gadget to Thea. "Go ahead," he said. "Type in whatever you need, then hit ENTER. It will be as though you're doing it on the N keyboard."

Thea took the keypad gingerly. "Wow," she said, staring at it. "This is awesome."

"It's safer, too," Humphrey said. "You know how you leave your shadow self behind at a computer when you do this? Well, with *that*, you don't—you're carrying it with you, the computer on which you typed in the commands. Your shadow self is never left behind to be vulnerable or exposed. Nifty, eh?"

Thea lifted her eyes to stare at him. "They'll

never let me *keep* this," she said. "You *did* say you'd brought it for me, didn't you?"

"If I make you a secret agent of the FBM, it's legitimate equipment," Humphrey said, "and trust me, in order to work on that cube, you're going to need clearance. Pretty high clearance. High enough for that."

"Hang on," Thea said. "Let me try this."

She pecked out a series of letters with her right index finger, and then hesitated, poised above the tiny button marked ENTER. Humphrey nodded encouragingly. Thea closed her eyes and stabbed the button.

"Where did *you* come from?"

At the sound of Terry's astonished voice Thea opened her eyes and looked around. She and Humphrey were right beside the desk in the secret Nexus room below Principal Harris's office. Humphrey wore a proud grin; Terry's face was a mask of bewildered confusion.

"New toy," Thea said, brandishing her keypad. "Humphrey brought it."

"Nice to see you again, Terry," Humphrey said, sticking out a hand.

Terry reached out and shook it reflexively, still

blinking at the two of them. "I don't get it—which computer—?"

"Yours," Thea said, enjoying herself enormously. "The Nexus. Remotely."

Terry let his breath out with an explosive sigh of denial. "That isn't possible," he said, spinning his chair back to stare at the monitors. "I would have *known*. And you'd need the password to get—"

"Terry," Thea said, "it's *Humphrey May*. From the Federal Bureau of Magic. He has the password."

"But I would have noticed," Terry said obstinately.

"It would have been a blip, if anything," Humphrey said.

Terry turned around to face him again, his eyes huge. He had actually gone white. "If I can't even tell when the Nexus security has been breached . . . How many of those things *are* there?"

"Only two: the one that Thea's holding and another, locked in a safe somewhere back in Washington," Humphrey said. "Relax, Terry. I have a special password; you would have known if anyone else had tried to actually hack in there."

Terry was still shaking his head. "But the security risk . . ."

"My responsibility," Humphrey said. "And I honestly don't think Thea is about to go showing this thing off."

"You're *leaving* it with *Thea*?" Terry squawked.

"Are you?" Thea said, glancing up.

"As I said," Humphrey said, nodding. "We need you for the cube. I will have your word that you will be responsible with this thing. It doesn't leave your side, and *nobody* knows what it does, outside of this room."

"Not even my parents?" Thea asked. "When I go home . . ."

"I will speak to your parents," Humphrey said. "But that's it. Not your brothers. Not *anybody* else. Are we clear?"

"Absolutely," Thea said.

"One more thing—I will have your word on it that you will not be using this to go on any solo trips for fun and adventure. It isn't a toy."

"I *never*—" Thea began defensively, but Humphrey shook his head and lifted his hand in emphasis.

"Thea. You came to get me last spring, from that hell-place I had got myself locked up in by picking up that stupid travel spellspam. I am grateful, but I will *not* have you use it to get yourself killed. You must promise me—no matter what, you come get me *first,* before you use it for anything. Do we have a deal?"

"I promise," Thea said.

"Fine, then. I officially entrust the prototype to you—and remember, it's my head if you misuse it. Now, Terry. I want to know what you think of these."

He fished in an inside pocket of his jacket and brought out a small envelope from which he extracted a computer printout and an opaque CD case.

"If I were anywhere else on this planet I'd just snap my fingers and I'd have the papers I wanted in my hand, straight from my office safe," he grumbled. "This is some of the data we got from those tapes that were retrieved with the Elemental cube, back in the summer," he said. "Everything we have is on this disk—we don't keep any of it on a permanent hard drive; it's been transferred onto a closely guarded handful of disks. We don't want a trace of this anywhere that it can be potentially hacked, no matter how many layers of security we wrap it in. You can look at the whole thing later—on the disk, don't copy anything—but take a look at these, in the meantime."

Terry flipped through the papers. The first page was densely covered with type, but Thea could glimpse plenty of blanks in the rest of it. Some pages were mostly blank, in fact; one of them had just a single line of text that went from edge to edge of the paper, as though it had got in the way of some slithering snail-like creature leaving letters for a trail.

"What is this?" Terry said, his attention caught. "Some of it looks . . . almost familiar." His head snapped up suddenly. "Some of this looks like the code I've just been tweaking to get Twitterpat back online. I mean, Mr. Wittering."

Humphrey laughed. "I know of the nickname," he said. "You're talking about the holographic image of your former computer teacher I saw when I first came here, right?"

"Yeah," Terry said. "All I could get him to do back then was to ask you to repeat whatever it was you said to him, because he insisted his faculties were limited, but I found that there was a loop in the system. I'll show you."

He piled Humphrey's papers on the edge of the desk and started typing something on the keyboard in front of him. Thea reached out curiously and picked up the papers, riffling through them as Terry typed. It meant nothing to her, a mess of gibberish words, out-of-place punctuation marks, lines of what looked like mathematical formulae.

"There," Terry said suddenly, dragging her attention away from the papers. "Look."

On the other side of the computer desk, the air shimmered slightly and then snapped into an image. It was slightly blurred around the edges, but recognizably Twitterpat. Thea caught her breath.

"Good afternoon, Terry," the image said in Twitterpat's own voice.

"Good afternoon, Mr. Wittering," Terry said. "We have visitors today."

The image blurred and then re-formed, this time facing Humphrey and Thea. "Patrick Wittering," it said courteously, apparently by way of introduction.

"Humphrey May, Federal Bureau of Magic. We met a number of times when you came out to Washington on Nexus consultations. And this is one of your former students at the Wandless Academy, Thea Winthrop."

The image did its blur-blink-regenerate thing again.

"Why is it doing that?" Thea hissed into Terry's ear.

"Processing," Terry whispered back. "It's capable of responding, but it doesn't have independent vision sensors, so it can't 'see' you. It can just be aware of your presence."

"There's something *wrong* with it," Thea said.

"Hands," Terry said briefly.

The characteristic hand motions that had partly earned Twitterpat his nickname were missing. The hologram's appearance was perfect, and his voice was Twitterpat's down to its nuances, but those expressive hands were still, hanging down beside him. The rest of him was almost enough to make anyone believe that Twitterpat was not, in fact, dead, but those motionless hands made Thea acutely aware that this was just a copy, a high-tech "living" puppet.

"Can I be of assistance in any way?" Twitterpat inquired, still facing Humphrey.

"Terry, is it possible for the entity to offer independent insight?" Humphrey said in a low voice.

"It's . . . helped me with things, once I knew how to ask, and what to ask," Terry said. "I've typed in questions, or scanned in things—and there *is* an analytic ability."

"Real intelligence? Rudimentary AI?"

"I am perfectly capable of answering those questions, Humphrey," Twitterpat said. "When I was created, it was with cutting-edge holographic and fuzzy logic algorithms. I am very much 'intelligent,' if you wish to phrase it that way. It is what I was created for—interactive intelligence that might be useful for providing insight into machine logic, at a speed and precision that is still beyond an unassisted human brain."

"Well, I'll be," Humphrey said. "I never knew that Patrick Wittering had fine-tuned it this far."

"Can I be of any assistance?" Twitterpat asked again.

Terry glanced at Humphrey. "Is it okay if I let him at the disk?"

"Can't hurt," Humphrey said.

"Let me see those printouts again," Thea murmured as Terry slipped the CD out of its case and fed it into the drive for Twitterpat to examine. She had noticed something in those incomprehensible pages that now tugged at her memory and understanding, though she couldn't quite put it into context. Terry glanced at Humphrey and passed over the papers; at the same instant the Twitterpat image began speaking again.

"The data is incomplete," it said.

"I know. We are still trying to rescue more material from the tapes, but this is the best we can do right now. If you recognize any of it, perhaps you can fill in some of the blanks."

"My own code has roots in some of this," Twitterpat said. "I do recognize some of the algorithms. However, there is an anomaly."

"What anomaly?" Humphrey said, his attention suddenly focused on the holographic wraith before him.

"The data is, as I said, incomplete, but I can begin to understand what the material behind it is about," Twitterpat said. "Some of the working methodology appears to be obsolete. Some of it resembles what I know of the current state-of-the-art data on artificial intelligence and fuzzy logic. And the rest of it appears to be of unknown provenance. I would—" He blurred rapidly, and then blurred again. "I'd be grateful if you could rephrase the question. My abilities are limited at this time," it said after a moment, its voice gone oddly flat.

"It's gone back into the loop," Terry said, striding back to his main keyboard. "Whatever you fed it, Mr. May, you scrambled its brain again."

"What's this?" Thea said suddenly, pointing at the page with the single line of type. Humphrey glanced over.

"Your guess is as good as mine," he said, shrugging. "That page, as it happens, was the product of one of the attempts to open up the cube—one of the better ones. The consensus is that we asked the thing its name, and it told us."

Thea drew her finger along the line of type. It appeared to be a single word, repeated over and over:

SLATE SLATE SLATE SLATE SLATE SLATE SLATE SLATE SLATE

"Slate," Terry said, peering over Thea's shoulder. "The cube says its name is Slate?"

"No," Thea said, staring at the page.

Humphrey turned sharply to look at her. "What?" he said.

Thea reached out for a pen that Terry had left lying on the computer desk and underlined five letters on the page:

SL<u>ATE SLA</u>TE SLATE SLATE SLATE SLATE SLATE SLATE SLATE

"Not Slate," she said slowly, looking up at Humphrey. "Tesla. The Elemental mage who created the professor's house. Nikola Tesla. It's *his* cube."

## 3.

HUMPHREY STARED AT THE paper in his hand with an expression that was equal parts astonishment and furious indignation.

"I cannot believe I didn't see that," he said. "It goes a long way to explaining why we haven't made much headway with the thing. Tesla was the only quad-Element mage in the history of the human race—the only one that we know of, anyway. It stands to reason that a uni-Element mage couldn't even begin to make a dent in it, and even bi-Elementals were out of their depth."

"Where's the cube now?" Thea asked.

Humphrey glanced at her, his eyebrow raised. "In a safe back at the Bureau," he said. "Why?"

"Have you tried taking it back to the professor's house? The house, too, was Tesla's doing. Maybe something in there could help unlock the cube."

"That is not a bad idea at all," Humphrey said. "I simply stopped at the professor—it never occurred to me that the *house* might be helpful." He pulled a silver-gray cell phone from a pouch at his waist. "No good," he muttered, staring at the phone screen, "no signal in this underground bunker. Thea, can you get us out of here? I need to make a phone call. Terry, I'm really sorry about screwing up your hologram, but if you can make anything of those scanned pages, I'd appreciate knowing about it. If I missed the obvious clue in *slate*, who knows what else I might have passed over."

"Will do, sir," Terry said, sounding mystified.

Humphrey glanced over at Thea. She nodded imperceptibly, and in the next moment they were back in the drizzly woods of the school grounds.

Humphrey immediately punched a speed-dial key on his cell phone and stood tapping his foot impatiently.

"Rafe?" he said abruptly. "No time to explain now, but get Slate and 'port immediately to Professor de los Reyes's house. . . . Yes, in San Francisco. . . . *Yes*, I know the professor is still in the hospital. Just do what I say, *quietly*. I have access to the house; everything is cleared at the highest level. If anyone does try to stop you, tell them you're acting on my authority—but avoid attention if you can, and most particularly try not to trip any of Luana's wires. Certainly if I were Slate I would think twice about manifesting with her waiting to pin me out on an examination board like a rare butterfly. Yes, *now*, Rafe. I know it's late. I'll meet you there."

He flipped the phone closed and turned back to Thea.

"What are you going to do?" Thea asked.

"I don't have a clue," Humphrey said frankly. "I don't think we're dealing with anything remotely familiar here. I might have to go back into the archives and read up on things that nobody's needed to know in decades. I need to get to the professor's house myself, in a hurry."

"Can I help?"

"I've a car here; I can drive down to the nearest public 'port and I can—" He broke off as Thea lifted her wrist, her new gadget still strapped to it, and gave him an innocent smile.

"I can get you there faster," she said.

"And then we'll both get into trouble," Humphrey said, chuckling. "I've no wish to add kidnapping to my list of sins."

"But it wouldn't be *kidnapping*, not really. You said that you had an idea about what I can do."

Humphrey hesitated, but only briefly, then flipped his phone open again, and punched in another number.

"John? . . . It's Humphrey May. Listen, something's come up. I need to borrow young Thea for a couple of hours. Yes, off-campus." He listened for a moment, and then sighed. "All right, sure. I can take Mrs. Chen with us. I'll swing by the residence hall now. Could you alert her? . . . It's on FBM authority. I can have a letter to you by the morning. Thanks, John. Good night."

Thea grimaced at him as he put the phone away. "Mrs. Chen?"

"Well, I didn't *think* he was going to let me just whisk you out of here on my say-so. There's a limit to how far FBM's writ runs, and he's responsible to your father. Now come on, we need to get going."

"No, we don't," Thea said, grinning. "If you're worried about getting there in time to meet Rafe— who's Rafe, anyway?—I can get us there at whatever time you want, remember?"

"Raphael Wynn. One of my assistants. He's an intern at the FBM. You'll like him. Let's go."

"Um . . ." Thea said, hanging back.

Humphrey, who had already taken a few long strides, paused to turn and look at her. "What's up?"

Thea lifted her wrist again. "Do you want anyone *else* to know about this thing?"

"Point," Humphrey said. "She has a computer in her office, doesn't she?"

"Yeah."

"We'll use that, then, for this time," Humphrey said. "Sooner or later you'll have to let the cat out of the bag, but I'd rather it was later, under the circumstances."

"Are you *sure* you want to leave it with me?"

"I think it will prove useful. But for the time being, let's follow the rules."

Twilight had started to shade into full dark by the time they got to the residence hall. Mrs. Chen flung open the door to her office almost before Humphrey had a chance to knock.

"The principal just called," she said. "What's going on now, Thea? Mr. May . . . ?"

"We need Thea's help with something that turned up last summer at Professor de los Reyes's, Mrs. Chen. I promise we won't keep her long."

"Fine," said Mrs. Chen, in a tone of voice that

signified that it was anything *but* fine. "I'll just get my coat. . . ."

"I don't think that'll be necessary," Humphrey said, ushering Thea past Mrs. Chen and stepping into the office. "Time being of the essence . . . if we could borrow your computer . . . ?"

Mrs. Chen rolled her eyes but stood aside. "I might have known."

"You might want to lock your office," Humphrey suggested, as Thea, receiving a reluctant nod of approval, began pecking at Mrs. Chen's keyboard. *The Elemental house*, she typed in, and then added, *just in time to fling open the front door as Humphrey's assistant 'ports in.*

She glanced around, saw the other two waiting on the other side of the desk, and hit ENTER.

The great tiled hallway of Professor de los Reyes's Elemental house in San Francisco suddenly blinked into existence around the three of them, and Margaret Chen clutched at her shoulders with both hands.

"I don't know how you do this on a regular basis," she said to Thea.

But Thea had already turned to the door.

"He's here," she told Humphrey.

Humphrey reached over her shoulder and pulled open the door.

On the front step, one hand half-raised to knock and the other curled protectively around the handle of a reinforced security-locked briefcase, stood a young man with dark hair falling a little untidily over his collar and eyes of such incandescent blue that Thea found herself staring.

"Good timing," Humphrey said easily. "Don't just stand there; come inside, we have work to do. This is Margaret Chen, from the Wandless Academy, and Thea Winthrop. Margaret, Thea, this is Raphael Wynn."

"Raphael," Mrs. Chen said graciously, extending her hand.

"Rafe," said the angelic young man, stepping inside and allowing Humphrey to close the door behind him. He shook Mrs. Chen's hand and then turned to nod companionably at Thea. "Hi."

"Um . . . er, hi. I'm Thea."

"So I understand," Rafe said, smiling.

Humphrey reached for the briefcase. "All clear back at the office?"

"If you mean Luana, she's long gone. She had a hot date or something. In any event, nobody was in the way. What's up? You found something new?"

The two of them fell into step, leading the way to the professor's office, with Humphrey turning to signal Mrs. Chen and Thea that they should follow.

"*Um, hi, I'm Thea,*" Thea muttered furiously, mimicking herself, staring at Rafe's back. "What a wonderfully intelligent thing to say."

"He does have striking eyes," murmured Mrs. Chen, smiling.

Thea glared at her, and Mrs. Chen quickly schooled her features into a serious and serene expression.

"Mr. May . . . Is that you, sir?"

Madeline Emmett, the housekeeper, came hurrying out of the dining room.

"We need access to the Nexus, Mrs. Emmett," said Humphrey. "I don't think we will be too long."

"I see. Will you be requiring anything?"

"No, we're fine. Thank you, Mrs. Emmett."

The others had come to a stop outside the closed door to the study. Humphrey approached the door and laid a gentle hand on the handle; after a moment, the door made a small clicking sound and swung open a crack.

"The keys in this house," Humphrey said, looking up to meet Mrs. Chen's raised eyebrow, "are a little different from other keys."

"Do *you* have an Elemental gift, Mr. May? I never knew that."

"No, that is not my talent. But this house has been instructed that I am allowed access to this room. Come on in. Rafe, put that thing on the desk."

Curious to see the white cube again, Thea watched Rafe carefully pass a hand over the briefcase's complicated locking mechanism. He placed it on the leather desk pad so as not to scratch the gleaming wood of the professor's desk and flashed Thea a quick, friendly smile. Once again she found herself struck dumb, and was barely able to smile back as Rafe flipped open the final catch manually and lifted the lid of the briefcase. Inside, nestled in a padded cocoon of protective dark blue velvet, the white cube seemed to glitter with a light of its own.

Thea said the first thing that came into her head. "I'd forgotten it was so white."

"From what I heard of the commotion when it arrived, I'm surprised you remember it at all," Rafe said easily.

"Doesn't look any different than at the office," Humphrey grumbled, coming over to take a closer look at the cube. "Thea, what do you think?"

Rafe looked a little startled, and Thea flushed a bright scarlet. What was she doing here with these adult mages, all trained in their craft? What could she possibly achieve here?

She reached out toward the cube with one hand.

"Hey," Rafe said softly, "look at that."

Thea's hand, hovering over the top face of the cube, made it brighten just a little. And a symbol came swimming to the foreground: a small equilateral triangle.

She snatched her hand back, startled.

"Fire," Humphrey said. "That's the symbol for Fire. There are other Element symbols on the other faces."

He gently took the cube out of its nest. "Fire," he repeated, pointing to the faint outline of the symbol visible on the cube's top face. "And then, going around, the next face has two wavy lines—Water. The next one has two straight lines, like the Roman numeral II—Air. The next one is a circle with a dot inside it—Earth. And that's the circuit around the edges: four Elements."

"What's on the top and the bottom?"

"*Which* is the top, and *which* is the bottom?" Humphrey asked, turning the cube in his hands.

"All I can tell you about the two remaining faces is that one of them appears to be blank, and the other has a symbol that isn't used to identify any Element that we know of: a five-pointed star."

"Can I . . . hold it?" Thea asked diffidently.

"That's why we're here," Humphrey said, and held out the cube.

Thea heard Mrs. Chen draw in her breath sharply somewhere behind her. She was dimly aware of Rafe, watching her with close attention. She reached out for the cube; Humphrey released it; and then the smooth, white, glowing thing rested in her own cupped palms.

It weighed almost nothing. She felt as though she held empty air. But air with a light inside it, as the cube brightened in her grasp and light spilled between her fingers. The uppermost face held the triangle sign—Fire again—and that edged itself into a white brilliance. Thea could also see that the bottom face, which represented the Element of Air, was pouring brightness between the crack of her cupped palms. The other two Element faces glowed, but did not shine. However, one of the mystery faces had brightened also. It was the one with the star symbol, which she had held facing inward toward her body, and it shone bright enough to make the folds in her clothing cast sharp shadows of themselves.

"You *are* an Elemental!" Humphrey said, and his voice was triumphant. "And a poly-Elemental, too. Look at those Fire and Air symbols!"

"And the star?" Thea whispered, rapt in the wonder of what she held.

"Damned if I know," Humphrey said. "But you're young; we have your entire lifetime to find out. At least we have an answer for what you are."

"Actually, what we have is another question," Mrs. Chen said. "I'm *far* from certain that this should have been done in this way, Mr. May. If Thea is indeed not just an Element mage but one with poly-Element abilities, and you had any inkling about this, it should have been done under controlled conditions so we could establish parameters."

"Mrs. Chen," Humphrey said, looking up with a wide grin, "the whole point of Elemental magic is that it functions under its own rules. What parameters? No two Elementals that we have today—and we have precious few as it is—function in quite the same way. And now we've got a brand-new one to learn from."

"And do you realize that you could have lost her

by doing a stunt like this?" Mrs. Chen said. "Even if you knew she was going to pass this test, she could have had a combination of Elemental gifts that might have been wholly incompatible with the cube. It could quite easily have killed her in the backwash. I've seen Elemental magic at work, and it's not something to treat lightly. Not at all."

"I can take care of myself," Thea said, finally lifting her eyes off the cube. "What *does* the star mean? You really don't know?"

"Yes, and that's another thing," Mrs. Chen said. "That star. That was a wild card, even for Elemental magic."

"There is indeed truth in what you are saying," Humphrey said, suddenly serious. "But there is more riding on the possibilities of this cube than you realize, especially now that I'm aware that it might be Tesla's own work. And what we *have* done here, after all, is found the needle in the haystack that Thea's gift has always been. Why was Thea not tested for Elemental magic long ago?"

"You know that it manifests when it chooses," Mrs. Chen said. "That's the real test for Elementals. They just . . . start doing."

"Like I did," Thea said softly.

"The more I think about the cube and what those wretchedly fragmented tapes told us . . ." Humphrey hesitated. "This thing could be bigger than anyone knew. And it makes sense to me now why the Alphiri want it so badly . . . except they lack the capacity required to open something like this."

"But they have no way of knowing that, do they?" Thea said. "The Alphiri probably know it's valuable, but they have no real idea why. They have no idea that even we are having trouble cracking it. It holds the very magic they've been searching for—but you need that magic to get at the magic."

"If you succeed in getting that thing cracked open, Thea, then you and this cube—and its possible contents—become the most valuable things that the Human Polity has possessed in a very long time." Humphrey turned toward Mrs. Chen. "That was partly my reason for the whole behind-the-scenes approach," he said. "I could not do this in public, in the blaze of inevitable publicity. In one sense I was working against the Bureau itself on this. Rafe, you never heard this conversation."

"No, sir. I certainly haven't," said Rafe instantly. "Not a word of it."

Humphrey flashed him an approving grin, and

then turned his attention back to Thea.

"Can you sense anything at all? Do you know how to open it?" he asked.

Thea stared at the cube, which still glowed in her hands with a pale, milky light.

"It's . . . as though I'm missing vital senses," she said at last, and let out the breath she had not been aware she had been holding. "I keep losing something—if I think I can see the cube clearly I cease being able to touch it, and it feels like I'm not even holding anything; it's got a faint music to it, but the moment I think I hear that, then I lose a certain scent that it had just a second ago, and then *that* becomes the key. . . ."

"Some schools of thought have connected the human senses to the Elements," Mrs. Chen said, nodding. "It's never been direct—there are five senses and only four Elements in Elemental magic, so there's been a bit of crossover and fudging—but there *is* a connection."

"It's, like, too *big* for me to take in," Thea said. And then her head snapped up and she stared at Mrs. Chen in thoughtful silence.

"What did I say?" Mrs. Chen said, raising an eyebrow.

"*Senses*," Thea said. "Humphrey . . . I have an idea. But I don't think you are going to like it."

Thea walked into the cafeteria of the Wandless Academy less than an hour after she had winked out of Mrs. Chen's office. It was the tail end of supper, with a few stragglers still lingering over the shattered debris of their meals. Thea swept a glance across these scattered groups of students, and finally found the group she sought—four people sitting by themselves at one of the tables in the far corner of the room, looking variously curious, bored, mutinous, and mildly expectant.

"You're all here," Thea said, as she reached the table. "Good."

"This had better be good. Terry said that you made it sound, like, life-threatening or something," Magpie said. "I have plans—I'm already late."

"I've got piles of homework," Ben muttered.

"What is it, Thea? You sounded awfully mysterious on the phone," said Terry.

Magpie looked up, frowning. "The *phone*?" she echoed. "Where were you calling him from?"

"Humphrey May was here earlier," Thea said. "It's a long story; I'll fill you in on the details later."

"This is about that cube," Terry said.

"Terry, I've held it," Thea said. "It's . . . in some weird way, it's alive. It has a presence."

"I remember it," Tess said. "I was there. Humphrey May said he had no clue what it did. He did say it was an Elemental cube. I remember that."

"It's Tesla," Terry said suddenly. "It's something to do with Tesla, isn't it?"

"He's the only quad-Element mage known," Thea said. "And they think he built that cube. They got other Elementals to try and get into it, but it's locked down tight. It needs four Elements to open it. And I can really control only two."

Ben sat up. "What's that?"

"Apparently that's the whole mystery," Thea said, with a small self-conscious smile. "I'm an Elemental. A *bi*-Elemental. The cube says I'm a Fire and Air Elemental. And maybe something else."

"What else is there?"

"There's another symbol and they don't know what it means, but it responds to me too. But I don't know anything about that. The thing is . . . it needs *all* the Elements. In concert. I don't have that."

"You're a bi-Elemental?" Ben said, staring at Thea.

"Or something like that," she said, trying to turn it into a joke.

Nobody laughed.

"Look," Thea said, "remember the time we all jumped into the rain forest?"

"Yeah, when Ben stepped on a slug," Magpie said with a grin.

"You put it there," Ben said.

"Hey, *focus*," Thea said. "Seriously, they need you. They need us *all*."

"We're not Elementals," Tess said. "None of us."

"Not individually. But together, all of us are. It's like this: Mrs. Chen says there's a link between the senses and the Elements. It's something that is not completely understood, but it's the best idea we've got right now. She says Earth equals touch, Fire equals sound, Water equals sight, and Air equals scent."

"But that's only four—there's taste. What's that linked to?"

"It's not explored yet. It can *all* be wrong. But I've tried, and I can't hold it all in my own head. I keep losing one thing when trying to latch on to another. I need you guys. You supplied all the other senses back in the forest. The five of us might be enough to match one Tesla. Just barely."

"When were you planning on this little experiment?" Ben asked.

"Now. They're waiting for us back in San Francisco."

"You've been flitting about again, haven't you?" Tess said, grinning. "Well, I'm in."

"Hell, yeah," Terry said. "I've been poring over some of those notes that Humphrey May left behind. It's confusing and there's a vast amount missing, but what there is . . . I want to know more. I'm in."

Magpie and Ben both hesitated, and then spoke more or less at once.

"But I promised I'd go . . ."

"I don't want to go on this wild goose chase if . . ."

They stopped, glancing at each other. Ben tilted his head in a signal that Magpie should go first. "Really," she said, "but we do make plans sometimes, you know. You might have given me a few days' warning. I need to organize my life before I can just flit about, lending you my senses."

"I don't see why I should," Ben said. "I'm the one who doesn't quite fit in here, anyway. It was . . . different last year—the Whale, the Nothing—but then this summer you went off chasing ghosts, Thea, and you didn't need us then."

"That's not fair," Tess murmured. "She did call us all in."

"Not really," Ben said mulishly. "We weren't a part of anything then, not together, and I—"

"Oh, get *over* it," said a sixth voice unexpectedly, in a tone of such exasperation that the five at the corner table all sat up sharply as though stung.

The girl sitting at the next table suddenly scraped back her chair and whirled to face them.

"You're just put out because she hasn't asked you properly," Kristin said, pointing at Ben, who gaped at her in complete astonishment. "And *you*"—she turned sharply toward Magpie—"you're just scared that you'll lose your place in the hot set. And *none* of you has any idea how wonderful it is to have *friends* who are just your friends and whom you can just call up out of the blue and say, hey, I need your help with something weird, and you don't ask questions and you just do. Because you're *friends*."

"Kristin," Thea began, but Kristin turned on her next.

"To have someone you can trust," she said. "Just like that."

"Good grief, what set you off?" Ben said. "Did that Faele that handed you the tooth spell make you prone to unexpected temper tantrums?"

"No," Kristin said. "I get the temper from my mother. That's probably how she managed to annoy the Maledicent who cursed me in the first place— by sassing her back when she shouldn't have. Other people get to be pretty or successful or rich. My Faele gifts are snaggle teeth, and other useless stuff. Like, I can find things. Big deal. You should just see how grateful my grandparents are when I 'find' stuff they've mislaid—they just think I'm making constant fun of them—every time they start with 'Where's my . . . whatever . . . ?' and there I am, holding it in my hand. At least you guys might actually achieve something *useful*. But no—*you*'re sulking," she said, pointing to Ben, "and *you*'re playing the homecoming queen"—the finger swung to Magpie—"and *you* are interested in the logistics of it, pure and simple, and aren't even thinking about what it might mean." The final point was at Terry, who looked startled to be included in this tirade.

"I am *so*, interested," Terry protested. "I've been working with—" He shut up abruptly, glancing around.

"There's too many secrets," Kristin said. "You should all just *trust* each other."

She turned on her heel, her cheeks suddenly scarlet, and stomped away with her shoulders hunched around her ears.

"*She* was *eavesdropping*," Magpie said, outraged.

"And then she has the gall to give us a lecture?" Ben muttered.

But Tess, still staring at Kristin's retreating back, looked thoughtful. "Who was that and what did she do with the Walrus?" she murmured.

"It's Kristin. Kristin *Wallers*. Those teeth really aren't her fault."

Magpie turned to glance back at Thea. "Faele gifts, eh," she muttered.

"I've had a few of those," Ben said, without taking his own eyes off Kristin.

"If I could bring everyone back to the matter at hand," Thea said.

"Like I said, I'm in. And so's Terry," Tess said. "When do we leave?"

"Right now," Thea said.

"You gonna use your gadget?" Terry said.

"Gadget?"

"Humphrey May gave her a secret agent toy," Terry said.

"Oh?" Magpie said, craning her neck. "Let's see . . ."

"You coming?"

"Oh . . . all right," Magpie said. "Come on, Ben. Your homework isn't more important than my social life. Let's get it over with. That's what friends are for."

## 4.

"THERE YOU ARE," HUMPHREY May said. He was sitting in the armchair by the window, sipping a mug of steaming coffee, as Thea and her friends blinked into existence in the middle of the professor's study. Rafe, engrossed in perusing the professor's bookshelves, turned and gave them a grin and a small wave.

"And who's *he*?" Tess whispered into Thea's ear. "You didn't mention there'd be perks."

Thea glared at her, and Tess dropped her eyes, a smile playing around the corners of her mouth.

"Mrs. Chen just stepped out for a moment, but she'll be right back," Humphrey said, putting aside his coffee and getting up. "In the meantime . . ."

"Is that the cube, sir?" Terry asked, eyeing the briefcase on the professor's desk.

"Yes, come and have a closer look. Thea, how

did you want to play this?"

"By ear," she said. "Can I . . . ?"

"Pick it up. You know it isn't as fragile as it appears," Humphrey said.

Thea lifted the cube out of its nest again, her touch gentle. She turned it over a couple of times until she found the blank face, and then took the cube between her two hands. One palm was flat against the bottom face, the blank face, and the other lay across the top face, the one with the star, which immediately brightened into a white glow at her touch.

Magpie sucked in her breath.

"What do you want us to do?" Terry asked, craning his neck.

"There's four faces. There's four of you," Thea said. "Back in the rain forest, each of you brought in one of the physical senses—Terry, sound; Magpie, touch; Tess, taste; Ben, scent. I have no clue which sense fits best with which of the Elemental faces, but I have a feeling it's a question of . . . finding the face, the Element, that best matches your own contribution. I *know* I heard a sound the last time I held it, Terry. You go first. Hold your hand over each face. When you find the one you think responds best to you, lay your hand on it. Open palm, like mine."

"Are you sure you know what you're doing?" Ben said, watching Terry begin to circle the white cube in Thea's hands as though he were stalking it.

"She's the only Elemental in the room," Humphrey said laconically.

"But will you be able to stop things if—" Ben began, but then Terry halted abruptly, his hand hovering over the face with the Fire symbol on it.

"Wait," he said, "I think I know what you mean. I can hear . . . stuff. There's a crackle to it . . . and a hum, something that sounds rather like distant city traffic . . . and someone's *singing* . . ."

"Wow," Tess breathed as Terry's hand made contact with the cube, and the Fire face's shade marginally deepened into a hue that was almost pink.

"Your turn," Thea said. "Same thing. Find the face that speaks to you."

Tess reached out for the cube in the same way that Terry had done.

"I'm not sure," she said. "I think I can taste something, right at the back of my throat, over by the Water face—but it's faint, so faint . . . And I didn't see it light up, the way Terry's did."

"Water is usually associated with sight," said

Mrs. Chen, who had slipped back into the room. "*Usually*. But I think from what you've told me, Thea, *you* were the sight component of this grouping, and you've chosen to attach yourself to that unknown symbol instead. So that sense might have migrated."

"But it was Fire and *Air* that lit up for me, before," Thea said. "Not water."

"As I said," Mrs. Chen said, "it isn't an exact science. Tess, if that seems the best fit . . ."

"No, wait," Thea said. "If she's unsure, let's see if the other two have a stronger reaction to anything. Magpie?"

Magpie reached out with her right hand, biting her lower lip. "I'm not sure I know what—*oh!*"

"What is it?"

Magpie stood transfixed, her eyes wide, her hand hovering just above the Earth face of the cube. "I can feel . . . it feels like . . . tree bark, under my fingers," she said. "And . . . silk. And . . . and . . . *feathers?*"

She touched the face, and it too changed color very subtly, shading into a coffee-with-a-lot-of-milk shade of white.

"Between you and Tess, Ben," Thea said.

"I so don't want to do this," Ben said, staring at the cube. He had wrinkled his nose several times already, as though in anticipation of a sneeze that never came, his usual allergic reaction to the faintest whiff of magic. He did so again as he spoke, scrunching up his face into a grimace and shaking his head. "It's like that infernal feeling when there's a sneeze just *hovering* in the back of your nose, tickling, but you never quite sneeze and it drives you bananas."

"Try it. I think yours is the stronger link," Thea said.

Ben sighed and reached out for the cube. His hand hovered briefly over the Water face, but then he shook his head and glanced back at Tess over his shoulder.

"You were right, I think. This one does nothing for me." He shifted his hand over the Air face, and then, suddenly, let go of an explosive sneeze that made Rafe, halfway across the room, jump and jolt a book off the professor's shelf. "Oh, yes, I think this one's mine," Ben said, after he sniffed a few times and rubbed at his watering eyes with his free hand. His fingers touched the Air face, and it, too, changed color into pale, pale blue. "I can smell ozone," he whispered. "Like you sometimes can in a thunderstorm. And apples. Yes, apples."

"I think that's the taste I had," Tess said, reaching out resolutely toward the Water face, which began to shade into a pale green as her fingers got closer, the color of shallow water over white sand. "Apples . . ."

She touched the Water face.

And everything went away.

Thea found herself standing alone in a thick, roiling white fog. She looked down at her hands, but she wasn't holding the cube, not in this place, wherever it was. But the new gadget, the wrist-computer that Humphrey had given her, was still on her arm. She squinted at it through the drifting mist, flicked it on, and typed *Cube 1: white fog, starting place.* She didn't have a clue where she was or what had happened, but it was obvious that she was no longer in the professor's office holding an Elemental cube with her friends.

Speaking of whom . . .

"Marco!" Thea called out experimentally. Her voice

sounded muffled by the fog, unable to carry very far. But almost instantly there were several responses.

"Polo!" Magpie called out from somewhere to her left.

"Likewise," Tess's voice came floating from somewhere behind Thea.

"Where are we?" Terry asked.

"What did you *do*?" said Ben at the same moment.

"Oh, great, you instantly assume it was me," Thea said, pitching her voice to carry.

"Your idea," Ben said.

"Well, thanks for the vote of confidence."

"Seriously," Terry said, "where are we? I can't see my hand in front of my face in this fog."

"Don't move, let me find you," Thea said. "Whatever else happened, I'm still the anchor, so don't drift off by yourselves. One at a time. Terry, keep talking."

"I think your voice comes from somewhere over to the right of me, and you also sound like you're in front of me," Terry said.

"This fog muffles everything," Tess said. "Feels like cotton wool. I can't see anything past my nose."

Magpie suddenly yelped sharply. Thea froze in place, whipping her head around, trying to place the sound.

"Magpie? Say something! What's the matter? Are you okay?"

"Sorry," Magpie's voice came back from the fog, sounding shaken. "Something brushed past my face. Like wings. I couldn't make out what it was. Could you hurry up?"

"Don't move," Thea said. "Terry, *talk to me.*"

"No, I think I see him," Ben's voice said. "Remember the colors that cube turned? I see a reddish area . . . it's just off to the left and the back of me. I think that might be where he is. Terry, look to the right and ahead—can you see anything other than white?"

"Not . . . really . . . wait . . . Yes, I think so . . . . There's a greenish—"

"That would be me," Tess said. "I got green. Ben was blue. Magpie was . . . brownish."

"I have no color, I'm white on white," Thea said. "Stay *put.* I think I see that pink tinge, Terry. Keep talking. Put out both your hands. I'll see if I can't see something sticking out of the fog when I get closer."

"Thea," said Magpie, and her voice quavered, "there's something out there. It's brushing past me constantly, and I can't see anything."

"Hold it together," Thea said. "I'm closest to Terry. We'll head your way as soon as we hook up. . . ."

She suddenly gasped as her outstretched hand brushed past something solid in the mist, which was shading into a pale pink around her, but the touch was instantly followed by a familiar voice.

"Thea?"

And fingers closed about hers: Terry's hand.

They clung together for a moment, and then Thea shifted her grip so that she held Terry's hand in a firmer grasp and stepped closer into the mist. Terry's physical form materialized as the mist seemed to shred from around him; he looked reassuringly solid, real, familiar.

"Are you all right?" Terry asked, squeezing her hand.

"I think so. I don't know." She shook her head. "I don't know what I was expecting. Not this. Magpie, I've got Terry. We're coming to get you."

"Hurry up," Magpie said, and this time Thea could hear tears in her voice.

"Hang on, we're coming. Keep *talking*! Your

color is the hardest to find!"

Magpie started singing instead, something slow and sad, in a language none of the others knew. It was the song that led them to her in the end; they practically tripped over her. She had not held out her hands, as Terry had done—she had crouched down into a tight little ball, hugging her shoulders with her hands, her head laid across her folded arms.

Without letting go of Terry with her left hand, Thea dropped down on one knee beside Magpie.

"What is it? What did you see?"

"Birds," Magpie whispered. "I think there's birds. Can you hear it? I think it's cooing. Like a pigeon. And that rustle of wings . . ."

"Hey. Sound's *my* province," Terry said.

"I felt them brush past me," Magpie whispered. "Wings. Like they were . . . looking for something. Lost birds."

"Magpie." Thea shook her shoulder gently. "Come on. We need to get the others. Come on. Look, there's no birds here now."

"Is everyone all right?" Tess called out, her own voice developing an edge.

"Yes, we're coming. Just keep talking."

"Oh, *fine*," Ben said, off in his own pocket of

mist. "Leave me till last."

"I need you to bring up the rear," Thea said. "You think the fastest of all of us."

"Survival tactic," Ben said, "except I'm not sure what I'm supposed to be surviving. Hurry up, would you?"

"Tess is over there," Terry said, nodding in what seemed to be an arbitrary direction in the white mist.

"How can you be so sure?"

"Twins count for something," Terry said. "Magpie, take my other hand. Thea, go forward . . . left . . . left . . . left . . ."

Tess stepped out to meet them from her own island of greenish mist as they came close enough for the mist to change color.

"I told you not to move," Thea said.

"Twins," Tess said, shrugging.

"Grab Magpie's other hand. Ben? You said you could see the greenish mist pocket—can you still?"

"No . . . yes . . . well, it's green and all other stuff . . . I guess you're all there . . . should I just . . . ?"

"No!" said Terry and Thea at once.

"Stay put. We'll come and get you. Tess, stick out a hand, grab him," Thea said. "Don't any of you let go, or we'll just lose each other again."

"Got him," Tess said after a moment.

"About time," Ben said. "Stuck in this completely impenetrable . . ."

"Actually," Terry said, "I think the fog is lifting. I can *see* all of you now; when Thea first approached me, I couldn't see her before our hands actually touched. But now . . ."

"I think you're right," Tess said, looking around. "I think . . . I actually grabbed Ben's hand, and that's when it started to—"

"Somehow we got split," Ben said. "Even if we're all still holding on to the cube, back in the professor's office, here we got scattered—and just as it took all of us to get through the first barrier of that thing, it took all of us to get through the second. Some defenses, this thing's got."

"Terry," Thea said, "does it feel anything like the Twitterpat holo to you?"

Terry turned a startled look on her. "It's nothing of the sort. Whatever made you ask that?"

"I don't know. All of this is weirding me out a little."

Terry sniffed. "If that's what this is, it is several orders of magnitude more sophisticated a mechanism than what Twitterpat used," he said. "That was built to interact with our own world on our terms—it isn't real, but our world is. This actually feels almost the exact opposite—what the Twitterpat hologram might perceive *us* as. That's an interesting idea, actually."

"Never mind *what* it is right now. What I'd like to know is *where*—" Ben began, but Magpie suddenly gasped.

"Look," she whispered. "Look down. *Look!*"

It was becoming obvious as the fog thinned that they hadn't been so much *in* it as *on* it—inside a cloud, perhaps—because what revealed itself underneath their feet was a whole lot of nothing, and then what looked like the surface of the Earth, a very long way down.

Tess let out a small shriek, but that was all anyone had time to do because all of a sudden they weren't standing still anymore but flying, or more precisely plummeting, down toward that distant ground.

"Dooooo somethiiiiiing!" yelled Ben, flailing uselessly around with his free hand as though he were trying to flap a nonexistent wing.

"I'm open to ideas!" Thea flung back, her hand clutching Terry's in a convulsive grip.

"I hate heights!" Magpie wailed. "I'm closing my eyes now! Someone let me know when we smash into the ground!"

"Oh, I think you'll know," Ben said, and then fell quiet as their descent assumed quite a different aspect. All of a sudden they weren't falling like a stone but gliding in a manner that felt controlled, although none of the five was aware of controlling anything. They actually began to angle and turn as they descended, in the manner of a raptor riding thermals.

After a moment, Thea, who had stopped feeling terrified and was now peering down at what seemed to be their destination with rapt interest, shook her head in puzzlement.

"That's New York," she said. "At least, I *think* it's New York. It doesn't quite look right, but I'm not sure why."

"It isn't New York," Ben said quietly. "It *was* New York. If you're right and this whole thing is Nikola Tesla's work, then that's New York in the 1880s. I read a little about him after last summer. He came to New York from Europe around 1885."

"Wow," Tess said, craning her neck this way and that for a better view as they approached the city laid out beneath them, a gridwork of streets and docks and bridges. "Look at those ships!"

"I'm not looking at anything!" Magpie squeaked. "Are we down yet?"

They swept closer to the city, still banking sharply, and flew down a street at the height of the first or second story windows, straight out toward the docks and the harbor area. There seemed to be a lot of noise, and wires, and people, and steam, and smoke.

"Oh! The gloves!" Tess exclaimed, looking down at the people scurrying beneath them in the crowded streets. "And my *word,* the hats! I mean, I know people used to wear that stuff, but can you *imagine* getting up in the morning? It had to take an hour to get dressed and properly turned out for the street!"

"Watch out—you're going to kick someone's hat off with your feet if you aren't careful," Terry said.

"Are we low enough for that?" Magpie said, finally opening her eyes. What she saw just underneath her own feet startled her so much that she gasped and relaxed her hold on the hands that were holding her own; if Tess and Terry hadn't strengthened their own grips to compensate, Magpie would have slipped out of their grasp and tumbled down into the street below.

"Don't do that," Terry said sharply. "I nearly dropped you!"

"What do you think would have happened? I don't think they can *see* us or anything." Tess said.

"Oh, don't be silly—we aren't actually *here*," Terry said. "We can't have just hopped off back to the 1880s. All of this is probably a memory projection."

"You can too go back to whenever you want," Thea said. "I'm living proof of that. Cheveyo, remember?"

"Look," Ben said suddenly. "We're coming up to the docks—and look, right by that ship, just stepping off the gangplank . . ."

"That's Tesla, isn't it?" Terry said. "I've seen pictures . . ."

And then the city beneath them, so thoroughly three-dimensional and real, suddenly and shockingly flattened into what looked like a grainy black-and-white photograph, which then winked out. They were briefly stationary, and a thin film of fog or cloud roiled around their feet. Then it cleared again, but this time something quite different was underneath them.

"Aaaaiieee!" Magpie wailed, closing her eyes again.

They were as high up again as they had been above the New-York-that-was—except this time they appeared to be above a different city, straddling a river that snaked between two banks lined with majestic baroque buildings—and then they were falling toward it again, just as they had done the first time. But now that they knew what to expect, they weren't quite so startled, and all of them, with the exception of Magpie, who still had her eyes resolutely closed, were examining the new city with great interest.

"Thea?" Terry said. "Clues?"

"Haven't the foggiest," Thea said. "Europe, obviously. But that means it's *before* New York, if these are Tesla's memories. Where was he before he came to New York? Paris, France? That isn't Paris down there."

"How do you know? It's got a river, doesn't it?"

"I've *been* to Paris," Thea said. "There's no island down below. No cathedral. No Eiffel Tower."

"Yeah, but when was *that* built? Would there be an Eiffel Tower in this time?" Tess said.

"I don't know. It doesn't *look* like Paris, anyway."

They had dropped down low again, skimming the ground, and they were rapidly coming up behind a dapper gentleman walking in a park. He was wearing a hat and they could not see his face, but Terry nodded.

"Tesla," he said. "No mistaking that frame. They said he was really tall. Look at that guy."

"He still can't see us," Ben said. "Oh, open your eyes, Magpie, nothing bad is going to happen and looking at you is making me dizzy. What's he doing now?"

"I haven't a clue, but he looks like he's in *pain*," said Magpie, who had opened her eyes.

She had barely finished speaking when Tesla looked up, *straight at the five of them.*

"He can *see* us," Thea gasped.

But that was all there was time for. The picture underneath them went two-dimensional again, with Tesla doubled over in what seemed to be agony. He had fallen onto his knees, and his hands were over his ears as though he had been assaulted by a sudden cacophony of noise.

"Oh, God, was that our fault?" Thea said, appalled, as they found themselves standing ankle-deep in white mist one more time.

"He did see us," Terry said. "We might have triggered something . . . or . . ."

"Did he see us back in New York?"

"I don't think so. I don't remember if he even looked up or not. Here we go again . . ." Magpie said.

They swooped one more time, and this time there was no city at all—just an open field with a barn-like object in the midst of it, a strange tower with a bulbous top protruding from the middle of it like an antenna. The field was surrounded by mountains, and the house or barn on the field was surrounded by a wire fence. The five of them skimmed over the fence, so low that they could read a sign tacked onto it: ABANDON HOPE ALL YE WHO ENTER HERE.

"Oh, lovely," said Ben.

"Shut up," said Terry, his eyes suddenly alight. "I know what this is. It's Tesla's laboratory in Colorado. This is where he did some of his most amazing work. Are we going to be able to see inside that . . ."

The building's roof gaped open underneath the tower antenna. For a moment it looked as though they might swoop right underneath the tower and through the gap, but just as they banked toward the side, the onion-shaped bulbous covering on top of the tower suddenly woke with a crackle. A bolt of bright blue-white lightning whipped around the outside of the bulb with a sizzling sound and then snapped together into a column of fire as thick as Thea's wrist, shooting off sparks and reaching straight from the top of the antenna into the sky.

The friends veered away abruptly, as though this lightning had been accidental and unplanned for, and circled the building slowly until they came to a half-open barnlike door on the side. They slipped in through the opening and hovered just inside the door, gaping with their mouths open at what was going on inside.

Tesla, bareheaded, his hair in wild disarray, stood with one hand stuck straight into a pillar of fire that must have been the root of the lightning bolt they had seen outside.

As they watched, a bird circled in through the gap in the roof, just barely sidling between the lightning bolt and the edge of the roof beam, and dropped into the room where Tesla's apparatus stood. Despite making the effort to avoid the fire as it entered, it then flew straight into the pillar of flame.

And disappeared.

They all saw Tesla recoil; they saw his eyes widen as he stared into the fiery circle before him; they saw his other hand rise, apparently reaching for a switch.

Then they saw him freeze as the bird reappeared in the fire. No, *two* birds.

"What's going on?" Ben whispered.

Both birds hung suspended in the fiery circle for a moment, and then they both vanished.

Tesla appeared to be saying something—his mouth was moving, but Thea and the others could not make out what he was saying over the snap and crackle of the pillar of flame.

The two birds reappeared.

No, *three*.

And then vanished again.

Tesla's hand was inching upward, toward the switch, as though he was fighting a great resistance, but before he had a chance to reach it, the birds were back.

Four of them.

With a superhuman effort, Tesla touched the switch. The pillar of fire instantly died.

Where it had been, a bird lay on its back on the ground, its feet in the air. Quite dead.

They saw Tesla fall to his knees and take the bird into his cupped palms with infinite gentleness. He lifted it up toward his face, and they could see that his blue eyes were full of tears. His lips were moving, but only the faintest of sounds came out—a whisper that might have been, "Please . . . oh, please . . ."

And then he threw his head back and screamed, a cry of inconsolable loss, of devastating pain, of something too deep to be put into words.

"It's a pigeon," Magpie said, staring at the bird cradled between Tesla's hands. "It's dead."

This time, the scene didn't fade into a two-dimensional image of itself, as the previous ones had done. It *shredded*, as though something had clawed through a piece of tissue paper and sent ribbons of it flying into a sudden high wind.

The wind exploded like a tornado, slamming into the five of them, and they were torn apart by the unexpected force of the gale. They scattered like autumn leaves even as the wind dropped and a solid white fog descended on them all—the same impenetrable fog that had been there at the beginning.

"Where are you guys? Hey? Anybody?" Thea called out after a moment of breathless silence.

There was no reply. It was as though they were far apart now, too far apart to gather themselves up again as they had done the first time around.

Suddenly afraid, Thea glanced at her wrist. She had to bring it practically up to her nose before she could see the gadget's keypad and its tiny screen.

*The professor's office*, she typed in as fast as she could, with a trembling hand. *All of us. Back in the office. Right now.*

Something changed in the fog around her. It began to grow damper, more solid, as though she were pushing her way through a substance that was more water than air, and then she was lifted off her feet as if kicked.

She landed against something hard, and heard her head crack against a solid object. Pain flooded her consciousness; she realized her eyes were closed, and made herself open them.

Thea was lying against the professor's bookshelves, with a couple of books scattered on the floor around her. Mrs. Chen swiftly crossed the room and knelt beside her.

"Are you all right?" Mrs. Chen demanded, reaching to touch Thea's temple, slipping her hand to the back of Thea's head. "I don't think you broke anything, but you . . . you *flew* over here as though you'd been kicked by a horse."

"The others?" Thea asked, trying to struggle upright.

"They're fine. They're here. Sit quiet for a moment."

"Thea?" Humphrey May, looking very white, came down into a half crouch on Thea's other side. "What happened? We saw you get inside. And then—you suddenly—you— Are you sure you are all right?"

"Now you ask," Mrs. Chen muttered.

"I'm fine. Really. Where are the rest of them?"

"Everybody is here," Humphrey said, mystified. "They're all—"

"We're okay," Terry called from across the room.

"I've got such a *headache*," Thea said, reaching to rub her temples with both hands.

"I don't doubt it," Mrs. Chen said, eyeing the

bookshelf behind her. "You're lucky you didn't crack your skull open. Do you need a glass of water?"

"No. I think . . . let me sit up."

The two adults moved back, allowing her to get into a sitting position; Thea blinked, trying to get her eyes to focus properly.

"Thea," Humphrey said, and there was a tone in his voice that was almost pleading.

"Will you let the child have some air?" Mrs. Chen snapped. "Perhaps you'd better get her that glass of water. And let's get her to that armchair."

"I feel as though it's all my fault," Humphrey said, scooping Thea up and carrying her over to the armchair that Mrs. Chen had specified.

"You don't *say*," Mrs. Chen muttered.

The twins came hurrying around the great desk to the armchair in the window; Magpie followed, and Ben brought up the rear. Rafe materialized from somewhere else with a glass of cool water in his hand.

"Here," he said, bending over to hand it to Thea. "I've got hot tea coming. With plenty of sugar. In the meantime, take a sip of that."

Thea flushed as her fingers brushed Rafe's; he didn't notice, or pretended not to. Thea took several large gulps of the water, dropping her eyes from the concerned expression on Rafe's face. She saw Terry biting his lip; glanced at Magpie, who had tears in her eyes; saw the apprehension that hovered on Tess's and Ben's faces—saw the concern, the fear, the open questions in both Humphrey May's expression and Mrs. Chen's.

She drew a deep breath, her hands tightening on the armrests of the chair.

"Something's very wrong," she said.

## 5.

"Makes sense," humphrey may said. "By all the accounts I've seen, Tesla was given the opportunity to go to Colorado and pursue his work there after his New York workshop was lost to fire, and when he eventually returned to New York from Colorado he was . . . changed. Different. Some even say marginally insane. The things that had interested him before suddenly didn't anymore. It was as though some of his most extraordinary achievements in Colorado—had diminished him."

"But how does a dead pigeon diminish him?" Magpie asked.

After the five Academy students had returned from their journey to the inner spaces of the white cube, Humphrey suggested that they adjourn for an early dinner at which they all discovered that they were hungrier than they thought. Now they were back in the professor's office after dinner. Any ordinary room would have felt crowded, but the Elemental house seemed to have taken care of that problem. The room, which definitely had not boasted so many chairs before, provided a comfortable seat for everybody present, and Thea could have sworn that the room had somehow gotten *bigger* since the last time she had been in it.

"Well, he did go a little nuts for pigeons later, when he returned to New York," Humphrey said. "Apparently he fed them for years. Until the day he died, actually."

"He was looking for his dead pigeon? In a different *state*? In a great big city?" Ben said, frowning.

"How long do pigeons live, anyway?" Tess asked. "Surely if he was looking for any specific bird it would have been long gone by the time he died?"

"He was in his early forties when he went to Colorado," Humphrey said. "He was nearly ninety when he died."

"No way a pigeon can live fifty years," Ben said.

"Did Tesla?" Thea asked unexpectedly.

"Did Tesla what?" Humphrey said.

"Live. Really live. Or was he just marking time?

Maybe he wasn't looking for a specific bird, but instead . . ."

"Yes?" Humphrey said when she petered out in midsentence.

"I don't know. I thought I had something, but now I'm not sure."

"Well, that's more than enough for today. We might all get a few more ideas if we take a rest and think about it. Margaret, do you want to take them all back to the school tonight?"

"No!"

That was a chorus of four: Thea, the twins, and Magpie. Only Ben said nothing.

"We've only just started to figure it out," Thea said. "Maybe we could try—"

"The computer angle," Terry said at the same time. "I could try and track down—"

"You can deal with the computer stuff back at the school," Ben said. "That's a Nexus too."

"I thought maybe we could go back into the cube at some point," Thea said. "If we could find out how to control the flying, perhaps we could stand still long enough to actually talk to Tesla. Find out if he really is in there."

"That would be valuable information," Terry chimed in.

"Uh-oh," Magpie said. "We'd have to skydive again?"

"You have classes in the morning," Mrs. Chen said.

"We can make the work up," Thea said. "It's just another day."

"Cutting school, eh?" Humphrey May said, with a grin.

"I'd have to clear it with Principal Harris," Mrs. Chen said. "And if he okays it, it's one day, mind. Tomorrow we're back at school."

"I'll get Mrs. Emmett to show you to your rooms," Humphrey said. "I'm certain that the house has already taken care of what's necessary."

"It's an Elemental house," Terry said, in response to Ben's obvious confusion. "It takes care of your needs as soon as you utter them out loud. And sometimes all you have to do is *think* them."

"And you spent the summer in this place?" Magpie said, her eyes sparkling. "Awesome!"

"Ah, Mrs. Emmett," Humphrey said smoothly as the door of the study opened to reveal the housekeeper hovering on the doorstep. "I'm afraid we'll all be imposing on your hospitality a little longer."

"I'm already aware of that," Madeline Emmett said. "I just wanted to let you know that your rooms upstairs are ready."

"Well, then. We'll pick it up after breakfast tomorrow," Humphrey said.

They filed out of the office and followed Mrs. Emmett up the stairs. Thea, the last out the door, turned to cast a lingering look at the white cube that sat on the professor's desk. The sense of wrongness persisted in her, with that last image they had seen replaying itself over and over in her head. There was something very important about those pigeons. About Tesla's connection to them. About the fact that one had died.

Something *very* important.

If only she could pin any of it down to something—anything—specific.

Mrs. Emmett showed them to their rooms. The boys were in the room that had been Terry's the previous summer, the girls in the one that had been Thea's. The Elemental house had rearranged and refurnished the rooms to accommodate its visitors.

"This is so cool," Magpie said, coming back into

the girls' room after an inspection of the entire area. She kicked off her shoes as she settled cross-legged onto her bed. "I just went into the bathroom, and I saw five brand-new toothbrushes arranging themselves on the vanity counter. It's as though the place was expecting us!"

"It does even weirder things than that," Thea said.

"Like what?"

"Shoes," Thea said.

Magpie glanced down to where her shoes had been. She did a double take as she realized that they had been neatly placed on the floor by the foot of her bed.

"But I didn't . . ." she began, perplexed.

"This place tidies up after you," Thea said, laughing. "Your half of our room back at the school would send the Elemental house into a complete tailspin. It wouldn't be able to rest until it had found a place for everything."

Magpie grimaced. "I don't know if I'd survive here for long if it insisted on putting things where *it* thinks they should go—but it's still awesome."

It seemed to Thea that her roommates fell asleep almost before they were fully horizontal in their beds. She herself could not seem to go to sleep that easily, haunted both by the memories of the past summer and by an insistent gnawing sense of having missed something important in the visions the cube had showed them.

When she finally did drift off to sleep, she had a chaotic dream in which she stood talking to a young man whom she recognized instantly as the young Tesla. Then she was standing by the bedside of an old man with white hair whose thin skin stretched tightly over his high cheekbones, revealing the shape of the skull underneath—and this, too, was Tesla. Then Tesla was a little boy, standing beside a home-made water mill in a tumbling creek, a large cat padding in his wake. Then it was the old Tesla again, his astonishingly blue eyes flickering open and looking straight at her. A slow smile spread across the wasted, skeletal face, and his lips moved as though he was speaking to her. But the dream didn't come with audio, and all she heard was silence, the deep white silence of falling snow. Indeed, when Thea flicked her gaze to the nearby window, there was snow coming down outside, drifting white veils of it. And there, on the windowsill, sat the shape of a luminous white pigeon, glowing with a strange inner fire.

Thea woke with a start.

Her roommates were sound asleep, faces buried in soft pillows. Magpie was snoring gently. Thea briefly considered waking them, and then thought better of it. It would be better if she didn't drag anyone else into it.

She reached out to her bedside table for the wrist keyboard gadget that Humphrey had given her, grimacing at the thought of his inevitable reaction when she eventually had to confess that she had gone off on her own again. She pulled the keypad back under the covers with her as she toggled the on-switch, and the screen filled the blanket tent with a soft greenish luminescence. It reminded her forcefully of the light with which Diego de los Reyes had filled his world in an attempt to trap her there, as well as the light she had used to weave herself an escape route, the light that she then walled in with him when she turned the mirrors in on him and buried him alive in the world of his own illusions. She felt queasy at the memory. But this wasn't the same, and she firmly told herself to pull herself together.

Somewhere in the memory of this little machine she had saved a few phrases she had typed in when the five of them had been inside the cube. Her original idea had been to *weave* herself back to that place, but as she stared at her tiny screen, she frowned in indecision.

It had taken all five of them to get the white mists to dissipate enough for something to actually happen. Thea hesitated at the thought of being stuck in the mists by herself. There was the Barefoot Road, which had taken her to hard-to-get places before, but this time she didn't think she had anything specific enough to give the Road as a pointer to where she wanted to be.

Which left only the computer-linked worldweaving: the purely creative effort of re-creating the space she required through sheer force of will and imagination.

Space and *time*.

If she needed to talk to Tesla, if there was a trace or remnant of the real Tesla left behind at all in the cube-universe, it would have to be a time-weave. The last time she had tried that, she had gone back only a few moments to reverse the immediate effects of a spellspam. This time she would have to go back years, and she would have to be extremely specific about it. Failure could mean becoming unstuck in time, much like Tesla himself might have been trapped—and there was nobody at all to send after her.

"I'll just have to take the risk," she muttered to herself, strapping the keypad to her wrist. She could barely make out the keys in the green-tinged gloom underneath her bedclothes, and she had to type slowly and carefully and then double-check what she had written, because computers were literal and unforgiving and she might find herself transported to some screwy part of the universe with no clue how to get back.

*Maybe I should have left a note for the others. . . .*

The thought was there and gone, even as her index finger touched the ENTER key and she felt the room begin to dissolve around her. Just before it all winked out, she thought she heard a small voice, very far away, that might have been Magpie's.

"Thea? Thea, you okay? What are you doing?"

And then it was gone. She was standing in a city street, in the cold light of early morning, staring up at a brownstone. A tendril of black smoke curled out of one of the windows. Fire. Or the aftermath of one.

Beside her, bareheaded, his long-fingered hands hanging by his side in a manner that spoke far more eloquently of his devastation than any anguished hand-wringing might have done, stood a man who could only have been Nikola Tesla. His hair was dark, and his features smooth; Thea judged him to be somewhere in his thirties at this point. This was the famous New York fire, the one that had driven Tesla from the city and into the mountains of Colorado.

"That's half a lifetime's work destroyed," Tesla said, his voice quiet. Quenched. "I have no means of rebuilding most of the things that were in that laboratory. It was irreplaceable."

"I'm so sorry," Thea said.

Tesla glanced down at her. "Have we met?"

"Not yet," Thea said, without thinking.

Tesla frowned delicately. "Not . . . yet?"

"It's complicated," Thea said helplessly.

"Indeed," Tesla murmured. "Most things are. However, your face is very familiar—as though I remember it from a long time ago."

"I'm fifteen," Thea said.

"Quite," Tesla said after a moment. "That would make it . . . unlikely."

He stared at her for a moment longer, his brow furrowed as though he was astonished or puzzled. Thea instinctively glanced down, belatedly realizing that she might have been standing in the middle of the New York street wearing just the T-shirt she had worn to bed, but her subconscious or some aspect of her gift that she had not yet figured out had taken care of that detail. Partly, anyway. She was not dressed in period clothes, but in something nondescript and dark that resembled a tracksuit.

Or at least that's what *she* saw herself as wearing. Her companion might have been seeing precisely what he expected to see.

"What will you do now?" she said, rather abruptly.

"I am not certain. I will have to consider my options carefully." He sighed, contemplating the façade that concealed his personal tragedy. "There should have been a plan. I should have done something . . . something exceptional, to protect what was worth protecting. I should have remembered Kaschei's needle."

"What's a Kaschei needle?" Thea asked.

"Not *a* Kaschei needle. *The* Kaschei needle. There was only one," Tesla said, correcting her. "Kaschei is the evil sorcerer from the Russian fairy tales. You have never heard of him?"

Thea shook her head, every instinct aquiver. This

was somehow very important, though she could not for the life of her figure out why.

"Tell me," she said.

Tesla cast another long, mournful look at the building. "It isn't as though I have anything else to do right now," he said. "Kaschei . . . was immortal, or was reputed to be. Until Prince Ivan found out that he *could* be killed, if a certain needle was pressed into his forehead between his eyes."

"He'd hardly let someone just walk up and do that," Thea said. "If he were really an evil sorcerer—"

"Oh, that would not have been the problem," Tesla said, frowning up at the brightening sky as though the imminent presence of sunlight spilling down the streets of New York City left him distinctly uneasy. "The problem, you see, was *finding* the needle. Because the needle was inside an egg. The egg was inside a duck. The duck was inside a rabbit. The rabbit was inside a wooden chest. The wooden chest was buried at the foot of an oak tree. And the oak tree was on an island that was impossible to get to. In order to get Kaschei's needle, you would have had to find the island, find a way to go there, dig up the chest, catch the rabbit, which would escape when you opened the chest, catch the duck, which would escape if you caught and killed the rabbit, and catch the egg that would roll out of the duck and away from you if you managed to catch and kill the duck—and only then could you get the needle. Then you could find Kaschei as he slept, and push the needle home between his eyes. But you had to *get* the needle first. And it was in a safe place—a place where no harm could come to it."

"But your lab isn't a needle," Thea said, glancing up at the smoke still wafting out of the window. "You could hardly hide all that inside an egg on an island."

"Ah, you don't understand, child," Tesla murmured, and then shook himself. "I must go. It will soon be full day, and I have always found the sun intolerable if I am out in it unprotected for long. Good day to you."

"Good luck," Thea said, but she already spoke to his retreating back.

*Kaschei's needle.*

The idea hung in front of her eyes, tantalizing her; she knew it was essential that she understand precisely how the concept was linked to the rest of the things she had seen in the cube-world, but she couldn't connect the dots into a picture that made sense to her.

She glanced down at the keypad on her wrist, frowning.

"I wonder what would happen . . ." she murmured, and tapped something new into the gadget. *Nonspecific place and time; somewhere/when where Kaschei becomes important enough for me to understand significance.*

It was risky, but then again, it was no more risky than some of the things she had already done while walking the Barefoot Road of the ancient Anasazi, the Road that led anywhere and everywhere if you knew how to use it. Cheveyo had taught her that it was possible to reach a destination on that Road with just an *absence* in her mind, shaped like the thing she sought. By weaving a world that filled the absence, and then letting the universes realign themselves so that she could step from one world into another, she could find herself in the same place as the thing she was seeking. She had done it before— she had found Signe Lovransdottir that way, back in the early days of the spellspam epidemic when Signe had been lost to the Alphiri. The only difference was that now, with Tesla's words and images vivid in her mind, she was chasing an idea, not a person or a place. There was no reason that it shouldn't work the same way.

Her finger hovered above the keypad for a moment, and then she pressed her lips together and jabbed ENTER with rather more force than she intended.

The change was immediate, and disconcerting.

Instead of the brownstone-lined New York streets, she stood beside a small stream. She wore the same loose dark clothes that she had worn back in the city, but this time her feet were bare. She wiggled her toes luxuriously and felt the cool grass brushing her ankles. Slightly upstream from her was a jury-rigged mill wheel, turning with remarkable evenness, and beside it crouched a boy.

The boy from Thea's dream. The boy that Nikola Tesla had once been.

He might have been about seven or eight years old, but the promise of his height was already there in the two long, lanky legs folded up about his ears. He stared despondently at his wheel and at the water, poking at both every so often with a long stick. There was a sense of tragedy about him, much as there had been in the city street on a different continent and many years in his future, but this felt like a deeper, more personal grief.

"Hey," Thea said helplessly. And then thought, *This is silly. I am talking to him in English. He's seven—he doesn't even speak it yet.*

But apparently language was not a barrier here, because the boy looked up at the sound of her voice.

"Hey," he said. "Who are you?"

"You're Nikola Tesla, aren't you?"

"Niko," the boy said laconically.

"What are you doing?" Thea asked, coming closer and squatting a few steps away from him to peer at the mill wheel. "Did you make that?"

"Yeah. But it isn't right. It's sticking."

Thea stared at the perfect smoothness of the wheel's motion in perplexity. "How? I can't see it sticking."

The boy gave her a shriveling look. "*I* can tell," he said. "It isn't good enough. I'm just not good enough to make it work right. Dane would know."

"Dah-ney?" Thea said awkwardly, trying to mimic his pronunciation.

"My brother."

"Does he help you with these projects?"

"He used to. He's dead."

The bluntness of that statement took Thea's breath away. She sat cross-legged in the grass without taking her eyes off Niko.

"I'm sorry," she said slowly.

Niko's eyes flicked up to meet hers, very briefly, and then he resumed staring at the wheel. "Two years ago, come next month," he said.

"How . . . how did he . . ."

"The big black got him," Niko said, without changing the tenor of his voice at all. "The horse. He was twelve. The horse threw him, and then stomped him." He paused. "I saw."

"You watched your brother die?" Thea said, appalled.

"Yeah," Niko said, and tossed the stick he still held into the stream. It was there, in that small motion— all the violence of the pent-up guilt and sorrow that he would not allow to bubble to the surface of his demeanor, his expression, his attitude, his voice. "It should have been me," he said, and each word fell into the water like a stone, and sank beneath the surface.

"It wasn't your fault," Thea said.

Niko glanced at her again, swiftly, and then away. "Maybe not," he said. "Makes no difference. I should have . . . He should never have died. There should have been a way to keep his life somewhere . . . safe. . . ."

He was blindly feeling his way toward something, something that he could not name, that he did not even realize he was searching for. But in Thea's mind something suddenly came together, like two magnets clicking.

"Kaschei's needle," she murmured.

Niko turned his head. "What?"

"You think you could have hidden your brother's own equivalent of Kaschei's needle so that death didn't find him?" Thea said gently.

"How do you know about that?" Niko asked. His voice had changed at last, a tinge of wonder mixed with fear creeping into his tone. "How do you know about Kaschei?"

"You told me," Thea said, tears in her eyes. "Far, far away and many years from now."

A girl's voice came drifting over to the creek; apparently the cross-language communication applied only between Niko and Thea, because all she could make out in the girl's call was the name *Niko*. The boy turned to look, lifted his hand in a half wave, uncoiled from his crouch.

"That's my sister," he said. "I have to go."

"So do I," Thea said. "It was nice to meet you."

"Are you going to come back?"

"Someday," Thea said. "Sure."

"Good. I might have fixed the wheel by then. Maybe. So that you can see when it runs properly."

"Okay. I'll look forward to that."

He turned without another word and loped away across the grass. Thea watched him run up to his sister, and then they both turned around to look at her and Niko lifted his hand in a self-conscious little wave. His sister merely stared warily in Thea's direction. Then they both turned their backs and trotted off.

Thea sighed, looked down at her wrist, typed *Home*, and then hurriedly erased that before she turned up at her real home and freaked out her parents. *My bedroom, Elemental house, San Francisco*, she typed instead, and pressed ENTER.

Niko's mill and the creek it was on melted away into the familiar bedroom in Professor de los Reyes's house. Thea threw back her covers and realized that the Tiffany lamp beside her bed was bathing the room in radiance and a small council of war appeared to be going on.

Magpie sat on her bed, kicking her heels against the side. Ben stood by the door with his arms crossed, looking mutinous. Terry was hovering by Thea's own bed, and Tess perched precariously just on the edge of it. They all turned to stare.

"Kaschei," Thea gasped.

"Gesundheit," said Tess. "Where have you *been*?"

"You haven't run off to tattle on me, have you?"

"Just about to," Ben muttered.

"Don't tell Humphrey just yet. He'll take this thing away from me," Thea said, lifting her key-padded wrist.

"Not a bad idea," Ben said. "Tess crashed into our room about ten minutes ago, after Magpie realized that you'd somehow *gone*, and here we all are. Lucky for you that you came back of your own free will just now. We were about to call in the cavalry."

"What *happened*?" Magpie wailed.

"I figured . . . we had to talk to the Tesla who was in that cube . . ."

"Which one?" Magpie said. "We saw at least three of them. I would like to ask him about the pigeons."

"I didn't get to the pigeons," Thea said. "Not directly. But I think I may have an inkling as to what happened."

"*Did* you talk to him?" Terry asked, leaning forward.

"*How?*" Ben demanded. "I thought we all had to go into the cube before it would allow us access to any of it."

"But she's an Elemental," Tess said slowly.

"All the same, Ben has a point," Magpie said. "How come we all needed to pitch in the first time and now all of a sudden you can sail in by yourself?"

"Because it was sealed, before," Thea said. "What the five of us did was break the seal. We needed to do that together—there *needed* to be more than one sense, more than one Element, in there, because Tesla was a quad-Element mage and he would have used all of his skill to lock that thing down tight. If it is what I now think it might be. But it's open now—to us. Perhaps only to us."

"To you, anyway," Ben said. "How did you get back in without going through the cube?"

Thea lifted her wrist. "I wrote myself in. I wove it."

"Back up," Terry said. "You sound as though you went in looking for something pretty specific."

"Well, yeah," Magpie said with a grin. "She was after Tesla. Did you get him?"

"Twice," Thea said. "But it was the dream that pointed me to—"

"What dream?" Magpie said, suddenly serious.

Thea turned, narrowing her eyes. "Tesla. First young, then a child, then an old man . . ."

"And there was snow," Tess said, nodding slowly.

"And there was a pigeon," Magpie said. "A white one. On the windowsill."

"Trust you to notice that," Thea said with a quick grin, and then stared at her friends. "Are you telling me we *all* had the same dream?"

"Uh . . ." said Ben, and his arms had unfolded, his hands hanging by his side. "Yeah, actually. I remember the old man."

"Me too. And the snow," Terry said. "Weird. But what suddenly lit a fire under *you* to start chasing it down? You did that way before we knew that we'd dreamed the same thing."

They stared at one another, wide-eyed.

"Could it be . . . the house?" Magpie finally

ventured, sounding spooked. "Could it have made us dream that?"

Terry and Tess exchanged a look. "It's happened to us before," Tess said. "But that's different—it's the twin thing. Not five completely unrelated people having *exactly* the same dream."

"Was it the same, really the same, or are we all just bouncing off details that sound familiar?" Ben asked.

Terry shook his head. "Sounds like the same thing to me. Down to that pigeon that Magpie remembers. I saw it too."

"I think I'm starting to figure it out," Thea said. "Humphrey keeps calling that thing 'Tesla's cube,' but I don't think it's so much Tesla's work as it is *Tesla*. Himself."

"What, like Twitterpat? Back in the other Nexus?" Terry said.

Thea shook her head. "That's just a hologram, a piece of software. I think this is much bigger than that. I think he somehow . . . preserved himself in that cube. Kaschei's needle."

"There you go again," Tess said. "Who or what is this Chai fellow?"

"It's a Russian fairy tale . . ." Thea began, and

then the door of the bedroom opened. Ben jumped two feet into the air; the others whirled, startled, and Thea's face and neck were suffused in a sudden vivid blush.

"*What* is a Russian fairy tale?" Humphrey May said, pleasantly enough, from the doorway. But he wasn't smiling, and his usually limpid blue eyes were hard. "Can we all play, or is it a closed Midnight Snack party? Don't look so trapped, Thea—the house told me you were all awake. I told it to alert me to anything out of the ordinary in these bedrooms." He tied the sash of his robe more securely around his waist, and came all the way into the room. "Well. Now that we're awake, and seeing as I'm personally responsible for all of you while you're out here, perhaps someone could fill me in?"

## 6.

IT TOOK THE BETTER part of an hour to explain everything to Humphrey, and then quite a while longer to mollify him, once he realized just how the keypad had been used without his knowledge or sanction. He postponed the rest of the confrontation until after they had all had a chance to sleep on it, having threatened Thea with dire consequences if she attempted to use the keypad again. He ordered everybody back to their rooms, and the rest of the night passed uneventfully, with no further shared dreams.

But they slept fitfully, and woke earlier than they thought they ought to have. They drifted down to breakfast in self-conscious isolation instead of as a group. Magpie beat Thea to the bathroom by a split second, and then hogged it for what seemed like hours, finally emerging and flicking her blond streak back with a dramatic sweep as she descended the spiral staircase; Thea, growling, skimped on her own ablutions in her haste to get some breakfast.

The prevailing mood was one of wary anticipation, but the house had its own ways of defusing tensions. By the time Thea finally made it down to breakfast, the others were in the midst of a raucous game of stump-the-house.

"Wild berry jelly," Magpie was saying as Thea entered the breakfast room. Magpie's eyes were closed, her expression a mask of rapt remembrance. "Wild berries gathered by hand in the woods behind my grandmother's house, and the spread she made from them—no extra sugar, just the berry sweetness, dark red, almost purple . . ."

"Something's there," Tess said. "A jar on the table, look. Is that it?"

Magpie opened her eyes and stared at a small cut-glass jar with a silver lid.

"Looks about right, but let's put it to the test," she said, reaching for the mysterious jar with her right hand and grabbing a spoonful with her left. She took a spoonful of the dark red jelly, and a slow, satisfied smile spread across her face. She licked her berry-stained lips and dug her spoon in for a second helping. "Oh, yes! Oh, I haven't tasted this for *years*."

"I've got one," said Ben. He started describing a pastry he had once had for breakfast in a Paris café when his family had been visiting France. It had been years ago, but the pastry had obviously left an impression because his description was so vivid that the others were salivating just listening to it. It was Magpie who yelped first, pointing to the pastry plate behind Ben's elbow, where a piece of custard-filled pastry precisely matching Ben's description had just popped into existence. Ben scooped it up and bit into it, custard squirting out of the sides.

"Amazing," he said, through a mouthful of custard and flaky pastry.

"Give us a taste!" Tess said, reaching for the rest of the pastry still in his hand.

He snatched it away. "Get your own!" he said.

So Thea did, and then Tess, and Magpie couldn't resist, and soon they were all licking custard off their fingers like a bunch of toddlers.

At last Thea wiped her fingers on a napkin and crossed over to the sideboard to pour herself a mug of coffee while the rest of them began to mop up the shattered remains of the French pastries.

"What are we supposed to be doing today?" Magpie said, pushing her plate away.

"Going home," Ben replied. "You know. The real world."

Thea glanced at him and he dropped his eyes. Then Terry pushed his chair away from the table.

"We'd better go find Humphrey then," he said. "If there are things I ought to be doing back at the other Nexus, I'd better figure out what the FBM wants."

Tess and Magpie fell into step beside him, still discussing ideas for highly unlikely dishes they could try and get the house to provide for lunch. Ben hesitated, as though on the verge of saying something.

"You coming?" Terry called.

"Just getting coffee," Thea called back, stirring cream vigorously into her cup.

She was far behind the others, when she finally drifted out of the breakfast room—and then she came to an abrupt stop in the midst of the main hall, her eye suddenly drawn to the library door, which stood invitingly ajar.

*Elemental house. Tesla built this house—made this house. The professor's grandfather knew Tesla personally. Is there anything in that library* about *Tesla?*

With a guilty glance after the other four, who had apparently marched straight off to the professor's study, Thea slipped into the library, scanning the floor-to-ceiling shelves. They were neatly stacked with books that ranged from paperbacks that looked almost brand-new to great square folios of embossed leather.

"Where would I even begin?" she muttered to herself with a sinking feeling in her stomach.

But this was the Elemental house, after all, and she had thought her desire even if she had not expressed it out loud. A closer look at a side table revealed several books neatly stacked there; the cover of the top book bore a face that Thea recognized.

It was a biography of Nikola Tesla, a much-worn paperback that had clearly been read many times. The second was another biography, much newer, a glossy hardcover with a dozen pages of grainy black-and-white photographs inserted in the middle. The third and largest was a coffee-table book of Tesla's life and achievements, lavishly illustrated. The fourth seemed to be another biography, but the alphabet was different—curlicued Cyrillic letters, perhaps

Tesla's native Serbian. This, too, had photographs bound in the middle, so even if Thea could not read it, the book was still potentially valuable. The book at the very bottom of the pile was a leather-bound journal that bore dated entries and looked like a private diary. That would have been the prize—except the contents of the notebook were in Spanish.

She nodded her thanks to the room at large as she reluctantly put down the diary and flipped through the four published volumes in turn. She quickly laid aside the Serbian biography and the two glossier books, and picked up the paperback for a closer look. It had been annotated in pencil, in the same firm, florid handwriting that graced the Spanish diary . . . and, alas, in the same language. The meaning of one of the comments, though, was clear to Thea—an emphatic, scribbled *Sí!* in the book's margin, right next to a passage that drew her immediate curiosity. It appeared to be a direct quote by Tesla himself, about his great rival Thomas Edison:

"If Edison had a needle to find in a haystack, he would proceed at once with the diligence of a bee to examine straw after straw until he found the object of his search. With a little time and calculation I would have saved him ninety percent of his labor," Thea read out in a voice barely above a whisper.

Somehow this seemed to be an important insight, although Thea could not immediately say why. She realized with a start that the others must be wondering what had become of her, but she felt an urgent need to spend more time with these books, to learn more about the man who had made this house and had somehow—whether accidentally or intentionally—transferred the essence of his living self into a white cube that had survived the death of his body by more than half a century.

She gathered up the five volumes and, feeling self-conscious, addressed the library shelves.

"I'd like to borrow these, if that's okay, House," she said. "I will make sure that they are returned as soon as possible, but please don't whisk them away and put them back until I'm done with them. And if it's okay, I'd like to take them with me when we leave here today. I'll get them back here as soon as I can." She paused, glancing around. "I'll take silence as assent. If you don't want me to take them for some reason, I'm sure you'll find a way to let me know."

She gathered up her half-full coffee mug, clutching

the books to her chest with her free hand, and made her way hastily to the professor's study.

"We were wondering what had happened to you," Humphrey said as she entered.

"I paid a visit to the library," Thea said. "The house showed me these five books, and I asked if I could borrow them. Apparently it was okay with the idea."

"You've only got four," Ben said, tilting his head for a closer look.

Thea glanced down at the books in her arms. The four published volumes were still there; somehow the old Spanish diary had disappeared from her arms.

"There *were* five," she said. "The fifth was apparently too precious to lend. It was a diary, handwritten. It makes no difference, really, because I couldn't have read it anyway—it was all in Spanish. But it seems it's okay for me to hold on to these."

Humphrey sighed. "Well, I guess that's okay. The house seems to know what it shouldn't let out of its sight—and I must say, I wouldn't mind taking a look at that diary myself. I'll have a look in the library later; perhaps the House will be kind enough to leave it out for me. But in the meantime, we'd better conclude our business so that Mrs. Chen can whisk you back to the Academy."

"I'll keep on working on those printouts, sir," Terry said.

"It is almost too much to credit, but if Thea is right and it's somehow Tesla himself within that cube world . . . I don't suppose I have to tell the five of you that what you've learned here shouldn't be discussed beyond these four walls."

There was another knock on the door, and Rafe stuck his head into the room.

"Kay has everything running smoothly back at the office," he said. "Luana wants to see you about some results, but Kay told her you'd be in touch when you got back. Have I missed something?"

"Who's Kay?" Tess said in a low voice, close to Thea's ear.

Humphrey glanced up at that. "Not that it's any of your business, young lady, but Kay is my other assistant, the one holding down the fort in Washington. And no, Rafe, you haven't missed anything huge. We're still looking for a needle in a haystack."

Thea frowned slightly, as the Tesla quote from the book under her arm swam back into her mind.

*Kaschei's needle.*

Tesla had transferred his mind and spirit into a vessel other than his body. Thea had been thinking about that in terms of the layered Kaschei story, and assuming that the "needle" had been Tesla himself. But suddenly things shifted in her mind, and she was presented with a series of memories in quick succession. Tesla in the Colorado lab, his hand in the column of flame. Humphrey's voice—*His most extraordinary achievements in Colorado seemed to have diminished him.* Four birds. One dead pigeon cradled in Tesla's hands, a keening cry of unspeakable mourning raised over the small body. The white pigeon in the window of Tesla's room, there at the end, the one they had all seen in their dream. Tesla's famous feeding of pigeons in the parks of New York.

Pigeons.

The needle in the egg in the duck . . . in the *duck* . . .

"Oh my God," she said abruptly, out loud.

Everyone swiveled to face her.

"What?" Humphrey said sharply.

"I've been thinking of *Tesla* as the needle. What if I'm wrong—what if he tried to preserve himself even further? It's the Kaschei story all over again. . . ."

"What was that, now?" Rafe said.

But it was Magpie who made the connection.

"The pigeons," she said, gripping both arms of her chair tightly. "It's the pigeons. You said he was a quad-Element mage—*there were four pigeons.*"

"He transferred the Elemental magic out of himself," Thea said faintly. "Into the birds."

"But something went wrong," Tess said. "One of the birds died. We saw it die."

Humphrey's head was snapping from one to the other as though he were watching a tennis game. "Are you suggesting that Tesla drained his magic from himself?"

"To preserve it. To keep it safe. Yes. You said he came back from Colorado different."

"But if one died, what happened to the rest of them?" Magpie said. "Where are the other three pigeons?"

"A Kaschei maneuver that went wrong," Ben said. "He thought he could keep the part of himself that he treasured most safe—in whatever way—but then something went awry and one of the four was permanently lost. The other three disappeared while he was still too distraught with the death of the first one to deal with the rest, and then he was stranded."

"Do you think that's why he kept feeding the pigeons, the rest of his life?" Tess said. "When he got back to New York, I mean?"

"So what you're saying is that all we have to do is find a couple of specific pigeons in New York City?" Rafe said, his hands in the pockets of his chinos. "Very funny. I come from New York. Do you have any idea how many pigeons we've got per square inch there?"

"But surely the original pigeons are long dead already," Ben objected.

"If Thea's right, they aren't regular pigeons anymore. They're, I don't know, *Elemental* pigeons— they can live forever, or certainly for many times a normal mortal pigeon's lifespan," Terry said.

"But even given that Tesla's Elemental pigeons may still be flapping around this world, what possible use would finding them be now, even if they were findable? Tesla—the real Tesla—has been dead for fifty years!" Ben said obstinately.

"Maybe not," Thea said. "If he really is alive in some sense, inside that cube—"

"*Wait* a minute," Ben said. "It's an *Elemental* cube. You said he was a quad-Element mage. It took all of us to break the seal. That cube was made when he had all his powers. But we saw him as an old man, and that means he didn't transfer into here until right at the end of his life. He must have had his powers to make the cube, to make the transfer—but if his Elements were scattered to the four winds, literally . . ."

"Make the cube, yes, but not necessarily the transfer," Terry said. "That's pure mechanics."

"And you should know . . ." Humphrey began, then stopped. He sighed. "You may remember, the first time I came to the Academy, back in the early days of the spellspams, I told you that there had been *three* Nexus computers. That one had been lost."

"I remember," Terry said.

"The first one . . . was around a long time before the others. It was very, very primitive—in fact, it was something that you, Terry, would probably not have called a computer at all. But it was a harbinger, and it was Tesla's work. He, if anyone, would have known exactly how to do this. He might have made this cube long before he conceived of transferring his Element powers into birds, but in the end, if he set it up right, the mechanics of the thing were not . . . Elemental in nature."

"You might call it software," Terry said. "The

process. It wasn't something he did, but a method of getting him to where he wanted to be."

Humphrey blinked. "I didn't think of it in those terms, but you're right," he said. "The magic needed for the transfer itself was minuscule, and even without the Elemental base, Tesla would have had enough knowledge and power to have achieved this."

"But maybe *we* found the pigeons," Magpie said doggedly, her attention with the animals and focused on neither the hardware nor the people. "We all dreamed him. Maybe we found them, and got them back to him, and it was in time to trigger that transfer—"

"But if we did, then why did we see him mourning the dead one?" Tess said. "And even if we found all the rest, that fourth one—wouldn't that loss have mattered?"

"Even a tri-Element mage is very powerful," Ben said.

"And what about that bird that we all dreamed about?" Magpie said. "Could that have been the fourth one?"

"The *dead* one?" Ben said, perplexed. "We're

supposed to bring it back to life?"

"But maybe it transferred out into another bird before—"

"Stop. You are giving me a headache," Mrs. Chen said. "Humphrey, I'm taking them back right now, before things get too far out of hand. I think the FBM can take it from here."

Humphrey raised an eyebrow. "We'll do our best," he said, and then turned to the five students. "You guys have been wonderful. I remind you again not to talk about that cube outside your little group, and if you have any more shared dreams, let me know! Thea . . ." He glanced at her wrist, where a long sleeve covered her keypad bracelet, and then deliberately gestured at the professor's computer terminal. "Be my guest," he said.

Thea hefted her borrowed books, walked over to the computer, and leaned over the keyboard long enough to type in a couple of words. "Ready," she said after a moment.

"Come on, then," Mrs. Chen said.

"Will you let us know what happens with the cube?" Thea said, turning back to Humphrey.

"Absolutely," Humphrey said, and allowed his

glance to rest once again, for just a fleeting moment, on her wrist. The implication was unmistakable: *You know how to get a hold of me if you need to.*

Thea gazed for a moment at Rafe, who wore a noncommittal, pleasant smile; then she sighed and hit ENTER.

The professor's study blinked out, and Mrs. Chen's office at the Academy rose up around them. This was no Elemental house—this room definitely felt crowded with six people. Mrs. Chen quickly took charge.

"Your teachers know you've a day of work to make up," she said. "Please speak to them directly about any assignments you may owe. You did well," she added, almost as an afterthought. "Now get out of here, all of you. I have work to do."

"She doesn't know about the keypad, does she?" Ben said, the moment they were out of the office and the door had closed after them.

Thea shook her head.

"Why do I get a bad feeling about that?" Ben muttered, staring down at his shoes. "Thea, back at the house . . ."

Magpie stirred, raking the hallway with a suddenly

feverish gaze. "I'd better go find Fi or Bella or Gary before class," she said. "They can tell me what I missed."

"I should go back to the computer and see if I can't make sense of those printouts of Humphrey's," Terry said. "I'll report back tomorrow. You coming, Ben?"

Thea watched Ben and Terry duck out the entrance of the girls' hall on the way to their own quarters. Magpie took the stairs two at a time, the long bleached strand of hair suddenly glaringly obvious again.

"I gotta go too." Tess, standing beside Thea, stirred and gave Thea an apologetic grin. "It was nice, though. The dream was freaky, but the rest of it was cool."

"What if they need us again?"

"It's the FBM," Tess said, shrugging. "They probably won't. Pity. I'd like to go back to that house for breakfast sometime."

Thea managed a quick grin. "If the chance comes up . . ."

"Gimme a call," Tess said. "Maybe Rafe will be there again."

"*Hey,*" Thea said.

"Later, then," Tess said, and left the residence hall.

Thea climbed the stairs slowly and headed to her own room. Her mind was still roiling with every-thing—the cube world, her encounters with Tesla, even the brand-new parameters of being an Elemen-tal mage herself. Instead of grabbing her schoolbooks and racing to class, Thea kicked off her shoes and curled up on her bed with the Tesla books, poring over improbable photographs of him holding balls of fire in his hands or reading tranquilly while behind him a wheel of fire spun with the fury and splendor of a fireworks display, showering his dark hair and sloping shoulders with sparks.

*Fire mage.*

"How could he bear it?" Thea whispered hoarsely, her finger tracing the wheel of fire in the photograph. "How could he bear to rip this out of himself?"

A couple of hours spent poring over the books left Thea with a handful of answers, a bunch of new questions, and a headache. Magpie was still not back. Feeling lonely and bereft all over again, Thea decided to go out for a breath of fresh air before the late-November twilight extinguished the day completely. A sky full of low clouds, like a smeared watercolor painting in shades of gray, had already caused the outside lights to turn themselves on, but Thea decided against the lighted paths laid out across the grounds and took a sharp right into the wilder woods behind the hall instead.

It was even darker under the trees. Leaves lay in soggy drifts on the ground; the cedars stood green-black in the half-light, rustling with shadows. It was in these woods that Thea and Magpie had first heard Mrs. Chen and Principal Harris talking about the Nothing and the havoc it was wreaking on their world, even at this school that everyone considered so safe and protected. It was the memory of this, with Mrs. Chen's voice already echoing in her mind, that made Thea nearly blunder into another secret conversation. She reined herself in and ducked out of sight behind one of the larger cedars, less than fifty yards from two shadowy figures huddled in the shelter of another cedar. One of the figures was, once again, Mrs. Chen. The other was Humphrey May.

They did not look as though they had noticed

her—but their voices were curiously indistinct and blurred for their being such a short distance away. It was as though the air between Thea and the two mages had thickened into an invisible soundproof barrier.

She suddenly realized what the matter was. *Of course—they must be warded.*

She chewed on her lip, frustrated, straining to hear, before realizing that she was still wearing the keypad.

There was more than one way to get around magic shields. Humphrey himself had given her the means.

*Situation identical,* she typed in lightly when her wrist gadget lit up at her command, *minus the wards.*

She pressed ENTER. The world, still shadowy and dark in the twilight, didn't look like it had changed at all—but quite suddenly the sound of that secretive conversation taking place fifty paces away became clear and pure.

"You were once Bureau," Humphrey was saying. "You of all people ought to understand this."

"I *retired,*" Mrs. Chen said.

"You don't retire from the Bureau," Humphrey said. "Your abilities are with you always; it isn't something you can shut off or disavow at will. You may have stopped being directly employed by the FBM when you came here, but that doesn't mean that you no longer fall under its jurisdiction."

"Back when I was working for the Feds, we didn't need to throw children to the wolves," Mrs. Chen said. "She's done enough for this round, Humphrey. Can't you leave her alone, at least until she graduates?"

Thea's ears pricked up harder. Under the circumstances, the mysterious *she* could only be herself.

And Humphrey confirmed it in the very next sentence.

"I use what tools are given to me, Margaret, and Thea Winthrop is the sharpest sword I have right now."

"One you are willing to destroy in order to get to your prize?" Mrs. Chen said. "How much of this can she take?"

"What she needs to. Weapons are honed, after all. I told you, she is a poly-Elemental, and that cancels everything else out. But she's still a child, still untrained, and probably dangerous if left unguided. If she can help us get back Tesla, fully in control of his considerable powers—*Nikola Tesla*, Margaret, the only quad-Elemental known to man—good *God*, do I really have to spell it out?"

"The ends justify the means?" Mrs. Chen questioned softly.

Humphrey's voice dropped a bit, losing a little of its frightening intensity. "I *like* her," Humphrey said. "I will do my best to deal with the situation so that she is kept as safe as possible, but if she is the only weapon I have, then I will use that weapon, and I will not apologize for it."

"She trusts you."

"And so she should. I am her shield; she is my sword. We are working together on this, for the most part."

"Except when you toss her in at the deep end and expect her to find her own way home," Mrs. Chen said. "*You* were the one pushing her to go after Diego—"

"Because she was the only one that could," Humphrey interrupted gently, but Mrs. Chen would not be derailed.

"The point is, Humphrey, I'm watching you. She's

my responsibility, in this place at least. I know you aren't involving her parents in any of this."

"I will, if I need to," Humphrey said. "Paul Winthrop is a friend."

"Don't push the friendship, when it comes to his child," Mrs. Chen said. "I'm warning you. I have my responsibilities, and I will not fail them."

"So have I," Humphrey said, and the edge was back in his voice. "And neither will I. And don't forget that your ultimate responsibility is still to the powers behind the FBM. We all have those."

"The children . . ." Mrs. Chen began, rousing to her full height, but this time it was Humphrey who lifted both his hands in a gesture of silencing, and for some reason it suddenly frightened Thea to see Mrs. Chen subside.

"Protect," Humphrey said. "That is what I am sworn to do. And I will, as I have always done. Whatever the cost."

Mrs. Chen turned her head away in a sharp little motion, and then, without looking back at Humphrey, walked away toward the lights of the residence hall. Humphrey waited for a long moment, and then reached up to pull the hood closer around his face, before plunging into the deepening night shadows.

Thea leaned back against the rough comfort of the cedar and fought the urge to burst into tears.

*Whatever the cost.*

What if the cost of Tesla's triumphant return to this world was Thea herself?

## 7.

THEY HAD BEEN A team only twenty-four hours before, but as soon as they returned to the Academy, Thea's friends scattered. Magpie flounced off with her other clique; Tess took up residence in the library; Terry effectively vanished into his Nexus world once again; and Thea glimpsed Ben every so often across the campus or across a classroom, looking troubled if he caught her eye, but apparently determined to keep those troubles to himself.

Thea supposed she could have discussed the Humphrey May incident with Mrs. Chen, but it was not the same as having friends, people she trusted, who had been in the same adventures that she had. She did not realize how much she needed a support group until hers disintegrated.

Perhaps it was that that drove her to break Humphrey's dictum about discussing any issues concerning the cube. That, and a glimpse of the Walrus, alone as usual, picking desultorily at her lunch nine days after Thea had eavesdropped on the conversation in the woods.

Kristin looked up in astonishment as Thea crossed over to her corner of the cafeteria and slid her tray on the table.

"Hello," she said carefully.

"Hey," Thea said, picking up her fork. "From the looks of your tray I don't think I will like this stuff much."

"I wasn't really hungry," Kristin said, but she picked up one of her wilting French fries and stuffed it into her mouth anyway.

"I missed a couple of biology classes," Thea said. "Anything I should be doing this weekend that I don't know about yet?"

"Mr. Crow didn't give you the assignments?" Kristin asked.

"Yeah, I guess . . ." Thea stared down at her food. Suddenly she wasn't so sure that this had been a good idea, after all. But then Kristin said something, and she realized that she hadn't been paying attention at all. She looked up, saying, "Sorry, what?"

"I said, where'd you go?" Kristin said. "Look,

it's not as though we covered huge swathes of new material or anything, there wasn't even a quiz you missed, there's one next week, just before the Christmas break, but you know about that already—and you wouldn't be asking me for school stuff anyway . . ."

Thea stared at her for a moment. "You can be scary," she said at last.

Kristin shrugged. "I'm a Finder, remember? That extends to finding what people *don't* want to talk about. Why do you think I always eat alone? I'm not what you might call comfortable company. Even without taking the Walrus teeth into account."

"I'm not supposed to talk about it with you," Thea said.

"Just me?" Kristin queried, lifting an eyebrow. "What did *I* do?"

"Not just you. Anybody. Anybody who . . . doesn't already know." Thea sighed, looking around at the packed cafeteria. It seemed the only table that wasn't overflowing with chattering, laughing, flirting, squealing, jostling students . . . was the one she was at. She, and Kristin. Thea suddenly felt as though a spotlight had been turned on her.

"Where's the rest of them? Your friends?" Kristin

asked, following Thea's gaze around the room. "That's your roommate over there, isn't it?"

"Yeah, Magpie and that stuck-up Fi Halloran and Bella Baldacci," Thea said venomously.

"She seems to be having a good time," Kristin said, crossing her arms and leaning forward.

"I can't . . . talk to her," Thea muttered, chasing a stray pea around her plate with her fork.

"Thanks," said Kristin sourly. "It's always great to know that you're the last port of call when someone's run out of all other options."

Thea turned a startled gaze on her. "It isn't like that," she said, and knew it came out sounding lame. "It really *isn't*," she added after a moment.

Kristin looked around again, indicating the rest of the student body with an eloquent shrug of her shoulders. "Me," she said. "Of all of them, me. You picked me. Forgive me if I'm finding that hard to believe."

"You were kind to me," Thea said.

That seemed to bring Kristin up short. "When was I . . . uh . . . *kind* to you?"

"Oh, a while back. Couple of weeks ago."

"When you were feeling sorry for yourself," Kristin said.

"Seriously. I'm *not* supposed to talk to anyone other than Terry or Tess or Magpie or Ben, but none of them are *here*. But the person who didn't want me to talk is precisely the person I need to talk *about* . . . and perhaps it would be best if I did that to someone who *didn't* know the whole story, whom I could trust."

Kristin stared at Thea with her mouth hanging open. The expression brought the snaggleteeth into painful prominence, but somehow those had ceased to have the usual repelling effect on Thea. Her instincts were telling her that this really was someone she could trust. What she had seen and heard in the twilight woods had occurred nine days ago—she had been carrying it alone for too long. Agonizing over whether *Humphrey May* was in fact someone whom she could trust. She was not immune to a sharp pang of guilt; thus far, Humphrey had always seemed to be on the side of the angels.

She gave Kristin a small wan smile. "So, how much time do you have?"

"We could always skip biology," Kristin said, with an entirely straight face.

They caught each other's eye again, and suddenly both of them laughed.

"So you noticed I've skipped a few of those lately, have you? Oh, but there's so much . . . I don't know where to . . . Oh, they'll have me for truancy," Thea managed at last.

"Fine. Then let's go and listen to Crow turn our stomachs with how we're digesting this stuff, and if you still feel like talking afterward . . ."

It was, already, an instinctive step back, a half-hearted raising of the shields that had been allowed to drop—but the smile that Thea turned on Kristin was real, glinting in the back of her eyes.

"After, then," Thea said, gathering up her tray, her lunch still mostly uneaten.

Thea spent the better part of biology mulling over what she was going to tell Kristin. She fingered the wrist computer Humphrey had given her, concealed under her sleeve. After the spellspam epidemic of the previous summer, nobody was left in any doubt that computers were not secure against magic, but that was all Kristin knew, and revealing Thea's magi-cal ability with computers would be huge. And yet, without that revelation, everything else would come across as wildly improbable.

It was a question of either trusting Humphrey absolutely or completely betraying everything—Thea could not see a middle ground. If Humphrey was right, and Thea was indeed a new Elemental, everyone would know that soon enough. It could not be kept under wraps for much longer. But the specter of the Alphiri was still haunting Thea, and after her secret had leaked out to a chosen few, she had been content to let Humphrey dictate the further timetable of things. If she took Kristin into her confidence, she would be changing the equation, and the Alphiri would still be waiting.

Grandmother Spider had once told Thea that Thea had made the choice not to perform magic in this, her own world, because she had been instinctively aware of the danger. Would this be breaking that pact with herself?

*Of course it wouldn't,* Thea told herself firmly. *It's no more than I've already done. I've used magic to travel, to tweak my reality, to change the world's parameters so that Terry could talk about magic without choking, and to take us all through to San Francisco. . . . The first time I did it with the five of us, it was revealing it to people who did not know about it before, the first time I did it to show Aunt Zoë that I could weave light, there was a first time I showed it to a lot of people . . . what's different . . . ?*

By the end of class she had decided to simply trust her instincts. She waited, pretending to fuss with her bag, until most of the rest of the class had left. Out of the corner of her eye she saw that Kristin, taking her cue from Thea's actions, was likewise procrastinating about leaving the classroom. They glanced at each other; Kristin nodded imperceptibly, and Thea suddenly reached a decision. Under the cover of the flap of her bag, she hitched up her sleeve a little and toggled her keypad on.

*This classroom. Empty but for us.*

Just as her finger touched the ENTER button, she felt a hand clamp onto her left wrist, and a familiar voice began to hiss something into her ear.

The room blinked and reconstituted according to her specifications . . . except for one small change. The voice hissing into her ear, the hand around her wrist, belonged to Ben—who had, by virtue of being in direct contact with Thea, been pulled into her sideslip world with her.

". . . think you're doing?" he finished saying, and then straightened, looked around. "What did you do? Did you do anything? What's going on?"

"You did something?" Kristin said from across the room, sitting up and looking around.

"*You* weren't supposed to be here," Thea said with a sigh, lifting her head to meet Ben's eyes.

"That . . ." he said, jerking his chin at her keypad bracelet. "What's she doing here?"

Kristin's eyebrow shot up. "Well, excuse me," she said. "If you two have something to talk about, I'll just see you later, Thea."

"No, wait," Thea said. "You can't go. There's nowhere to go *to*. I brought us here to talk. He wasn't . . . planned."

"Brought us here." Kristin echoed flatly. "What's that supposed to mean? It's Crow's classroom—what would happen if I opened that door and went out into the corridor?"

"I have no idea," Thea said. "Technically, there *is* no corridor."

Kristin shook her head. "I don't understand."

"Of course you don't," Ben said. And then, turning back to Thea, "You could have figured out that she would have no clue what was going on."

"I saw Humphrey May. Here on campus. The night we came back," Thea said. "Kristin, give me a moment. I'll explain. But since Ben's here . . ."

Kristin sat back down, dropping her bag at her feet. "By all means," she said. "I'm all ears."

"So?" Ben said, crossing his arms. "Thea, we can't discuss this . . ."

"There—is—no—corridor," Kristin intoned, waggling her hands at Ben in a mockery of a spell-casting gesture. "I can't tell anyone, remember?"

"Not *here*," Ben snapped. "But we all get to leave."

"Humphrey May—he's from the FBM, isn't he?" Kristin said. "One of those three that the Feds sent in during the spellspam?"

"Yes," Thea said. "But since then, he's been around. He's helped, he's a friend . . ."

She stopped, both because her misgivings about Humphrey were what had brought her here in the first place, and because Ben winced when she described Humphrey as her friend. When she glanced over at him, his shoulders were hunched defensively and he looked guilty, as though he had been caught out at something. Thea gave him a sharper look.

"You already knew," she said.

"No. I didn't know," Ben said. Too quickly. "What did he want this time?"

"I didn't say *I* talked to him," Thea said slowly. "I . . . overheard him talking. To Mrs. Chen. And it was about me. About how I'm a means to an end.

It's Tesla they really want."

"Who or what is Tesla?" Kristin said, fascinated.

"Not *now*, Walrus," Ben said. He looked down, hesitating. "Sorry. But—back at the Elemental house . . ."

"Back at the house what?" Thea prompted.

Ben glanced at Kristin once more and sighed, dropping his arms in a gesture of resignation. "I heard him tell Rafe that he'd have to continue acting as liaison, that he—Humphrey—would stay in the Pacific base until the situation was resolved, that Rafe should take the cube back to a Fed safe and keep it under lock and key, and that Humphrey would continue to monitor *you*."

"That's hardly inflammatory," Kristin said. "All he's saying is that he'll keep an eye on you. And Thea, you yourself said that he helped, that he was a friend. So why shouldn't he stick around? And what's this Tesla got to do with it?"

"She's an Elemental, you idiot," Ben said.

"Who?"

"Me," Thea said in a small voice.

Kristin stared at her. "An Elemental? For real? Is that how you do this no-corridor-out-there trick?"

"Maybe. It's part of it. But Nikola Tesla

was—*is*—the only quad-Element mage that's ever been known."

"Was or is? And what are you?" Kristin said, leaning forward.

"Was. Is. That's the point. There's this cube . . ."

"*Thea,*" Ben said desperately, "you know what they said about bringing in outsiders. You couldn't talk about this to one of *us*?"

"No," Thea said, losing her temper. "Apparently I couldn't. Terry's so tangled up in whatever he's doing, I couldn't even *find* him. Magpie's crossed to the dark side, Tess is too busy with her books to lift her head and say hello, and *you* . . . well, you were avoiding me."

"Well, I thought—"

"Tesla," Kristin said firmly. "What's this Tesla thing?"

Ben shot Thea another desperate look, but this was what she had brought Kristin here for. She turned away and started to piece together the story of Tesla and the Elemental cube. Kristin didn't say anything until Thea ground to a halt; then she sat back and started ticking off points on her fingers.

"Okay. First. How much about that cube did Humphrey May know when you started out?"

"He said that it was an Elemental cube as soon as he saw it."

"I don't think he knew that it had anything directly to do with Tesla, though. Not until later. Not until Terry—" Ben began, but Kristin turned on him with a scowl.

"I wasn't talking to *you*." She turned back to Thea. "Did Humphrey May know that *you* were Elemental? When all this started?"

"I'm not sure when he began to believe that, actually," Thea said. "But everything that happened with the spellspam . . . that gave him some clues."

"Humphrey May gave you that thing you're wearing? The keypad?"

"Yes."

"I don't get it—how come *he* gives you something like that, without even telling your parents?" Kristin said. "Nobody knows that you've got it, or that he gave it to you. And even if he didn't know about Tesla, quite, when he gave it to you, he did at least suspect what *you* are. And he certainly knew what you could do with it. And he knew that you *would*, because you've done it before. He was setting you up."

"Why?" Thea said blankly. "Why would he do that?"

"He was trying a few shortcuts of his own, probably. It seems to me as though he is after an Elemental mage of his own. He figured you for one, and gave you something that he knew you were going to use. You would either prove him right and take it and run with it, and he gets the credit for it. Or you would use it to help him retrieve Tesla, the *greater* Elemental mage, and he would still get the credit. Or nothing happens at all—but nobody knows about it in that case, because you aren't allowed to discuss it. Any way you slice it, he gets something out of being generous to you."

"Thea," Ben said, "are you *sure* about Tesla? What we saw could have been just a visual record, like a sort of home movie of a life. You seem to think that he's actually real in there, alive . . . and apparently so does Humphrey. What makes either of you so certain?"

"Humphrey said the first Nexus, the very first 'supercomputer,' was similar to that cube that we've got, which means that Tesla is more than capable of doing that. As for me . . . I *talked* to Tesla myself."

"Directly?" Kristin asked skeptically.

"At least twice," Thea said. "Once as a grown man in New York, after a fire in his lab—after he lost everything—and once as a kid. Where do you think I got that whole Kaschei idea from?"

"So you do believe that he's real, that he's still *alive*?" Ben asked.

"As alive as you or I," Thea said.

"Then you'd better be careful," Kristin said. "Because if you're right, and Humphrey believes you're right, something very valuable is at stake here. And if nobody except Humphrey knows what you are, then it's easy for him to use your talents to get what he wants. Tesla is a known quantity—his work is known, his potential value is huge. You . . . are an unknown. Your own potential is still only theoretical."

"Like hell," Ben said loyally. "She's proved what she can do. And others know what she's done. Mrs. Chen. The principal. Her parents."

"All of whom are subject to the FBM," Kristin said. "All the *rest* of the world knows for sure is that you're a failed Double Seventh, Thea. The seventh child of two Sevenths, who can't do magic. Not that you've come into any kind of power at all."

"That . . . was necessary," said Thea faintly. "The Alphiri . . ."

"Perhaps. But your shield can be turned against

you. You might have to choose—reveal yourself and deal with the Alphiri, or stay wrapped in your silence and maybe get sacrificed for something thought to be the greater good."

"Thea, do the *Alphiri* know about Tesla?" asked Ben suddenly.

"I have no idea," Thea said, startled. "How would I know that?"

"Why do you ask?" Kristin said.

"Well, how did we *get* the cube, again?" Ben said.

"It was retrieved with Beltran when we went to get . . . oh dear . . . well, Corey certainly knows about the cube . . ."

Kristin's head swiveled back to Thea, her expression confused all over again. "Who's *Corey*?" she asked plaintively.

"The Trickster. Coyote," Thea said. "He's an Elder Spirit of the First World. He's got his paws in this, and if he does, then the Faele do, because he uses them to do his dirty work when he can't— The cube. They stole the cube."

"Corey is of the Faele?" Kristin said, frowning slightly.

"No. He's older than they are—he was here when

the world was made and the first humans dreamed the first stories about it. There's probably a part of him in all of us; that's how we know him when he crosses our path."

"I don't know," Kristin murmured. "The Faele have been around for some time, too, as part of our stories—creatures we thought we had invented, or thought we had maybe glimpsed but then dismissed because they were too unbelievable, until they crossed the polity borders and revealed themselves to be real enough."

"The Faele were always the other, something outside of us," Thea said. "Corey is supposed to be an incarnation of our own oldest instincts. But he can learn, and he can adapt—it's one of the most astonishing things about him. When the Faele crossed his path, and ours, he took what he could from them—tactics, ideas . . . perhaps artifacts."

Kristin ran her tongue over her teeth. "The Faele are trouble."

"Duh," Ben said, rolling his eyes.

"Two things about the Faele," Kristin said. "They might seem mutually contradictory, but that's the Faele all over. The first is that they live absolutely in the moment, and don't care about the consequences.

If something sounds like a good idea at the time, they'll just *do* it, and leave someone else to deal with the fallout. The second is that they hold grudges like nobody's business."

"A grudge is a consequence," Ben said.

"I said they were contradictory," Kristin said. "They might have been recruited into this, either by your friend the Trickster, in which case anything they did was purely innocent and they were just having a high old time, or else by the Alphiri, who might have fed some old grudge to get them to throw a wrench in the works. Just because the Faele could. Just because it would screw up someone else's plans. If they disliked that someone else enough." She ran her tongue over her teeth again. "I should know," she added morosely.

"But if Humphrey knows the cube was stolen, or thinks he knows . . ."

"The question is, what would the Alphiri want with the cube?" Ben said.

Thea stared at him. "The same thing," she said, "that they might have wanted with me. If the Alphiri know what—or *who*—is inside that cube, they might be willing to pay any price for it. It's high magic; it's what they've wanted all along—and this time it comes in a conveniently prepackaged form. It's *buy-able*. Legally. We aren't talking about a person."

"I thought we were," Kristin said, blinking. "This Tesla guy."

"But he is real in a very different sense than you and I are real," Thea said. "The Alphiri are literal. They understand that the human polity will not sell a human being—that lesson's been driven home hard. But they could make a case that Tesla is not a human being. Not anymore, anyway. Not in this form. That it would not be slavery if they purchased what they could always represent as a hologram."

"And he'll never die," Ben whispered, his face suddenly stark. "Oh, God. It's *forever*."

"They couldn't make him do anything, though," Kristin said. "Like, what would they threaten him with?"

But Thea had suddenly gone quite white.

*He'll never die. Slavery. Forever.*

*Alone. Alone in his world.*

Suddenly the face she saw in her mind's eye was not Tesla's, with its piercing blue eyes and careful, old-fashioned center-parted hairdo. Instead it had deep-set dark eyes, smooth olive skin, and dark hair falling wild to the shoulder.

Diego de los Reyes. Whom Thea herself had condemned to just such a fate.

"But they don't know about the magic," Ben said. "About the Kaschei maneuver. About the fact that the Tesla locked inside that cube may be utterly useless for what they want of him."

"But he's in the *cube*," Kristin said obstinately. "That means that he *does* have the magic. Somehow."

"No," Thea said. "Terry said the actual transfer would be purely mechanical. That he had to have actually made the cube way back, when his full powers of Elemental magic were still intact. Whatever happened afterward didn't affect that."

"So he had magic, this Tesla . . . and then he didn't . . . and now he does again?" Kristin said, frowning.

"He doesn't . . ." Thea cocked her head to the side quizzically. "Wait a minute. What makes you think that he has it again?"

"Because it isn't just a transfer, if what you say is true," Kristin said. "If it was just a transfer, then it *would* be just a—what was it you called it earlier? A home movie of his life. If he transferred himself, and did it in such a way that his body died, in this world, it took more than a mechanical copying. He changed himself fundamentally with magic. And you said that the cube was sealed with Elemental magic?"

Thea nodded mutely.

"Well, *someone* had to have done *that*, in the end, didn't they?" Kristin said.

"Would it be possible to preprogram it?" Thea asked, turning to Ben.

"Don't look at me. You'd have to ask Terry that," he said, shrugging. "But she's right; it was sealed, and it took all of us to break that seal."

The same thought occurred to both Ben and Thea at the same moment, and she reached out and grabbed his arm.

"The Alphiri couldn't have gotten past that seal," Thea said. "They wouldn't have the first clue as to how to go about it, even if they had the Elemental magic, which they don't. And whatever was inside that cube . . . they didn't know about it. They couldn't. We *broke* that seal . . ."

"And they'll find out about that long before they find out about anything beyond that," Ben said. "It's information, and all information is for sale, and everyone knows that the Alphiri pay handsomely for it. It will leak. And they couldn't get at whatever was locked up inside the cube before, but now they can. And they'll want it."

"They'll try to buy it," Kristin said. "They always try to buy."

"They can't buy," Thea said. "They officially don't know it exists. And if they knew it existed, they would also know that it wouldn't be for sale."

"Not by the Human Polity, anyway," Kristin said.

"What do you mean?" Ben asked, but Thea was nodding.

"They buy from whoever's selling," she said. "And they don't ask where it came from. The cube was stolen before—it could be stolen again."

"The Trickster. The Faele." Ben sat up. "We'd better get back," he said. "We should tell someone."

"Who?" Kristin said. "Humphrey? Wasn't that the topic you came here to discuss?"

"There's got to be a way of dealing with this without involving Humphrey," Ben said.

"There might be," Kristin said.

The other two turned to stare at her.

"Well, the whole idea is to keep Tesla from falling

into the clutches of the Alphiri, in whatever form," Kristin said. "It seems to me that if there's anyone who's actually equipped to be in contact with him— real or not, at this point—it's you, Thea. Have you considered that it might be easiest all around if you were to steal the cube yourself?"

## 8.

"LET ME GET THIS straight," Terry said. "You want to *burgle* the FBM *headquarters?*"

The safest, most heavily shielded place in the Academy—and also one of the few where Terry could speak freely without worrying about accidental magical utterances and their consequences—was the Nexus room. As soon as Ben had blurted out to Terry the idea of kidnapping the cube, Terry had sent his sister to Thea with an urgent message to meet him there. It was late, and even outside the secret room the admin building was empty and quiet, with offices locked for the day.

"I don't want to steal trade secrets. I just want Tesla's cube," Thea said.

Terry shook his head in outraged disbelief. "Ben said this was the Walrus's idea."

"*Kristin,*" Thea said. "Please, those teeth really aren't her fault."

"But she put you up to this?"

"It sounds like a good plan," Thea said defensively.

"Do you have any idea just how insane this is?" Terry said. "Let me ask again—you want to burgle the Federal Bureau of Magic . . . ?"

"The cube—" Thea began, but Terry raised his hand to silence her.

"They keep it in a *safe,*" he said pointedly. "A safe, Thea. And it's a safe at the FBM headquarters, secured by physical means and by heavy-duty protection spells. Given those circumstances, why do you think the cube is in any danger at all? And even if it is, how do you think you can possibly get at it?"

"I can weave my way around things," Thea said. "Whatever barrier is thrown up, there's a world where that barrier doesn't exist. There's a world where the safe isn't locked at all. There's a world where the safe isn't even there."

"You think other people might find out how to get to that place?" Terry said, sounding startled. "Are you seriously telling me *nothing* is safe anymore?"

"In the place where there is no safe, there may be no cube," Thea said, shrugging. "But in *this* world, they both exist—one's merely an obstacle to the other."

"But the cube is already safely locked away in this world," Terry said. "Thea, it makes no *sense.*"

"What if someone with access to that safe is somehow tricked into opening it?" Thea said.

"Like who?" Terry said, frowning. "I don't get this sudden feeling you have against Humphrey. You aren't suggesting that *he*—"

"Not deliberately," Thea said. "But Humphrey isn't there. He's here, on this coast. That's what Ben overheard. That's what I think he was saying to Mrs. Chen. So who's guarding the safe with the cube in it?" She grimaced. "Sounds like a Kaschei needle all over again. Tesla, in a cube, in a safe, in an office, on the opposite coast of a continent."

"I don't get how you think you can guard it better," Terry said, perplexed. "Or from whom. I've heard nothing whatsoever about any danger in that quarter, and I've got an ear to the ground via the Nexus, and Humphrey May e-mails me regularly, and—"

"That cube was stolen at least once before," Thea said stubbornly. "Humphrey himself said so. And look where it ended up."

"Yes, in an uncrackable safe," Terry said.

"Before that. In a duffel bag in the desert. By way of Corey the Trickster. And the only reason the Alphiri didn't have it *then* is because they either weren't aware of what it was, or they knew they had no hope of getting at it. But the Alphiri live longer than we do. They think in longer terms. They might have let it come into our hands so that we could do the dirty work—and then they'll get the better bargain."

"They could not *possibly* know any of it," Terry said, shaking his head. "Besides . . ."

"I'm going to get it," Thea said, and crossed her arms across her chest.

"You're going to go against the Federal Bureau of Magic. The *FBM*. Because you don't trust them with a major magical artifact, which it is their business to study and protect. *Seriously*."

"They aren't above using whatever means necessary," Thea said.

"What does *that* mean?"

"Luana wanted to blanket the entire Academy

with an anti-spellspam spell, remember?" Thea said. "No matter what the fallout might be. No matter that people like Ben, like *you*, might have been seriously hurt by that."

"Yes, but that time it was actually Humphrey May who stopped her," Terry pointed out. "And now you're basically saying that he's turned into her?"

"No," Thea said, stung. She wasn't sure what she felt about Humphrey May at the present moment, but she was a long way from thinking he was like Luana Lilley. "And that's another thing, anyway. If Humphrey's over here—for whatever reasons— who's back there watching the safe? Can you really tell me you trust Luana with this? Come on, be honest."

"That's not fair," Terry said after a moment of silence. "She's hardly a proper yardstick to measure anything by. She might have her own agenda, and she might be a complete idiot, but she's FBM, in the end."

"But she's arrogant and vain and ambitious," Thea said. "Even Grandmother *Spider* wasn't totally sure about the Faele. She left me alone in the First World to go back and check on her dream catchers. What could we say about a fallible mortal like Luana?"

"You're making this up as you go along, aren't you?" Terry said, staring at her. "And just how do you think you can make that cube safer than it is now? Keep it *here*? That's insane—it'll be ripe for the plucking. And besides, do you realize what will happen if you get caught? You probably *will* get booted out of the school. It would mean burning quite a few bridges."

"I have a plan," Thea said. "And I don't plan on getting caught. I'm going in."

"*Fine,*" Terry said, uncoiling from his chair. "But you're not going alone."

"You think it's a terrible idea."

"*Yes*, but that's neither here nor there. You're going to do this anyway. You need someone to watch your back."

"But it's the FBM. It's your own family business; you've called it that plenty of times. You'd be burning those bridges too," Thea said.

He glared at her. "You said you had a plan," he said. "When were you planning on doing this insane thing?"

"No time like the present," Thea said with a small smile.

"You mean, before you've had a chance to sleep on it and realize just how wildly weird and unpardonable this is," Terry said. "If it had been one of us, Thea . . . but the *Walrus*? Kristin? Why on earth would you take her seriously?"

"Because she isn't tainted by knowing what we all think we know. Because what she said came out of a fresh look at the situation, by someone who had absolutely no agenda. Because it makes sense."

"Promise me one thing," Terry said, after a beat. "If something goes seriously wrong, promise me you won't try anything really stupid. We pull out."

"Sure," Thea said, with a grin, pushing up her sleeve and activating her keypad.

"I mean that, Thea," Terry said, craning his neck to see what she was typing. "You're already doing something rash. You don't even know where you're . . ."

The softly glowing walls of the Nexus room vanished, and they found themselves standing in what at first appeared to be utter darkness. But as their eyes adjusted to the meager light creeping in through a window with drawn blinds, the shadows around them began to assume familiar shapes—a desk, a chair, a computer monitor, a bank of filing cabinets.

"... going," Terry finished in a whisper. "Where are we?"

"This is Humphrey's office," Thea hissed. "I've been here once before, during the spellspam, but that was a while ago, and it was in daylight. Hang on a sec, let me remember the layout . . ."

She shuffled forward past what she thought was the corner of the desk and smothered an exclamation as she blundered into it.

"I don't suppose you thought to bring a flashlight with you," Terry whispered. "We need some light—Oh."

Thea had reached the window and opened up the Venetian blinds. Reflected light glinted dully off the surface of the monitor and the glass doors of a couple of cabinets against the far wall.

"Okay, now what?" Terry said. "The safe isn't in this room."

"So do you know where it is?"

"Are you kidding me? My uncle might run the place, but just because they handed me the Nexus doesn't mean they let me run loose in here."

"Okay, so we have to do it the hard way," Thea said.

Terry rolled his eyes. "I thought you had a plan."

"I do. Once I get the cube."

"Oh, *great*," he said, peering at where she stood by the window, her left wrist tilted so that the screen of the keypad caught all the available light. "What are you doing?"

"Asking a few questions. There's a map."

"Of what?"

"Of this place. Where the safe is. Except it looks really weird. Like it's in several dimensions beyond the physical."

"Not all of this place exists in the here and now, Thea," Terry said. "Didn't your father ever tell you about it? And are you still sure that someone else could steal that stupid cube, just like that? Just say when you're ready to quit. I'm quite happy to go back to the school without tripping any of the FBM's alarms."

"You're starting to sound an awful lot like Ben," Thea said. "Is that the only reason you came along? To be able to tell me 'I told you so, let's go home now'?"

"But it isn't . . ." He heaved a deep sigh. "Okay. You've got two problems. I'm relatively certain that getting to the safe is only done via a single approach corridor, not from just any arbitrary office. Not even Humphrey's or Uncle Kevin's. You need to find the entry point where the maze that leads to the safe actually begins. And just to make it more fun, there *is* security in this building."

"We can duck the muscle," Thea said.

"It's not just . . . ordinary muscle," Terry said tightly, and then tossed his head in frustration. "I can't," he said. "It isn't . . ."

"Okay, I get it. There are special security requirements, so the thugs come with special equipment. I'll take that into account. What's the second problem?"

"What you just said." Terry nodded at her keypad. "Does that thing tell you which dimension you need to chase the safe down in?"

"I'll figure that out when I get there," Thea said. "Come on."

He reached out and grabbed her right wrist, the one without the keypad, as she sidled past him. "Do you really know what you're doing? Once you get out into that corridor, there's no turning back. There's nothing you need to prove, Thea, not to anyone."

Thea jerked her arm out of his grasp with a violence that startled them both, making Terry step back and into the desk. In an attempt to keep his balance, he dislodged an in-box and upended its contents onto the floor. Terry started to reach over for the fallen papers, but suddenly realized that Thea's tense, rigid shoulders were quivering with what seemed to be stifled sobs.

"What is it?" he said quietly. "This isn't really about Humphrey May at all, is it?"

"I will not be responsible for that again," Thea said, and her voice was strange, muffled. "I will *not*. I can't do it. The Alphiri already think themselves cheated because of Diego, and what I had to do to Diego. If anything happens to Tesla, if Tesla falls into the hands of the Alphiri—if they get that cube—I *know* what they can do to him. I know, because I've already done it. I locked Diego away, alone, into a world from which he can never escape." She gasped, took a deep breath. "They'll blame me . . ."

It was a different *they* this time. Not the Alphiri. Her own kind.

Diego de los Reyes. The wraith-boy who had been like her. The one whom she had locked into an eternity of lonely isolation, because allowing him to be free would have been impossible.

"Nobody blames you for that," Terry said after a beat, his voice very low. "And this is not the same thing at all."

She shook her head, a small, despairing motion. "It is," she whispered. "It's *worse*."

"Tesla locked himself into that cube," Terry said gently. "Only he knows why. *You* didn't do it."

"But he lived," Thea said. "If anything happened . . . Tesla would be completely aware of what was going on. At least, before . . ."

"You were already dealing with a ghost," Terry said.

Thea flinched.

"I'm sorry," Terry said. "*I was there*—at least, I was on the outside looking in. I should have seen this coming. I could have helped. It isn't right that you took all this on yourself. Even Humphrey was more there for you than I was, and we all know what you think of *him* these days."

It was an apology, but it was also a clear attempt to lighten the mood, and Thea managed a smile, reaching up to knuckle at her eyes.

"Okay now?" Terry said quietly. "You seen enough? I think the FBM can manage to keep Tesla from falling into the wrong hands, Thea. That's what they're here *for*."

"What did you knock over?" Thea said, taking a step sideways and trying to peer at the pile of paper on the floor behind Terry's back. "We'd better pick up."

They both dropped into a crouch and reached for the same piece of paper; their hands brushed in the dark, and Thea felt herself blush. She let Terry grab the offending page and reached instead for what seemed to be a pile of memos held together by a large paper clip, and, underneath them, a manila envelope with something scrawled on it in marker pen.

"He hasn't been to the office in a while. There sure is a heap of paperwork to catch up on when he gets—*oh my God*."

Terry's head snapped up. He looked first toward the closed door, then back to Thea. "What? What is it?"

Thea, still staring at the envelope in her hand, handed it over to Terry. "Look," she whispered urgently.

*Humphrey May, c/o Kay Otis.*

The names were big and black and unmistakable on the envelope. Terry stared at it, and then at the inbox he had disturbed.

"Yes?" he said, squinting at the envelope and then looking back at Thea with a blank expression. "I think I remember Rafe mention a Kay back at the professor's office. Humphrey said something about Kay being his other assistant. What are you—"

"No," Thea said, pointing to the second name. "*Look*."

Terry squinted at the name Thea's finger rested on. "*Kay Otis*. Okay."

"Rafe said 'Kay.' Just Kay. Just the first name."

"I don't . . ." Terry began again, perplexed.

Thea sighed. "Say it fast three times."

"Kay Otis, Kay Otis, Kay Otis," Terry said, giving her a strange look.

"Kayotis," Thea said. "*Kayotis*. Coyote."

"Your Trickster Coyote? In this place? Come on, that's stretching! They do background checks, you know."

"When he was Cary Wiley he didn't have any problems getting the tutor's job with Professor de los Reyes," Thea said.

"But that doesn't mean—wait, where are you going?"

Thea had gotten to her feet again, and was tapping at her wrist pad. "Terry, I was right. This settles it. Now I know I must go in and get that cube."

"Thea, wait! *Wait!* This is nuts. You can't possibly be sure—it's just a name."

"And maybe I'm wrong. And it's just a name. And nothing is lost." Thea whipped around to face him. "But if I'm not wrong. And there's a great gaping hole right here in the midst of the most secure place in the world. And the Alphiri get what they wanted to have—access to magic. And this time it would be seriously heavyweight magic. If I let it happen, then not only do I have to live with the idea of Tesla being owned by the Alphiri, but *everything I have done to Diego will have been wasted.* I'm sorry, Terry. I may be wrong, but I can't risk being right and doing nothing."

"You don't think that anyone would have noticed that name?"

"Why would they? It's just a name, like you said." She paused, lifting her head as though she was trying to catch a scent. "And if Larry de los Reyes was here, he'd probably tell you that he could smell him."

"Can you?"

Thea shook her head. "I don't work that way. But I've always been able to recognize him—now *her*—and I can sense that he's been here."

"Because you've told yourself that Kay Otis is Coyote," Terry said.

176

"Fine, don't believe me," Thea snapped. "I'm still going."

She looked down at her wrist, tapped something on her keypad, and then stepped up to the office door and laid her hand on the handle.

"Where are we going?" Terry said.

She managed a small smile. "To rescue a wizard. Come on."

The door squeaked a little as Thea drew back the deadbolt from the inside and eased it open. She stuck her head out into the well-lit corridor with a degree of carelessness that made Terry suck in his breath.

"Will you be careful?" he hissed.

"I've specified empty corridors," Thea said, lifting her keypad-braceletted arm. "There's nobody out there. It's okay."

"Don't take that for granted," Terry said. "I told you, this place—"

"Yes, I got it, I got it. I didn't vaporize everyone in this building so that we can stroll down the corridor. But at the very least, even if we do meet someone, we won't be seen. We'll probably be able to notice anyone who's coming long before they get wind of us."

"Don't get cocky," Terry said. "That's all I'm saying. You have no idea what you're up against."

"You keep saying that. Do you see anyone about?"

He followed her into the corridor, looking both ways. The place was plush—polished wooden doors with gleaming brass handles opened off a wide passage painted a serene shade of forest green and floored with deep-pile carpet. There were no overhead lights, but frequent wall sconces left no place for shadows to linger. The eerily empty corridor curved into a gentle arc on their left, and stretched out straight to their right until it reached what looked like an elevator bank at the far end.

"Which way?" Terry said.

"Down," said Thea, after the slightest of hesitations.

Terry heard it, and instantly latched on to it. "You sure? And you aren't thinking of climbing into an elevator, are you? The first rule of breaking and entering is never to get into an elevator."

"'In case of fire, use the stairs,'" Thea said.

"There may not be stairs leading to where you want to—"

"Then we'll jump into that chasm when we get to it," Thea said impatiently. "Come on, already."

She was a couple of steps down the corridor before she realized that he was not following; turning, she saw him still hesitating by the door of the office they had just left, staring at it with an expression of dismay.

"Now what?" She followed the direction of his gaze and finally realized that he was looking at the shiny brass doorknob of the door to Humphrey's office, which was still ajar. Thea realized, belatedly, what he had just thought of.

"This," Terry said, "is fingerprint heaven. And if you get what you came for, this place will raise an unholy hue and cry. They will start with the obvious—and we left a trail in that office, Thea, as blatant as we could short of sticking around and confessing."

"Shh," Thea said. "Let me think for a sec."

After a moment she stuck her right hand into her pocket and pushed the door open a little farther so that she had an unimpeded view into the room. Then she shrugged her sleeve off the keypad, and typed a few words.

*All traces of us. Weave.*

Terry, craning his neck from behind her, was trying to read over her shoulder. "What's *that* supposed to . . ."

Thea glanced at him briefly, indicating the office with a jerk of her chin. "Watch."

He turned back to the office, and sucked in his breath. In the dark room, still only barely lighted by the trace of outside lights, a glimmering golden trail had appeared—two sets of footprints on the carpet, a scrape of gold-glint on the side of the desk where Thea had brushed against it, gold on the handle of the Venetian blinds she had turned to let in whatever light she could, spatters of gold on papers in the inbox. Thea waited a few breaths to make sure that everything had showed, and then *reached* into the office with her hand.

The gold streamed toward her fingers in ribbons, spooling off whatever surface it had managed to settle on. Thea wrapped her right hand around the ribbons of light, braiding them into a thin golden strand and coiling the strand in her palm as she wove, reaching for every speck of it that showed, from desktop, window, floor, doorknob. When she was done, she glanced at the supple length of bright gold braid in her hand and then closed her fingers around it and held it out to Terry.

"No fingerprints," she said. "Here. You take this."

"That was *cool*."

"That was the first thing I really figured out I

could do," Thea said. "Back with Cheveyo."

"Yeah, but . . . are you going to be sweeping up each footstep as we make it? That would be a royal pain." He was staring past the gold thread in his palm at the traces of gold footsteps that had also glimmered into existence just outside the office door, on the deep plush carpet of the corridor.

Thea rubbed her temples. "We'd need to walk on air for that not to show," she said morosely. And then her head lifted sharply, as though something wholly unexpected had suddenly occurred to her.

"What?" Terry said, stuffing the gold braid into his pocket.

"What size shoes do you wear?" Thea asked.

"Eh? Ten, but what . . . ?"

"Lift up your foot," she instructed.

Mystified, he obeyed, lifting his right foot off the ground. A gold size-ten footprint glowed where it had just been.

Thea hesitated before she typed the next thing into her keypad, then reached out with her hand, gathering the stuff she needed into her fingers.

*Size ten air cushion under right shoe.*

"Other foot. Be careful when you put your weight on the right."

He had wobbled a little even as she said that. "Weird," he said. "What are you doing?"

*Size ten air cushion under left shoe.*

"Try walking."

Terry took a couple of wobbly steps. "Feels like gel soles, actually," he said. "What did you—Hey. *Hey!* I'm not leaving tracks anymore!"

Thea looked at him, her expression equal parts astonishment and exultation. "I just wove air," she said. "You're wearing air overshoes—you're literally walking on air. *Their* air, the air that was already here. Nothing that we brought in. We'll be touching nothing now—leaving no trail. Why are you looking at me like that?"

"He was right," Terry said slowly. "Humphrey."

Thea had turned to close the door of the office, hand muffled in her pocket again. "Right about what?"

"You," Terry said, and then hesitated. "Is it safe to talk?"

Thea, in the process of creating her own air-shoes, paused in her typing, glanced up at him, and typed in a few extra words. "Is now," she said. "I probably should have done that first, before I did anything else at all."

"You *are* an Elemental," Terry said, with a grin so wide that it threatened to split his face in half. "For real. *You just wove air.* Not light. Not color. Air. You change the world around you. No wonder you 'know' that nobody will see us, even if we do run into an entire company of security—you're hiding behind air. This is *wild*. You know, I'm beginning to think you can actually do this crazy thing—come right into the FBM headquarters and walk out again with nobody knowing you were here."

"*Beginning* to?" Thea said, grinning.

"I still think you're overreacting. Sometimes a Miss Otis is just a Miss Otis."

Thea's grin disappeared. "Nuh-uh," she said. "I'm not wrong about that. Come on, let's go."

Careful now, they pushed open the doorway to the stairwell with a cushion of air between Thea's hand and the surface of anything she reached out to touch. They started down what seemed to be an unremarkable flight of stairs, bare concrete with institutional metal railings on the side. At first glance, Thea saw nothing strange about the middle of the stairwell except that it seemed to go down an awfully long way, but she kept glancing over the railing, frowning.

"Something's not right," she muttered. "It feels as though it's . . . backdrop. Scenery. Something we'd expect to see."

"What were you expecting?"

Her own words of only a few minutes before flashed back into Thea's mind just as she stepped off a level step and found . . . nothing.

*We'll jump into that chasm when we get to it.*

She caught herself on the railing by the crook of her elbow, did a graceful swing around, and scrambled back up the solid stairs where she had just stood, narrowly missing Terry, who was only a step behind her. They both teetered for a moment, then they steadied each other, and Terry turned to stare at her.

"What on earth . . . ?" he said, sounding aggrieved.

"There's nothing there. Nothing underfoot. I told you it looked wrong. It's just illusion."

"So what *is* there?"

Thea stared at the stair she had just tried to stand on. "It looks solid enough," she said, uncertain.

"It's in the way you look at it. It's a common trick. They just . . . find what's in your head, and continue it. *Stop thinking about stairs.*"

That was about as easy as being told not to think about elephants while standing at the elephant enclosure at the zoo. Stairs were all around them; they were in the stairwell of an office building. Thea could suddenly find nothing else *except* stairs in her mind. But she resolutely focused on something else—something completely unexpected.

The Walrus's teeth.

She couldn't help a small chuckle. When she looked again, what lay at her feet was no longer the FBM back stairs—it was a large, cavernlike space, with stairs coming in and out of it at crazy angles, some in a plane that was sideways to the one she was on, some frankly upside down.

"Whoa," Terry said. "What are we supposed to do? Pick a direction, any direction? It's like that Escher drawing they use in Ars Magica to teach improbability spells."

"I feel dizzy," said Thea, staring at the puzzle space before her. "It feels like I'm standing sideways."

"*That's* sideways. We're straight. We just came straight down."

"No," Thea said, with dawning comprehension. "We're *sideways*. And if we can figure out which way is really down, that's the way the safe is."

The stairs on which they had been descending now appeared to end only a couple of treads behind them, giving them no clues. Doorways opened off other stairs at crazy angles, leaving Thea's head swimming every time she tried to orient herself.

"There *is* no up or down," Terry muttered. "It's *all* sideways."

"What's that?" Thea said suddenly, pointing to a dark object lying in the middle of one of the landings at right angles to them, apparently held on by Velcro.

Terry squinted at where she pointed.

"I have no clue," he said. "It might be a feather. But then again, I have absolutely no idea how far that thing is from us. It might be a locomotive."

"A black feather," Thea said thoughtfully.

"I said it *might* be," Terry said. "What's the matter?"

"Raven feathers," Thea said. "Corey and I have a history with raven feathers."

Terry transferred his attention back to the object on the landing. "You think that way's down?" And then he hesitated. "But this is your Trickster spirit, no? So he might think that you wouldn't trust a hint, and that you'd go in the opposite direction, and go the wrong way. Or he might think that you might think that, and that feather's the right way after all. Or—"

"Stop, you're making me dizzier than the stairs," Thea said. "But are you starting to come around to the idea that there *is* a Trickster involved?"

He glared at her. "That's not fair."

"I think we'll go that way," Thea said, coming to a decision.

"You sure— *Heeey!*" Terry yelped as she suddenly bent her knees and leaped off the landing they were standing on, sailing straight across the empty space in the middle of the whole puzzle and coming to rest in a half crouch on the landing they had been looking at.

Now that Thea was there, the perspective was quite different; it didn't seem that far away. "It's this way," she said, bending to pick up the feather at her feet and running it through the fingers of her other hand. "Come on, jump."

"This gets worse at every turn," Terry muttered. He took a couple of running steps and leaped across to where Thea waited.

"Feel better now?" Thea said. "See, it is this way. Come on."

The stairs led down from the landing, and then took a sharp right under an archway, vanishing behind it. When Thea and Terry arrived at the archway and stepped through, there was a brief buzzing sound behind them—and when they turned to look back, they found nothing but a dirty whitewashed wall.

"Whatever," Terry said. "We're here now. There seems to be no going back."

"We're fine," Thea said, pointing with her feather. "Look there."

In front of them, a short stretch of linoleum-lined corridor away, stood a set of heavy oak double doors. They were closed, with no less than three heavy brass bolts, all locked down with large, old-fashioned padlocks.

"Okay," Terry said carefully. "I don't suppose you've got a key for that?"

"I told you," Thea said. "No keys are needed."

She was typing on her keypad as she spoke, and Terry suddenly realized that the double doors were at his back.

Open.

With another set in front of him. This time steel. Thea grinned and typed some more.

And then the steel doors were open behind them. And something that looked like a veil of pure energy rose ahead, crackling like high-voltage electricity and arcing tiny blue-white lightning.

"Ooh, that's actually pretty," Thea said, typing into her keypad. "Tesla would have liked that one."

And then they were past. The open maw of a great dragon faced them instead, its glistening, foot-long sharp teeth surrounding an entrance into what looked like the back of a throat.

Terry wrinkled his nose. "They didn't have to be quite so realistic," he muttered. "That thing is suffering from a thousand years of untreated halitosis."

"Hold your nose," Thea said, flashing him a quick grin. "And down the gullet we go . . ."

And then, with startling suddenness, the entire corridor appeared to end abruptly, with nothing in front of them except stars and faraway galaxies glowing dimly and double-spiraling in the distance.

"Thea," Terry said, standing on the edge of this vista and staring at it with wide eyes, "*how are you doing this?*"

"There is nothing in front of me," Thea said, "but air."

"This cube could not be safer if it was on Mars," Terry said. "Only you can get this far. You're using Elemental magic. How many people can claim to—"

"If someone has a key—a *real* key, be it iron or just spoken word—nothing stands between them and the cube," Thea said. "I'm not trying to hide it from the people trying to break the system, Terry. I'm protecting it from someone already *in* the system."

"But what if . . ."

Thea lifted the feather she still held in her right hand. "I know," she said. "There's the name. There's this."

Terry looked at yet another barrier looming before them. "How many of these . . ."

"As many as they thought they needed," Thea said. "I think it's geared to how good you are at getting past them. Without a key, that is. At seeing past the illusions. Or weaving past them."

"So the better you are at that, the more they fling at you?" Terry said, appalled. "We could be here until we die of old age!"

"Uh, no," Thea said, smiling at something ahead of them. "I don't think so."

They were standing before a narrow door, its top half paned into nine squares of dirty glass, peeling paint hanging in pitiful strips from the stained and cracked wood beneath. A spiderweb hung from the corner of one of the glass panes to the edge of the lintel, and a small mound of dust and debris was piled up against the door at the bottom.

"Looks like that hasn't been opened for twenty years," Terry said.

"I know," Thea said. "This is the only real one. The only one for which I *don't* have a key."

"All this way and you can't open it?" Terry said. "Now might be a time to try some more of that Elemental—"

"*That*," Thea said, "I don't know how I would hide from anyone. If this was opened by Elemental magic—by any sort of real magic—it would be better than a fingerprint, I suspect."

"So what, then . . . *Wait* a minute."

"What?"

"Something my mother said. 'You only need a key

if you believe that there is something worth locking away.'"

"Um, yes," Thea said, and then her own expression changed. "Oh, my," she said. "Mrs. Chen said the same thing, really, last year—the best place to hide something is usually in plain sight."

Their eyes met, in sudden comprehension.

"The only people the FBM would expect to get this far," Terry said, "would already have permission to enter. Anyone else would have dropped by the wayside, and would probably still be throwing up somewhere at the memory of that dragon breath. It's the illusion gates that are the key to this place."

"And this door?"

"This door isn't locked at all," Terry said. He shook down a bit more sleeve, enough to cover his hand, and touched the handle. At Terry's light tap it swung open, creaking just a little; the pile of dirt and the cobweb remained unaffected, leaning disconcertingly against nothing and attached to some point in thin air.

"Wow," Terry said, hesitating. "I wouldn't have believed . . ."

"You still sure that it would be safer here than

anywhere?" Thea slipped into the room behind the ancient door, carefully kicking it open a little wider with her air-booted foot.

The place was much larger than it had any right to be, stretching away into deep shadows in the back, with shelves upon shelves of boxes and scrolls and books, and an entire wall covered by a bank of computer monitors, currently switched off.

"This is amazing," Terry breathed, following her in and staring around.

Thea was typing something into her keypad, and as though in response, a small pale glow occurred somewhere far back in the stacks of shelves.

"That way," Thea said, pointing. As they approached the glow, they saw that it was emanating from a closed briefcase, suffused in a kind of dull white light.

Thea reached out for the briefcase; the light wound itself around her arm like a tentacle, wrapped itself around her shoulders, and hovered around her hair and face, eerily lighting up her features. With the briefcase in one hand, she reached out with the other and gently laid the raven feather she still carried into the space that the briefcase had occupied. Then she looked up at Terry, her face wreathed in pale light.

"One last stop," she said, "before we go back."

And the shadowy safe, the deepest repository of all the secrets of the Federal Bureau of Magic, sank into utter darkness around them.

## 9.

"I SHOULD HAVE FIGURED," TERRY said, after a moment of silence.

He stood beside Thea on the flat, hard ground that was the Barefoot Road. They had materialized at the foot of the mesa that held Cheveyo's home; it glowed russet and dark gold in the honey-colored light cast by a sun low in the sky, hurrying toward sunset. From somewhere far away the cry of a hunting raptor came echoing out of the open sky. Except for the bird, they appeared to be alone. There was no other sign of life stirring in Cheveyo's abode.

Thea shifted her grip on the briefcase. There was nothing extraordinary about it now, nothing to point to the treasure it contained. It had ceased to be luminous, or at least its pale white glow had faded into insignificance in the presence of Tawaha, the sun god who had once taken human form in these lands to speak to Thea.

"You planning on leaving the cube here?" Terry asked.

"It will be safe with Cheveyo," Thea said. "At the very least, nobody will be looking for it here."

"Uh," Terry said, "the moment they figure out who took it, this is the *first* place they will look. And isn't this where your Coyote friend actually lives?"

"But with any luck they won't figure out who took it," Thea said. "And besides, Coyote is watched here. Grandmother Spider and Tawaha said they would watch him."

"They might have meant anywhere. That includes our own world."

"Yes, but they have *real* power here," Thea said stubbornly.

"Are you sure Cheveyo will take this thing?" Terry asked. "Did you actually *ask* him?"

"He always said I ask too many questions," Thea said.

But she had hesitated a moment too long before she answered, and Terry picked up on it immediately.

"You're still making this up as you go along," he said. "Asking why the sky is blue is a question.

Wanting to know if he'll take on babysitting duties on a cube-bound wizard who's technically been dead for fifty years is hardly the same thing. What are you going to do if Cheveyo says no?"

"You return, Catori."

Cheveyo's voice, coming from above and behind them, made both Terry and Thea turn sharply to look. Terry, who knew enough about the properties of the Barefoot Road to be aware that the fact that he was standing upon it with shoes still on his feet was blessing enough, stayed where he was. He looked back over his shoulder to where Cheveyo stood beside a rocky outcrop, leaning on his staff. Thea, not constrained by any such considerations, had turned and already taken a step toward her old teacher.

"I come to ask a favor," she said. She thought she could hold his eyes, but under his shrewd, penetrating gaze, she dropped her own, suddenly uneasy.

"And so once again you come to my world with a burden that you carry," Cheveyo said softly.

"This time, it isn't just my own," Thea said. She hefted the briefcase. "There is something, some*one*, in here who needs protection. Perhaps just for a little while, maybe for longer; I don't know. But the place I took this from wasn't safe. If the Trickster has found a way to slip past the defenses . . . well, I did not want this falling in the wrong hands."

"And what do you say, friend of Catori?" Cheveyo said, turning his eyes on Terry.

"There are some things of which Thea seems certain," Terry said. "But they are not the sort of things it is possible to prove beyond any doubt—not to me. Not to anyone in our world, I guess. At least not yet." He paused, and Thea could feel his eyes resting on her. "But I trust her instinct," Terry said at last, making his choice, betting on Thea and friendship and gut feeling rather than pure logic and cold hard fact.

Thea, suddenly aware that she had been holding her breath, allowed it to escape with a small sigh and threw Terry a quick, grateful look. Then she turned to face Cheveyo again.

"When you first came to me, Catori, you came bearing nothing but that instinct," Cheveyo said slowly. "You had no way of knowing that it had been by your own choice that you were deprived of magic in your world, where magic matters so much. But you had your instincts, and your instincts were true—it was a time to hide rather than to reveal. Here, you could be protected. It was a place of awakening . . . but it was also a place to hide."

"They think they have figured her out at last, in our world," Terry said. "She isn't hiding anymore."

Cheveyo shook his head slowly. "True, but not completely true," he said. "That light you have glimpsed—it's something that escaped through the cracks. You are still locked away in your tower, Catori—the things you have done, you did in secret. Only a handful of people know of this; you are still hiding. And you cannot hide forever, least of all here." His eyes were luminous with a dark fire, a fire that was vision and dream and certainty and wisdom. "I will do this thing that you ask of me, for a short while. If you would protect something or someone dear to you in your own world, it will soon have to be your own power that does it—and that choice is coming for you, in a nearness of days. But until then, I will hold your treasure. And I will keep it safe."

Thea held out the briefcase without another word, and Cheveyo reached out and took it.

"Thank you," Thea said. She had run through a dozen phrases expressing her profound gratitude in her mind, but in the end nothing but simplicity would do.

Cheveyo, one hand holding the briefcase, lifted

his staff with the other in a gesture that was both blessing and dismissal. "Go, and pursue what destiny the Road takes you to," he said. "I will be here when you return."

Thea bowed her head in respectful acknowledgment, and turned back to Terry.

"Time we were getting back," she said, giving him a small smile as she lifted her wrist and tapped at her keyboard.

"I thought you didn't need that here, that the Road—"

They were back in the Nexus room, very suddenly, the mesas and the sunset and Cheveyo's dark eyes just fragments of a dream.

Terry shook his head sharply.

"Anyone ever tell you that you're weird?" he said. "How long have we been gone, anyway? It's always hard to tell, in here."

"Twenty-seven seconds," Thea said.

"What? But you . . . we couldn't . . ." Terry leaned over and stared in disbelief at the computer clock at the bottom of one of his monitors. *"How?"*

"We couldn't very well have come back tomorrow midafternoon," Thea said. "People would have wondered."

"Sometimes you really scare me," Terry said. "Thea, are you absolutely sure about all this?"

"You said you trusted my instincts."

"I do, but it all feels like an insane dream right now, and I'm not certain that I believe any of it actually happened. Exactly what do you want to do next?"

"Absolutely nothing, until I figure out what I already did," Thea said.

Terry stared at her for several long moments with his mouth hanging open, and then shook his head sharply. "I suppose you'll let me in on the secret, when you do."

"You'll be the first to know," she promised with a grin. "I'd better get back to my room now. It's been a long night."

"Yeah," Terry said. "All twenty-seven seconds of it."

She smiled. "I'll see you tomorrow," she said, and tapped ENTER.

Magpie wasn't in the room when Thea materialized there. Thea was grateful; there was far too much she needed to think about.

Thea slipped into bed with one of her Tesla books, and was quickly absorbed. Pigeons had played an increasingly essential part in Tesla's later life; when he could not make his daily feeding time in one of New York's parks, he sent other people to take his place. Tesla once disappeared from a formal dinner at which he had been the guest of honor, and was found a short time later in his favorite park, late at night, standing quite still, completely covered with pigeons, who had settled on his head and shoulders and outstretched arms.

It was an arresting image. Unable to read much past that point, Thea put the book away; it was very near to lights-out, anyway. Magpie still hadn't returned, and Thea lay awake for a while, but she fell asleep before she saw any signs of Magpie's return.

Her dreams were full of a rush of wings, glimpses of gray pigeon feathers, and the sound of distant cooing. At one point she stood in a rain of feathers, all gray and silver-pale except for one that was black as night and twice the size of the pigeon plumage, falling like an omen, a dark premonition. But there was nothing coherent in those dreams, nothing that she could have interpreted as a message of any significance. She woke suddenly, with a start. The only thing that remained was an odd sense of anticipation, and a fading memory of the rustle of many wings.

Magpie was in her bed, grumbling and knuckling her eyes. They were both late and didn't exchange more than a couple of words in passing.

It was one of those breathless days when Thea felt she was running as fast as she could just to stay in the same place. She simply seemed to be late for everything. Classes backed up and stacked up on top of one another, the few spare moments between them spent juggling books and notes and homework assignments and running down corridors with her backpack bouncing painfully against her legs as she rummaged through it for the things that she would need for the next class.

Somewhere during the third class of the day, mathematics, Ben passed a note to Thea while Mr. Siffer had his back turned for a moment.

*Can you tell the Walrus to quit making faces at you? People are starting to wonder.*

Thea looked up, startled, and looked around for Kristin. Ben was quite correct; her face was a mask of blazing curiosity, and her eyes glittered. She brightened as she realized she finally had Thea's attention, and mouthed something like, *Well?*

Thea, glancing at Mr. Siffer, who was starting to

turn, managed a swift and unequivocal gesture of drawing her index finger across her throat accompanied by a suitably ferocious scowl. *Cut it out. Not now!*

Mr. Siffer turned fully around, sweeping the class with a gimlet gaze, and Thea dropped her eyes and stared studiously at her notebook. But the escape was only temporary. After class, Kristin stuffed her books untidily into her backpack and made a beeline for Thea's corner.

"*Well?*" Kristin asked breathlessly.

"Not now," Thea said, glancing meaningfully at the other students. "You know I can't."

Kristin eyed Thea's wrist hopefully. "You could . . ."

"No. *Later,* Kristin!"

"That exciting, was it?" Kristin said with a grin.

"All right, what did you *do?*" Ben demanded, leaning across his own desk.

"Terry didn't tell you?" Thea asked carefully.

Ben's shoulders hunched up defensively. "Tell me what?"

Thea rolled her eyes. "Look," she said, "I promise I'll catch you up, but first I need to figure out a few things myself. I'm not holding out, and I'm not going to simply disappear, so you can stop watching me like a cat at a mouse hole, Kristin, because right now I'd rather everyone's attention was focused somewhere *else*."

"Yes, well, it was my idea," Kristin said.

"And full credit will be given, if you absolutely insist," Thea shot back. "But wouldn't you rather wait and see just how much trouble you'd be in?" She hoisted her backpack on one shoulder and turned to give Ben and Kristin one last indignant look before flouncing out of the classroom.

"Is she always that snippy?" she heard Kristin ask.

"Not before *you* turned up," said Ben.

But they both backed off, and she had a breather, a space in which she simply sat back and waited to see what would happen next. She *had* been winging it, as Terry had pointed out, and she had finally run out of impulses, waiting to see what the response would be to the things she had set in motion.

Nearly forty-eight hours later, crossing the quad on her way to the library, she saw Terry hurrying toward her across the lawn, waving urgently. Even as she slowed her pace, she saw his expression change to one of resignation, and another familiar voice spoke behind Thea.

"Ah, good," Humphrey May said. "Just the two people I wanted to talk to."

There had been no warning that Humphrey May was at the school, or on his way—no time for Thea and Terry to get their stories straight.

"I had hoped," Humphrey continued pleasantly as Terry reached them, "to just let you two get on with trigonometry and Shakespeare for a while, but I need to pick your brains."

He was smiling slightly, professionally, but the smile never reached his serious blue eyes. Thea stole a quick glance at Terry. Humphrey sounded as though he was simply there for a pleasant chat, not to confront them over breaking and entering. On the other hand, there was something to be said for avoiding a scene, and they had no way of knowing if FBM agents were waiting just out of sight to take them both in.

"What's up?" Thea asked. She managed to keep her voice level, but her heart was beating very fast and a flush was creeping into her cheeks.

"It seems," Humphrey began, almost unwillingly, "that somehow it was let slip that . . ." He looked Thea straight in the eye. "You'd better make sure we aren't overheard," he said, nodding at her keypad. "I could shield us, but in this place that would reveal rather than conceal if anyone was watching."

Thea obligingly tapped a couple of words into her keypad, hit ENTER, and looked up again without saying a word.

"I think we're in trouble. Again." Humphrey hesitated once more, and when he spoke again it was to utter a name that Thea had not been expecting—or at least not so soon. "The Alphiri," he said.

Thea felt the familiar sinking sensation in the pit of her stomach. "What about them?"

"Let me just say that I appear to have a somewhat loose-lipped assistant," Humphrey said, with a touch of acid. "One who has a weakness for a pretty face, at any rate. Rafe was there when we talked of . . . of what you and your friends had come to the professor's house to help out with. Mention was made of pigeons. Rafe was mightily amused at the idea of hunting down individual birds in New York City. He mentioned something along those lines to my other intern, a comely young woman by the name of Kay Otis. Next thing we know, Miss Otis has vanished. And as of yesterday . . . the Alphiri have been observed stalking pigeons in New York."

Thea stared at Humphrey, trying to imagine the Alphiri chasing down birds in the streets of New York. The image was ludicrous. But then she thought of the ramifications of the whole idea, and any notion of humor vanished.

"If they have figured out the same thing that *you* figured out, through Rafe's ill-advised confidence in Miss Otis, we might have lost this race already," Humphrey said. "Something was discovered back at Headquarters in the wake of Miss Otis's disappearance, something that hints pretty strongly that some of your old friends are involved here—the Faele, perhaps, and even the Trickster himself. Your Coyote spirit. The same one who turned up last summer as young Beltran de los Reyes's tutor. The same one who was involved in Diego's bargain with the Alphiri."

Thea flinched at the name. Terry saw it, and bit his lip; Humphrey did, too, and reached out and laid a hand on her shoulder.

"I'm sorry," he said. "We—*I*—gave you a heavy burden to bear in that matter. But Diego, however powerful he might potentially have been, was an untrained and ignorant child. If the Alphiri can actually harness Tesla himself—the only quad-Elemental in history—we are in trouble so deep that even I am not sure where it all might lead. Thea . . . we need your help, once more."

"The pigeons are his magic," Thea said. "His Elemental side. Without that power restored to him, he is not what the Alphiri seek. But he himself took that out of himself. Can that Elemental magic be restored? Is it even possible?"

"It's Elemental magic," Humphrey said. "You'd know more about the fine detail of that, even now, than I do. But with Elemental magic, everything is theoretically *possible*, even though a high price might be demanded for some things to occur."

"We need to find the pigeons," Thea said. "Before the Alphiri do."

Humphrey appeared to be on the verge of saying something else, but then apparently reconsidered. "But they're *pigeons*," he said. "Let's say they are truly Elemental in nature and not subject to the lifespan of an ordinary bird, and that they are still around. From what you've told me of your own vision of them, they still don't *look* any different from any ordinary bird out there. Rafe might have been a reckless fool here, but he does have a point— chasing pigeons in New York borders on lunacy.

And we have no way of knowing if there is even anything to find."

Almost a year had passed since Thea had rescued Humphrey from the lonely place he had allowed a spellspam to trap him into. He had been anxious back then, uneasy, concerned—but not frightened. This time, he was afraid.

"I've been working on some of the equations you left with me," Terry said suddenly, filling the gap of silence. "I think maybe I've found a few useful things. Can you give me another twenty-four hours?"

Humphrey hesitated. "If need be," he said at last. "But please understand—if there *is* something there that can be useful, you'd better find it before the Alphiri do. Time is of the essence here."

Thea's heart thumped painfully again. He hadn't mentioned the cube, but this might imply that he was waiting for them to own up, that it might go easier with them if they would simply step up and make a full confession. . . .

Terry cleared his throat and Thea drew a deep breath. She looked away, aware that she had been almost mesmerized, her mind snared by the myriad unpleasant possibilities.

"Are you going to be staying at the Academy for

a day or so? Or do you have to get back to the problem?" Terry said.

The question seemed almost artless, but Humphrey answered it.

"I'll be here for another day. If that's what it takes," he said.

Thea glanced at the two of them, and then at her wrist pad. Touching the ENTER key brought them back to the quad, with other people hurrying by. It was starting to look like it would rain again.

"I'll be in touch," Humphrey said, and turned away to stride across the quad in the direction of the administration building.

"He's afraid," Terry said softly, watching the FBM mage's retreating lanky frame. "It might have been Rafe who spilled the beans, but *both* of the people involved in this fiasco report directly to Humphrey. He's the one ultimately responsible. He took his eye off the ball back at the office, watching you, and now he's painted into a corner."

Someone was calling Terry's name, and he turned his head to see his sister running across the quad toward him. Trailing in Tess's wake, dragging her feet but with her eyes alight with unwilling interest, came Magpie.

"What did he want?" Tess asked breathlessly as she reached them. "What's he doing back here?"

Even as Terry opened his mouth to answer, another voice came from behind Thea.

"All right, *now* can you talk about it?" Kristin, trailed by a furious-looking Ben, was standing only a few feet away.

"What, are you two following me now?" Thea said, a little sharply.

"Not exactly, but I *was* going over to the library. I saw you heading there, and I thought maybe we could, you know, talk about stuff." Kristin shut up abruptly, suddenly going red, aware that everyone's eyes were on her. "Well, all right," she said, suddenly defensive, "I'm curious. So sue me."

Thea rolled her eyes.

"All *right*, since everyone's here, come on, then, all of you."

A quick tap on the ENTER key shifted the world around them for the second time in a handful of minutes. The air was suddenly a little warmer, and the school grounds around them were noticeably emptier than they had been moments ago.

Thea rounded on Terry. "Terry, what's going on?" she said, letting her wrist drop. "You look like you already know what Humphrey is here about. But it can't be that—they can't have found out anything already . . ."

"You *did* steal it, after all!" Kristin said. "Didn't you?"

Ben glared at her. "Haven't you done enough damage?" Kristin just shrugged, and Ben turned his attention back to Terry and Thea. "You didn't, did you? Tell me you didn't listen to her! I *told* you that was a preposterous idea."

"You'd be right," Terry said. He quirked an eyebrow at Thea, and received a nod in response. "We did go in."

Ben did a horrified double take. "*We?*" he said. "You actually went *with* her? Have you both gone crazy?"

"Well, it was that or blowing the whistle on the whole thing. I was hardly likely to let her go in alone."

"They got you, didn't they?" Ben said. "That's why Humphrey's here, isn't he? How much trouble *are* you in?"

Terry glanced at Thea again. "It isn't public, and that's only to be expected—they would never admit that someone waltzed in and out of their highest-security area at the Bureau headquarters," he said. "But I stayed behind at the Nexus after you left, just to keep an eye on things for a little while. By the time I went to bed, everything was still quiet. And there's been very little chitchat over the last day or so. But when I checked this morning . . ." He shook his head. "Nothing firm, nothing that can be nailed down, or actually pinned on anyone. But there was a definite sense of a hornet's nest being upset when I got back to the computer this morning. And one name kept popping up."

"Thea's?" Ben asked, appalled.

Terry shook his head. "A certain Miss Kay Otis," he said, very quietly. "Apparently she's gone missing in a very strange way. And so has a very important artifact."

"What did you do with it?" Kristin asked.

"With *what*?" Magpie asked, head swiveling from one to another as she tried to make sense of what was being discussed. "What are you all talking about?"

"They took the cube," Tess said faintly. "They actually walked into the Federal Bureau of Magic headquarters and stole the Tesla cube."

"Why?" Magpie said blankly.

"Because *she* thought it was a good idea," Ben growled, tossing his head in Kristin's direction.

"Not that I know much about it," Magpie said, "but even given that someone might have thought it was a good idea . . . *how*? It isn't like you can just wander into the heart of the FBM—"

"So who's this Kay Otis person, then?" Kristin interrupted.

"Actually, that name sounds awfully familiar," Magpie said, frowning. "Have we met her?"

"Kay Otis. Kayotis. Coyote," Terry said. "Thea says that it's the Trickster himself."

"In the midst of the FBM? You can't be serious! Do they have any idea?"

"Do they think *she* took the cube?"

"How did they ever let her in there?"

"Didn't they realize—"

"Everybody just shut up a sec and let me think," Thea said, exasperated. "What about Kay Otis, Terry? How do you mean, 'gone missing in a very strange way'?"

"Don't know, exactly. What information I have right now is sketchy at best."

"I don't understand, I really don't, how you two weren't nabbed in the first five seconds that you were there," said Ben grimly.

"They didn't *nab* us because she really is what Humphrey said she is," Terry said with a sudden grin. "If anyone else had tried to waltz in there, I swear it would have been alarms all the way. She just made the place . . . forget us."

"An Elemental," Tess said.

"Do you think that the place might have remembered you, just a *little*, after all?" Ben said. "If they *do* know it was you, Thea—if they have any idea what you two idiots did last night, you'll be lucky if it ends with you just being kicked out of school and not in court."

"Isn't he always the bright ray of sunshine," Kristin said.

"This is all your fault," Ben said, rounding on her. "You and your brilliant idea."

"Actually, if Kay Otis *is* the Trickster, I'm awfully glad she had the idea," Thea said. "We'd better get back. I'm guessing there's one person at the Academy right now who knows what's going on."

"Humphrey wasn't saying very much, if you mean him," Terry said thoughtfully. "But I think he screwed up. He was too focused on you, and trusted this Rafe fellow far too freely with what was going on back at Headquarters in Humphrey's absence. When Rafe screwed up, so did Humphrey, simply because he's Rafe's boss. But he came out here to find things out, not tell us what he knows. If he knew that we . . . that Thea took that cube, he would be out here with guns blazing. But he didn't come to demand, he came to *ask*. That was as much humility as I've ever seen in a senior FBM mage."

"How would you know?" Kristin asked.

Tess couldn't help a quick grin. "Family business," she said. "We've been around the FBM type all our lives. Starting with Mom and Uncle Kevin, and all the interns that come marching through the house beginning to cultivate the proper aura of arrogance and an air of invincible righteousness. You don't get far in the system without those—you have to think you're always right, or you can't expect anyone else to believe that you are."

"I know," Terry said, flashing a smile almost identical to his sister's. "Thea, I think this is a negotiation, and you've got the upper hand right now. Humphrey badly needs a victory, and really quickly, too. I think he'll be willing to give you almost anything you ask if you can guarantee one for him. For all he knows the Alphiri already have the cube, and all that's missing from the equation is the pigeons."

"Where *is* the cube, then, exactly?" Tess said.

"Safe," Thea said, "for now." She lifted her wrist, poising her left hand above her keypad. "Ready?"

They were suddenly back in the real world; the temperature had dropped a couple of degrees, and it had started to rain. Magpie flipped up the hood on her sweatshirt, and all of them scurried for cover.

"You think anyone saw us?" Thea said, scanning the grounds.

"This is so cool," Kristin said, grinning from ear to ear with those preposterous teeth on full display, hugging her elbows with glee. "I don't think anyone was paying attention, Thea, but if they were, they're probably thinking they're working way too hard and have gone off to have a nap."

Ben stared at her. "This isn't a game," he said.

Kristin turned to stare at him for a long moment. The ghost of a smile still hovered around her lips, but her eyes had gone serious.

"I know," she said.

"If anything does come down on Terry and Thea, it's all your fault," Ben said. "If you hadn't been so—"

"Cut it out, guys," Thea said. "Well, I suppose I'd

better go find Humphrey."

"I asked him to give us a day," Terry said. "You sure? You can make him sweat over this, just a little."

"No, I'd rather get it over with. I have an idea."

"You want me to come with you?" Terry asked.

"You want us all to come?" Magpie said unexpectedly.

"I'm hardly likely to be expelled or deported from this place on the spot, even if he *does* have a clear idea of what happened. But if he doesn't know anything, there's no point in putting anybody else in the cross fire just yet."

Terry was staring thoughtfully at the keypad on Thea's wrist. "Does that thing do e-mail?"

"I have no idea," Thea said. "I've never really tried it. Why?"

"Because, now that I think of it, you might need help at some point, and it would be a good thing if you were able to send out a Mayday message. But it might be set up so that it can communicate with only one outside port—Humphrey. And it wouldn't be hard for him to keep tabs on you, if it is."

Thea lifted her head sharply. "You think Humphrey knows where I go? When I do use it?"

"If he does, then he already knows everything, and then some," Ben said.

"Not necessarily. Thea, you write in your own shorthand when you do this stuff—things that mean something to *you*, and will take you to a place that only *you* know the precise details of. It isn't like you're writing in an exact set of directions. So even if he can keep track of your keystrokes, he still might not know where whatever it is that you've written down will take you. But all the same . . . you'd better use that thing very carefully."

Thea squared her shoulders. "Humphrey May knows what he knows," she said. "Let me go and find out just how much."

"How do you know where he is?" Ben asked.

"He wants to be found," Terry said. "He'll put himself in your way."

"He went toward the admin building," Kristin said helpfully, pointing.

"I noticed," Thea said. "Thanks. I'll get back to you guys." She caught Terry's eye once again, hesitating just a little. "Terry, about Humphrey . . . Are you sure . . . ?"

"We are," Tess said.

It had started to rain more heavily, and now Thea

flipped the collar of her light jacket up about her ears and dashed out onto the wet grounds, racing through puddles as she ran. It took her only a few minutes to get to the administration building, but her hair was plastered across her face by the time she got there, and she paused for a moment to push it out of her eyes.

"Oh dear," said a contrite but humorous voice behind her. "You didn't have to get *soaked*."

Thea pushed the wet hair behind her ears, shrugged down her damp collar, and turned around. "It's only water," she said. "Were you waiting for me?"

"I guess I was," Humphrey said.

Thea drew a deep breath. She was about to call his bluff, to throw down the gauntlet to a fully fledged, trained mage of the Federal Bureau of Magic, all on the word of a friend. But Terry had trusted *her* when it mattered. It was time to return the favor.

"If we aren't certain that those birds of yours can be . . . rejoined, then we can just sit back and watch the Alphiri chasing pigeons in the park, and laugh about it," Thea said. "The only person likely to have any kind of certain knowledge about this would be Tesla himself. Why don't you let me, or *us*, go back and ask him?"

For a moment she thought she had overplayed her hand, because his expression darkened into a thunderous scowl—and then the scowl vanished, and what was left was exactly what Terry had predicted would be there. Helplessness. A sense of vulnerability that bordered on outright fear.

"We . . . can't. The cube . . . I didn't quite tell you the whole story. The truth is, *they* might already have it."

It took Thea a moment to parse this, and when she did it was with genuine surprise. "You think the *Alphiri* have the cube?"

He really hadn't come to the Academy to ream Thea out for breaking into the FBM headquarters. Part of her was simply relieved; another part was slowly coming to realize that the foray into the FBM, and the theft of Tesla's cube, had been something quite different from anything she had done before. It had been a conscious, planned defiance of all the accepted rules. And she had done this under the very noses of the Federal Bureau of Magic, the highest authority in the land, and had done it without being detected.

"We don't know where the actual artifact is, right now," Humphrey said, the words all but wrung out of him.

Thea stared at him for a long moment.

"I can get your pigeons," she said at last.

Humphrey shot her a startled look. "But we don't know, not for certain, that the birds are even—"

"We do. *You* do. And if the Alphiri are out there looking, then *they* know it too. If the pigeons are out there, we can get them."

She had spoken with confidence. Something had shifted; they had suddenly been transformed from mentor and trainee into something approaching equals.

Thea could see Humphrey become aware of this; he looked surprised by it, and not entirely in a pleasant way.

"What makes you so sure?" Humphrey said after a moment, his voice suddenly darker and lower.

Thea looked at him steadily. "Because," she said, "I have a Finder."

"A Finder?" Humphrey echoed. "One of you five is a Finder?"

"No. Another."

"Someone . . . *else?* Here, at the school? We'd agreed that this whole thing would stay within the circle, that as few people as possible would know about any of it."

"Rafe told somebody," Thea pointed out. "On the whole, my Finder is probably a lot more trustworthy. If you want those pigeons, use what you've got."

A memory of Humphrey's own words came back to Thea, overheard on a damp night in a cedar wood. *I use what tools are given to me, and Thea Winthrop is the sharpest sword I have right now.*

"One of those pigeons has been hurt," she continued. "Or even killed. We know that, from what the five of us originally saw when we entered the cube. Between Magpie's connection to things that are sick or wounded and need healing, and Kristin's ability to find the others, we can do this."

"Who's this Kristin? Your Finder? How do you know that she is to be trusted with any of this? How did she get to be involved?"

"Things happen for a reason," Thea said.

"I'm not sure I like this. I need to meet this Finder of yours."

"You said time is of the essence," Thea said.

Almost unwillingly, he nodded. "This needs to be done quickly and quietly, before the Alphiri get it all together."

"We can do it," Thea repeated.

Cheveyo's voice suddenly came floating back to her—*You cannot hide forever.* If she did this—if she showed her hand at last—there would be no more hiding, in this world or in any other. And if the Alphiri failed in their quest to gather the Human Polity's greatest wizard and make him do their bidding, they would know, in no uncertain terms, that there was an alternative—Thea herself, coming into her own place of power at last. Once she cast aside the concealment that had kept her safe, she would be exactly the thing that the Alphiri had wanted in the first place, a mage who could give their race the magic that they craved, who could give them a legacy, could make their race immortal. And it would be she, Thea, who would be on the front lines next time.

"Are you all right?" Humphrey said. "You look very strange, all of a sudden."

"I'm fine," Thea said, coming back to herself with a snap.

"Are you sure you need to involve someone new in this?"

"She's necessary," Thea said. "Without a Finder, we would be doing exactly what Rafe found so amusing—blundering around New York catching pigeons on a hit-or-miss basis. Which is probably what the Alphiri are doing. But with a Finder who is focused on a certain thing or a certain idea, we can do it."

"Do you have a plan?" Humphrey asked, and there it was again—that change, the difference in his tone. He was frowning a little, but he had accepted her as a partner rather than an apprentice.

"Not yet," Thea said. "But Christmas break is coming up. I can pull all of us together, with no schoolwork to distract us from this."

"You can always reach me, through *that*," Humphrey said, nodding at her keypad device, answering Terry's question beyond any further doubt. "Let me know what logistics support you need. I'll do whatever I can to help. Go find Tesla, Thea. Thanks for doing this for us."

*I use what tools are given to me.*

*Thea Winthrop is the sharpest sword I have right now.*

Humphrey May had just shown his hand; the sword had been unsheathed. He had offered assistance, but he had also stepped back from the front line, leaving the battle itself to Thea. It was at once a gesture of trust, and a cold willingness to gamble Thea herself to win a game with much higher stakes.

*Protect. That's what I am sworn to do.*

Humphrey's words, again, but this time they resonated for Thea, too.

"I'm not doing it for you," Thea said. "I'm doing it for Tesla."

10.

"OKAY, ONE MORE TIME," said Ben, ticking his points off on the fingers of his right hand. "These so-called Elemental pigeons were somehow detached from Nikola Tesla; they're little magical Elements, and they are still potentially alive and flitting around New York City decades after any ordinary pigeon would have kicked the bucket. The Alphiri buy this idea and send a pigeon-hunting team to New York. Humphrey May, the highest authority on this subject right now in *our* polity, speaking straight from the heights of the FBM and all of its vast and all-powerful knowledge, buys this idea—to the extent of okaying a pigeon hunt of our own, before, quote, 'the Alphiri get them.' But not even Humphrey May is sure whether said pigeons, assuming they exist, and can be caught, can even be . . . what did you call it, Thea? . . . *rejoined* to the original Tesla entity.

And if they can, nobody has any idea what would happen next. How am I doing so far?"

"Pretty much covers it," Thea said.

They had gathered together, all six of them, in what Kristin called Thea's pseudo-classroom—a bubble-universe classroom emptied of its student population, shielded, warded, and made safe for Terry to speak his mind in. Thea had called them in to report on the outcome of her conversation with Humphrey May, and, with a twinge of guilty misgivings, to inform them that she had volunteered them all for the pigeon-hunting project.

And Ben, judging from the sharper-than-usual edge of sarcasm in his words and the tone of his voice, wasn't taking to the idea very well.

"And you agreed to help him find these . . . these . . ." Ben waved his hand in front of his face, helplessly searching for the right adjective. "It's a wild goose chase!"

"Wild *pigeon*," Kristin said, grinning.

Ben growled at her.

"Terry . . . it might come down to you, in the end," Thea said, turning away from Ben.

"You're thinking that anything remotely like a rejoining would somehow have to happen inside a cyber-environment," Terry said. "It makes sense; that's the only place where all the pieces can actually exist together without violating all kinds of real-world rules. But what do you want me to do about it?"

"You'd need to write something. Some kind of code that unifies the pieces that were scattered and makes it all whole again."

"That's quite a job," Terry said, a strange expression on his face.

"Well, you've had practice," Tess said. "The Twitterpat thing in the Nexus. You've worked with it for quite a while now."

"Yes, but Twitterpat wrote that. All I did was tinker."

"Yeah, right, and you're so bad at tinkering that they handed you the Nexus on a silver platter," Ben said.

"I thought you were against this whole idea," Magpie said, turning to him.

"I *am*!" Ben said. "I think the whole thing is getting weirder and more out of control. I'd like to see a *shred* of concrete evidence."

"Your father is a scientist, isn't he?" Kristin murmured.

"So?"

"Sometimes," Kristin said, "you have to have faith first and evidence later."

"Oohhhh," Ben said, turning away. "You started all this, you know. You and your bright idea of stealing the cube."

"Well, there *is* that," Thea said.

"What?"

"You wanted evidence. We can get evidence, of sorts. From the cube. From Tesla himself. He was the one that did the split in the first place; he, if anyone, will know if anything can be done to reverse it."

"And you're telling me that you can go back in there and actually talk to this Tesla spirit or whatever's trapped in there? If *he* tells you it's all a wild goose chase, will you go back to Humphrey May and tell him it's all off?" Ben said.

"Would that be satisfactory?" Thea said, and this time she couldn't quite hide the grin.

"You're just making fun of me now," Ben said, narrowing his eyes.

"Some," Thea said. "Ben, I don't blame you. I don't quite believe any of it myself. Still, we all saw what we saw. And then there's the Alphiri.

Something about all this made *them* believe that there's a bargain to be had. Whatever else I might think of them, I trust their instincts on that score. They must think there's something in this for them or else they'd be quite happy to let us do our own pigeon-chasing."

"Humphrey said that the *Alphiri* were seen chasing pigeons," Tess said slowly.

"Yes, and?" Ben said, turning on her.

"There's varying levels to this," Tess said. "If they didn't think it was worth their time, they would be doing nothing at all. If they were marginally interested, they might have contracted somebody to do this particular hunt for them, and just present them with the pigeons, if found. But no—they *themselves* were seen in New York chasing birds. This is important enough for it not to be trusted to underlings."

"Important enough to break cover," Magpie said.

"All right, so someone believes there's really something in it," Ben said, conceding that point at least, however unwillingly. "What possible use can *we*—"

"And how much attention would you give to a *kid* prancing around trying to catch a pigeon?" Tess said thoughtfully.

"We won't have to resort to random netting," Thea said. "Kristin is a Finder. If she can turn her talents to Finding particular birds . . ."

Kristin sat up. "You want *me* to . . ."

"I thought we were going to talk to Tesla first," Ben said.

Thea sighed. "All right," she said. "I need to go—"

"We might as well all go," Ben said. "It took all of us last time, and we would *all* be there to hear whatever he had to say."

"Skeptic," Thea grumbled, pushing up her sleeve and staring thoughtfully at her wrist keypad for a second. "Fine. Hold on to your hats."

The sudden appearance of open sky and flat-topped mesas around her made Kristin's breath whistle through her teeth as she gasped in astonishment.

Cheveyo stepped out from behind a stone outcrop, his staff in one hand, the Tesla cube held in the palm of the other.

"Catori," he said, acknowledging Thea. And then, with a brief nod at the others, "And to all of you: welcome back. I told you that it would only be a short while before you would return for this, Catori.

I did not realize myself just how short a span of days it would be."

"You may still need to guard it for me a while longer," Thea said. "But we need to contact the man who lives inside it. We need . . . a few answers."

"Your wizard. Tesla." The words were nothing less than the truth, but coming from Cheveyo, who had no way of knowing what the cube contained, they froze his visitors in their tracks.

"How do you know that?" Thea said, recovering first. "Were you able to reach him yourself?"

"I, no," Cheveyo said. "But Grandmother Spider knows. And after you left the cube with me, she came to tell me something of it, to make sure I knew how to protect it." He held out the cube to Thea. "This is your kind of power, your gift, not mine."

Thea took the cube, bowing her head in a gesture of respect.

"I will leave you," Cheveyo said. "If you have need of me later, you know how to call me."

"He's scary," Kristin said in a small voice, staring at the place Cheveyo had been standing a moment before.

"Only if you have reason to fear him," Thea said. She stared at the cube, frowning slightly. "I'm trying to figure out just how to go at this. The last time we all piled on was when we unlocked this thing, but we didn't get to talk to Tesla then. It was like we were watching a movie."

"But that's when we saw the pigeons," Magpie pointed out. "The whole thing started then."

"But when I got to *talk* to him, I time-wove myself a place in his own time and space, a somewhere and somewhen that he was real, touchable, able to have a conversation with me. But I was looking for fairly specific times, then, and I was able to choose . . ." She looked at the others, perplexed. "The problem is that we need to speak to him directly, or else it's all going to be hints and fancies again. But we need to speak to him at different times in his life. We probably need to speak to him in the immediate aftermath of what happened in Colorado."

"Are you sure about that?" Ben murmured. "He looked pretty strung out over that. Would he even be able to tell you anything coherent?"

"Well, as soon as possible after that event, then, when it was still fresh in his mind and he could offer ideas."

"It would probably be constructive to speak to him *before* he did what he did," Magpie said. "It would tell us far more about his motives, and if he even thought about the possibility of getting any of his Elemental abilities back, if he thought he could control them, outside himself. If he even *wanted* any of it back."

"And much later, to see if we succeeded in finding the pigeons," Tess said.

Thea turned to her. "How do you figure that?"

"He might know," Tess said. "It might be linked to *his time*, somehow. It might be our only clue as to whether we should go on with any of this."

"But we know that he didn't have the Elemental gifts back when his body died," Ben said. "Or he certainly took some pains over making people believe that at the time."

"But the cube," Kristin said, frowning at the smooth white cube Thea held cradled in her hands. "I'm sorry, but I just don't get how anyone could do that, transfer himself into that and let his body die . . . not without *some* magic. I don't think there are many people out there capable of making themselves immortal. Just like that, on a whim. And living on inside an artifact."

"But is he living on in there?" Magpie asked abruptly. "Or is it all just his dreams and memories and the things in his life he thought to be important?"

Thea sighed. "I think," she said, "that we should go as far forward as we can. Seek him when he is old, and perhaps wise, or at any rate wiser than the young wizard who thought that releasing Elemental magic into wild birds was a good idea. And then we can ask Tesla himself where to go from there."

"Sounds good to me," Terry said. "But that still leaves the method in your hands. Do you have to do this on your own, or can you take any of us with you?"

"That would be pretty awesome," Kristin said, her broad grin showing her preposterous teeth.

"Thea, wait," Terry said. "Perhaps at least one of us *should* stay behind. Just in case something happens here. Someone should keep an eye on things."

"He has a point," Magpie said. "I'll stay. You all go; you can fill me in when you get back. But you might need someone physically here in a hurry, and I'll stick around."

"You'll miss all the fun," Kristin said. "You sure?"

"Oh, please, can't *she* stay?" Ben said, staring at Kristin.

Thea, who had been typing on her keypad, looked up and skewered Ben with a glare. "Cut it *out*," she said. "Okay, Magpie. I've set things up so I can 'talk' to you. I have no idea if any of this will work the way I think it will, but . . . here goes."

The red sands blinked out, and all of them except Magpie found themselves in a hotel room furnished in a sparingly elegant and yet utilitarian manner. Three or four pigeons balanced precariously on the ledge outside a closed window, glimpsed through half-drawn drapes. A faint sound of their cooing came drifting through the glass, mingled with a murmur of distant street traffic—tinny honking of car horns, a deep rumble of heavy buses, and the occasional staccato counterpoint of horses' hooves and wooden carriage or cart wheels on hard tarmac.

"What—?" Ben began, his voice hushed, but Thea closed the fingers of one hand around his wrist to silence him and pointed. They were not alone in the room. A man sat in a boxy-looking leather armchair by the window, apparently lost in thought.

He was a striking figure—tall and gaunt, clean-shaven, his graying hair middle-parted in an old-fashioned style, his blue eyes distant and unfocused. He was dressed in a suit and a clean white shirt with a blue tie knotted under his collar. One long-fingered hand lay perfectly still on the leather armrest; the other held a half-full cut-glass tumbler containing an amber liquid. His index finger tapped against the side, gently, rhythmically, almost in perfect time to the pigeons' coos.

"Is that him?" Kristin whispered.

She had spoken very softly, but at the sound of her voice the man in the armchair turned and looked straight at them.

"I remember you," he said after a moment, staring at Thea. A slight frown creased his forehead. "Why do I remember you?"

"We first met . . . many years ago, for you. And then again, many years before that."

"That makes no sense," Tesla said. "And yet, it does. Give me a moment, I will find the moment."

Even as Thea drew breath to speak, Tesla sat up in his chair, his fingers curling tighter around his glass.

"Oh yes," he said. "When I was a boy."

"That was . . . the second time," Thea said carefully. "The first time was many years after that. Here, in the city."

"You are speaking of time shifts. I have never had

occasion to try them, myself, but I know they exist. The Alphiri portals needed to be configured for those, too. The theory is familiar to me."

*"The Alphiri portals?"* Ben said, staring at Tesla. "What do you have to do with . . ."

Tesla gave him a long, stern look. "They came to me with a basic idea," Tesla said, "and struck a bargain with me to improve it. I did so. They planned to use them to improve transportation of entities across space and time, much like the human 'ports that I later developed for our own use, but far more complex."

Kristin was slack-jawed, Ben's expression was one of both astonishment and outrage, and Terry looked chagrined, as though something very obvious had just been pointed out to him. But it was Thea, her instincts roused as usual at the mention of the Alphiri, who responded to his words.

"You mean you've already struck a bargain with the Alphiri?"

"For the portals. Yes."

"When did they come to you?"

"Years ago. Many years ago, now."

*"Before they came to the rest of the Human Polity?"*

"Perhaps. At that time I had no way of knowing

whom they had contacted, and why. It wasn't my business. They came to me with a problem and I turned my hand to solving it. And they paid well for it. Not like some of my own kind. People cheat and they lie, but the Alphiri always deliver on their side of the bargain."

Thea exchanged a frightened and bewildered look with the others.

"Are we too late already?" Kristin said in a small voice.

"I remember *you*," Tesla said to Thea, but his eyes were resting on Kristin, and he wore an expression of carefully controlled distaste as he took in the prominent teeth. "But the rest of you, I have not met. I am certain of this. Who are you and why do you come here? Why do you disturb me?"

"We're here because of the pigeons," Tess said abruptly.

Tesla turned his haunting eyes to her, very slowly. They were no longer distant and dreamy, but very sharp and piercingly probing.

"Pigeons," he echoed. "Continue."

"We saw you," she said, "back when you were in Colorado Springs . . . when you tried to take your magic . . ."

"Kaschei," Thea said faintly. "You once told me of this, long ago. How someone in a fairy tale took his heart, the essence of his life, and kept it in a place where nobody could ever find it or harm it, so that he could live forever, that he would be safe. Was that really what you were trying to do?"

Tesla remained silent for so long, Thea began to worry that they had lost him completely to some inner reverie of regret or old age, and that the entire visit was to prove useless except for the startling information about the Alphiri. But then Tesla stood up, turned to the window, and stared outside, both hands wrapped around his glass now. When he spoke, his voice might have belonged to a different man—someone more decisive, younger, and stronger—or someone still wrestling with unimaginable pain.

"That," Tesla said clearly, "was the worst mistake I ever made."

"Maybe we can help," Thea said after a pause. "If there is a way to help. Can it be reversed? What exactly did you do?"

He turned to face the five of them. His face was transformed, alight, glowing. But his voice had cooled, just a little.

"It would need," he said, and they heard the bleak edge in his words, "an Elemental mage."

"We have one," Terry said.

Tesla lifted an eloquent eyebrow. "One who will understand? Who will not judge? Who will do what is necessary, even though it may be hard?"

"Yes," Thea said, after a moment of silence.

"Well, who is it?" Tesla said. Then he blinked and refocused on Thea's face. "You? But you are a child."

"So were you. Once."

"My gifts came to me full-fledged later." Tesla cupped his fingers around Thea's chin, lifting her face; Thea met his eyes steadily and in silence as his intense gaze searched her face. At length he dropped his arm to his side, still not taking his eyes from her, and nodded once, slowly.

"Yes," he said. "Yes, I can see."

"I think you had better tell us everything," Thea said. Her heart was pounding; it was one thing for Humphrey May to tell her that she *might* be an Elemental, quite another to have Nikola Tesla himself, the greatest Elemental mage in the history of the human race, confirm it with just a searching glance. "Those pigeons of yours have suddenly become very important. And if the Alphiri find them before we do, you might find yourself in a position of being not the bargainer, but the bargain. And they *will* use you against humanity."

"I never have liked humanity," Tesla said, in a voice almost conversational. "I do, however, like human beings. And it would sit ill with me to allow one to come to harm through some action of mine." He settled back into his armchair as if into a throne, both arms laid along the leather armrests. "You have to realize, though, you are asking about troubled times. About times when I may well have been mad. This will not . . . be easy."

The story that emerged was one filled with passion and pain. Tesla had been an incredibly gifted and idealistic young man who tried to make his way in a world he never quite understood and that was quick to take advantage of him. He had been the only quad-Element mage in the history of the human race, and while he was alive that was something that everyone took for granted.

But he had to work for every achievement, and sometimes begged and scrounged for loans and for outright gifts, most of which ended up in the laboratories and workshops where he researched and honed his Elemental talents. When he lost his New York laboratory and office to fire, he thought he had reached rock bottom.

"When the opportunity came to go to Colorado—to have a free hand—I hesitated not for a moment," Tesla said. He kept his eyes on the birds, which still strutted and shivered on his windowsill. "And then, out there, alone . . . I lost my head. I panicked. I thought about how it would be to lose that, too, to some error of judgment or to accident beyond my control—and I remembered Kaschei. I came to believe that if I could keep the best of me safe, somewhere outside of me, then nothing could ever hurt me again."

He lapsed into silence, and it was Kristin who broke it—Kristin, the only one who had not seen with her own eyes what had happened in the Colorado laboratory, had not seen the dead bird in Tesla's hands or heard his keening cry of grief.

"But it went wrong," she whispered.

Tesla started as though someone had broken into a reverie. "It went wrong," he echoed.

"We saw it," Tess said quietly. "We were there. We saw the birds in the pillar of flame. We saw one appear, then two, then three, then four . . . then they were gone, all except the one."

"The Elemental birds," Tesla said. "And I had not taken into account that they would be free, and that they would be frightened, and that they would all go away. All except the one, as you say."

"Which one was it, sir?" Terry asked.

"It was the Fire Elemental," Tesla said. "The others were lost, but this one was gone. Gone. And I felt his absence inside of me like someone had ripped out my soul. I knew that Kaschei could never have felt like this. Or else the tales lied, all along, and I had believed that lie and I was now lost along with the best part of me."

"You lost *all* of your magic?" Thea asked.

"No. Enough remained, and I could fake it for the rest of my days on Earth. But my body grew tired and old, and my mind was always searching, and my soul was gone from me. When the time came for me to lay down my earthly shape . . . You see, I had made the cube that you now carry, an Elemental cube, years before I had torn myself apart, and I believed that when I grew too physically frail in the earthly plane I could endure in a different form." He paused. "But you already know this," he said. "It was the cube that must have brought you here. It was the only thing that could have done that."

"No, sir," said Thea. "It brought us into your existence that first time, the time that we saw you and the pigeons at the Colorado laboratory. And we saw other things too—we saw you in a park in a great European-looking city somewhere, and when we came close to you, you kind of collapsed. . . ."

"I remember that," Tesla said, sitting up. "It was Budapest, and they called it a nervous breakdown at the time, overwork, stress. But I remember that day, and I remember feeling as though the sunlight was suddenly too heavy for me to bear. Every sound was magnified until I could hear a fly buzzing a block away, and the sound of horses' hooves out in the street felt like cannon fire in my brain. It took me a long time to recover from that. They called it a breakdown, but it was after that . . . it was that day that really woke the Elemental. . . ."

The other five exchanged a puzzled look.

"You mean *we* made you into an Elemental?" Ben said.

"The powers must have been there all along, but it may well have been that encounter that woke them to fullness," Tesla said. "So you all were my blessing and my curse, you children."

"Do you want it all back?" Kristin asked abruptly.

"How can I have it back?" Tesla said. "At least a part of it has gone, vanished permanently, died a final death."

"But the rest," Kristin persisted. "The other three pigeons. We could find them. We're on our way to look for them. But first we need to know, do you want them back? *Can* you have them back? Can it be done?"

"Reintegration? As I said, it would need an Elemental mage and all kinds of other things. The kind of thing that wasn't even properly invented when I was still among you as a man of flesh and blood."

"You mean computers," Terry said, stepping forward. "There has been much done in that field. That part of the problem, you can leave up to me."

"You?" Tesla said, looking him up and down. "But you are so young."

"So were you, once," Terry said, with a quick look back at Thea.

"We would need your help," Thea said. "We don't know nearly enough. We can go out and seek your pigeons, but you would need to guide us. Perhaps it might be possible to return to a point that's early enough, to a place where your Fire Element pigeon might not have perished."

"And we'll do it before the Alphiri find them," Kristin said stalwartly.

"You would have to be in at least two different places at the same time, and so would I. And it would help if it was a different I for every occasion," Tesla said.

"Tell us what we need to know, and we can always come back and ask if we need answers," Terry said.

"No . . . wait," Thea said slowly. "I mean, are you actually able to do that? Split yourself into different . . . avatars?"

"He did it with the pigeons," Ben said.

"Yes, and it is not an experience I would repeat lightly, young man."

"But if you could . . ." Thea said slowly. "If you could, or would be willing to, it would help. And I think I know a way."

Tesla frowned. "I will listen," he said.

Thea looked down and spoke, apparently, to the floor. "Magpie, are you there?"

"Yup," a voice from nowhere replied instantly. The disembodied sound managed to be both distant and disconcertingly present in the same room, as though an invisible person standing right next to Thea had actually spoken.

Tesla's back stiffened, and he searched the empty air around Thea with wary eyes. "What was that? Where did that voice come from?"

"It's a friend," Thea said. "Would you excuse me for a moment?"

She reached out behind her with her right hand, and stepped *away*. In the next instant she was standing near Cheveyo's stone house, holding Magpie's hand.

"Did you find him? Did you talk to him? What did he say?" Magpie said breathlessly.

"Yes, yes, and yes," Thea said, grinning. "He said he'll help. He said he'll probably help best if a different him goes with different teams, and that we'll have to split up to try and cover all the bases. So I have an idea. I need to talk to Grandmother Spider."

"She's way ahead of you," Magpie said, and her own grin widened.

Thea turned her head and met the chocolate brown eyes of a dark-haired Grandmother Spider, sitting on a sun-warmed rock a few steps away.

"We've been talking," Magpie said, a touch smugly.

"Indeed we have, and we've had much to say to each other," Grandmother Spider said, getting to her feet. "What new venture are you planning, my child?"

"This is going to sound awfully weird," Thea said. "But I need to know . . . those spellspam dream catchers you sent us . . . can we use them to carry different splinters of a man's mind or spirit? So that the man could be in several places at the same time?"

"It is not," said Grandmother Spider, "a use I have ever put them to. But true dream catchers can do and be many things. This man—is this your wizard, Nikola Tesla?"

"Cheveyo said you'd told him about this," Thea said. "Yes. It is Tesla. I left him waiting for an answer."

"Do you have your dream catcher with you?" Grandmother Spider asked.

Thea fished it out of her pocket. "Always."

"Mine too," Magpie said, offering hers on the palm of her hand.

Grandmother Spider closed one of her hands around each small dream catcher and bowed her head over them. She began to hum softly, a gentle haunting melody that sparkled with ancient magic. Her hair, spilling over her face and her hands, turned shades of chestnut, wheat-gold, white, gray, and solid blue-black. A light began to seep through her closed fingers, as if she held a fistful of fireflies. Then she stopped humming, and the world sank into a silence; her hair turned silver-white, and stayed that shade. When she looked up, her eyes were dark blue, like a twilit sky.

"I have made them empty so that they will hold what spirit comes to fill them," she said, holding both tiny dream catchers out on the palms of her hands toward Thea. "Use them wisely. This can be a dangerous thing, this breaking apart of a man."

"He is already broken," Thea said softly. "We do this in order to try and heal him."

"Then go with blessings, and may you succeed in your quest," Grandmother Spider said. She turned her head a little, and smiled at Magpie. "And we two shall meet again, I think."

And then she was gone, and a small brown spider sat in the middle of one of the dream catchers. Thea carefully set the dream catcher down on one of the boulders by her feet long enough for the spider to scurry off it and into the shadows, and then gathered up both dream catchers in one hand.

"I'd better get back," she said to Magpie. "Do you want to come? I don't think there's any reason for you to wait here alone any longer."

"I'll wait," Magpie said. "I don't suppose you need to make that poor old man any more spooked than he already must be."

"Okay. Back soon."

Thea closed her eyes for a moment, and when she opened them again she was back in the hotel room, with Tesla staring at her.

"This is a new thing," he murmured.

Thea flushed, both with pride that she had managed to surprise someone like Tesla and with an anxious urge to explain herself, to justify the things she did to a supreme authority. "I have these," she said, holding out the pair of dream catchers. "Grandmother Spider has made them . . . empty. Empty and ready to be filled." She glanced at Tesla. "If we can figure out how to get some other version of you into these, a younger version with a better understanding of a special set of circumstances, these will hold those parts of you that we take with us. We will need the you that decided to split the Elementals, the you that knew how to do it in Colorado. Perhaps there's even a chance we can figure out how to go back to a precise moment, and rescue *all* the pigeons, even the one you lost."

"Not the me of the immediate aftermath of that," Tesla said. "I would not wish children to see me that way. The me that left New York for Colorado, perhaps. There is knowledge there. And the timing can be stretched so that a practical run at the process can happen for you to witness. But I beg you to remember that it was grief that made me as mad as you may get to see me."

"That's one," Tess said. "But the Alphiri are chasing pigeons in *New York*. Do they know something we don't? Why would the pigeons have gone to New York?"

"*Back* to New York," Tesla said. "I had started feeding them, in the city, before I left for Colorado. And then, when I returned, I continued to do this. The city is where they knew me best. That is where they very well might have gone."

"Two, then," Thea said. "One for Colorado, one for New York. One for each dream catcher. And if Terry needs to ask questions, for the computer, there is always the cube, directly."

"You're going to give *me* the wretched thing?" Terry said. "How am I supposed to keep it safe from anybody? What am I supposed to tell Humphrey?"

"You have the notes he gave you. If he asks, tell him you are working from those."

"So. Two. How?" Tesla said succinctly.

Weighing the dream catchers in his hand, Terry thought about the problem for a moment. And then his eyes lit on Thea's wrist keypad.

"Can I borrow that?" Terry said.

"First I need to get us to where we need to be, to find the two personalities that we need," Thea said, loosening the wrist-strap and dangling the gadget from her fingers. "Those parts of you, Tesla, that we need to get for this to work. But once we get there, Terry, say the word. The rest of you are going to have to wait for us here. I'll just take the three of us who need to be there."

"Fascinating," Tesla said, his eyes alight as he stared at the keypad. "May I examine . . . ?"

Thea fought the impulse to hold on to the keypad and relinquished it to Tesla, who turned it over in his hands, obviously rapt.

"Fascinating," he said again, "absolutely fascinating. What is this thing, and what is it that it does? Is that how you have achieved coming here to see me?"

Thea retrieved the keypad. "If you will tell me something about the moment where one of those two parts of you that we need to find exists, I'll show you how it works."

"What precisely do you need to know?" Tesla asked.

"Anything. Any detail. What your surroundings were like. What you looked like."

Tesla hesitated. "Shall we try the New York one first? I feel a little queasy at the thought of returning to Colorado . . . at that time." He took a deep breath. "The New York me is perhaps ten or fifteen years younger than I am at this moment. Take some of the gray out of my hair, make it darker. Give me a mustache." His fingers twirled a nonexistent one on his upper lip as he spoke. "Perhaps a little later than that. Make me . . . walk with a cane. I did, after my accident. A car hit me, and after that it was easier to have a third leg. Try . . . this very room."

Thea was typing as he spoke. "Okay," she said. "Ready."

The others appeared to fade from around them, and the three of them—Nikola Tesla, Terry, and

Thea—suddenly stood in the very room they had just left, except there was another Tesla present, a younger one. He looked much as he had described, down to a dapper wooden cane leaning against the armrest of his armchair, and he sat in almost exactly the same position that the elder Tesla had been found in when they had first seen him, cradling a glass of whisky.

"One of my little indulgences," the older Tesla murmured, at Thea's elbow. "I did not allow myself many. What is it that you need to do now?"

"Thea," Terry whispered, holding out his hand for the typepad.

Thea handed it over.

Terry typed for what seemed to be an inordinately long time; fortunately, the other Tesla in the room didn't react to their presence. But the elder Tesla's breathing was very quick and shallow as he stared at his younger self, and Thea, sparing him a swift apprehensive glance, turned her head to look back at Terry.

"Hurry *up*," she hissed.

"Done," he said instantly, handing her back the keypad and one of the dream catchers. "Hold that thing up—like this—so that you can see the whole figure within the circle," Terry said. "And then press ENTER."

Thea obeyed, squinting through the dream catcher until the Tesla in the armchair just fitted within the circle of the web, and then hit the ENTER key.

For a moment, nothing happened. And then, suddenly, the dream catcher started to spin in Thea's hand, very fast, and a strange bluish light began to stream from it. They all turned their attention from the man in the chair to the spinning dream catcher, and it was only the gentle thud of an object falling onto a carpeted floor that brought their attention back to the armchair.

The other Tesla was gone. The whisky glass had fallen from the armrest, its contents pooling in an amber puddle on the hotel carpet.

The dream catcher continued to glow faintly blue in Thea's hand.

"I think we have him," Thea whispered. And then, glancing up at Tesla, she added, "Are you all right?"

"It feels . . . strange . . . and yet terribly familiar," Tesla said. "It feels as though I've suddenly lost a memory I did not believe I could ever lose, stopped

remembering something I cannot believe I could forget." He drew a deep shaky breath, and ran a hand
through his hair—and then patted it back down
into place again, tidy and dapper. "Well," he said,
"I suppose we'd better go and get the other one."

## 11.

"CHEER UP," SAID KRISTIN. "It could be worse."

"I'm cold, I'm miserable, and I'm alone in a city I don't know, chasing pigeons that may or may not exist," Ben muttered into the dark green knitted scarf wrapped around his neck and mouth, his hands stuffed deep into the pockets of his jacket.

"You're not alone; you're with me," Kristin said. "And there's Tesla's ghost."

"You're right," Ben said. "It's worse."

They had all told their families that they needed to stay at the Academy over the short break. When they had broken up into teams, it had seemed obvious that Tess would stick around with Terry at the Academy Nexus during the Christmas break, holding down the home base, and acting as aide and a contact point for everyone else. Thea had taken on the thorny problem of the lost Fire Elemental pigeon, and if anyone could help out on that front it was Magpie, with her ability to commune with hurt animals and her healing touch.

It was clear, of course, that Kristin, their Finder, would have to go to New York to find the rest of the pigeons. It had come as a complete and unpleasant surprise to Ben that he would be expected to go there with her. It was only when he became aware that he was being a source of both amusement and exasperation to Tesla himself that Ben folded, sulkily and with ill-grace.

And that's where they were now, the two of them—bundled up in winter jackets, gloves, and sheepskin boots, late in the afternoon on Christmas Eve. Everywhere Ben looked, people were laughing, excited, enjoying themselves. Bryant Park, behind New York's Public Library, was crowded. Women were weaving enthusiastically in and out of the Christmas shops set up in brightly lit small kiosks along the park's outer walkways, followed closely by bags and packages floating in their wake; children were careening around and shrieking in delight; usually dour-faced businessmen wore benevolent smiles. The fragrance of roasting chestnuts mixed with spice, cocoa, pizza, and hot cider.

Above them, perching on statues, fences, and window ledges, or scurrying and ducking on the ground between people's feet, were the pigeons. Puffed up to twice their size against the cold, pecking hopefully at some bit of debris or another or crowding expectantly around some benevolent soul who had, in defiance of park ordinance, clandestinely started scattering bread crumbs or popcorn.

And in those crowds of birds and men, pigeons flocked to what seemed to be empty space, and perched in midflight as if they were resting on something that wasn't there—the incarnation of Nikola Tesla, whom Ben and Kristin had released from their dream catcher.

They had been given strict instructions by Terry and Thea. During the capture of the Tesla avatar the dream catcher has been spinning clockwise, and in order to release the spirit they had to spin the dream catcher counterclockwise, very fast. They could recapture their version of Tesla for the return journey by looking at Tesla's figure through the dream catcher so that he was contained inside its circle, and then spinning the dream catcher clockwise again.

The release instructions had worked perfectly, and a shadowy, half-transparent Tesla now stood under the light of a park lamp with a strange, dreamy smile on his upturned face. He was apparently a corporeal presence to the pigeons alone—nobody else, with the obvious exceptions of Kristin and Ben, seemed to notice or care about the presence of a hatless man with neatly parted hair, dressed in an old-fashioned and oddly formal pin-striped black suit and black patent leather shoes, oblivious of the time of year or the weather.

Tesla appeared to be equally invisible to half a dozen Alphiri who fruitlessly attempted to mingle with the human throng. The Alphiri were not necessarily a startling presence among humans—they were a common enough workday sight, often sitting politely at business lunches where they did not eat or at cocktail parties where they did not drink, mingling with humans in banks, in offices, and on city streets everywhere. But they stood out in this crowd, somehow—a head taller and slender to the point of looking emaciated when compared to the well-padded Christmas revelers. The Alphiri wore their usual assortment of not-quite-right clothes, although they at least tried to acknowledge the time of year and the occasion. One of them, whom Ben and Kristin had glimpsed several times, wore a bright red woolen hat with an enormous pom-pom, and a headband with reindeer antlers on top of it. At least two of the others sported Rudolph-the-Red-Nosed-Reindeer noses over their own bony proboscises, and one was wearing snowshoes attached to his long-toed bare feet.

The one with the antlers had just surfaced again, making his way through the crowds toward where Ben and Kristin stood, and Kristin glanced around for options.

"Let's go skating," she said, nodding at the rink set up behind them. "I seriously doubt any of *them* know how, and it might give us a bit of a chance to just observe."

"I can't skate," Ben said sulkily. "And what about Tesla? Are you just abandoning him there?"

"What, you never tried ice-skating? It's about time, then. Tesla will be fine. If he sees something, he'll let us know. Come on." She stepped away, and paused when he didn't follow, glancing back at him. "Or do you want to stand here by yourself and draw their attention to you rather than to me?"

"You just want me to make a fool of myself," Ben said, but he dragged his unwilling feet after her anyway.

Humphrey May had made sure they had enough money, and Kristin hauled a twenty out of her pocket as they came up to the rental pavilion beside the rink. They exchanged their shoes for two pairs of somewhat battered blue skates. Kristin tucked the claim tickets into a pocket before stuffing her feet into her skates and lacing them up in a brisk, businesslike manner. She glanced at Ben, who was still frowning at his laces.

"I think this has been done up wrong," he said.

"No, it hasn't. Honestly, you're such a dork." Kristin leaned over and expertly laced up the skate closest to her. Ben wiggled his foot experimentally.

"Hurts," he said.

"They're *rentals*, you can't expect heavenly comfort," Kristin said. "Make sure the other one's tight. You don't want a broken ankle."

"*Now* she thinks about that," Ben muttered.

Kristin rose to her feet, balancing precariously on her blades. "Ready?"

"Are you sure this was such a good idea?" Ben said, making no move to get up from the bench.

"We can shake the Alphiri, at least for a while," Kristin said.

She teetered from the bench to the edge of the ice

rink, turned once to give Ben another encouraging look, and launched onto the ice.

Ben almost missed the transformation, so intent was he on wobbling on his own unsteady feet to the edge of the rink, but when he looked up from his efforts he almost failed to recognize Kristin. The only reason he knew who she was at all, in fact, was her vivid yellow jacket, a bright spot of color in the rink. Gone was the awkward girl who was always on the edge of things. In her place was someone confident and graceful, who threaded her way through the circling skaters into the less crowded center of the rink, pirouetted twice, and then drifted back through the crowd until she hovered beside the entrance, beckoning Ben in.

"Come on, the water's fine," she said.

"The water's *frozen*," Ben retorted. But he took a deep breath and stepped out on the ice.

His feet immediately threatened to slide straight out from under him, and he hung on desperately to the plastic barrier fence, which was scarred from many previous encounters with nervous beginners.

"Not fair," he said. "You didn't tell me you've been doing this from the cradle. I'm going to make a complete idiot of myself. And look, there's that wretched

Alphiri again. All we did was draw attention to our-
selves. You're brilliant, and I'm a clown."

"I'll teach you," Kristin said breezily. "You have to
let go. You can't take the fence with you. I Find best
when I'm not actually concentrating on what I'm
looking for. You wait—it'll come popping straight
at me as soon as I take my eyes off it."

"What will?"

"The pigeon, you twit. What we came here for,
remember? Now come on—move your feet. One at
a time. Just a little bit. You have to forget how to
walk and learn how to *glide*. Watch."

She left him once again, took off through a gap in
the crowds into the center with long gliding motions,
then took off from the back inside edge of one skate
and landed smoothly on the back outside edge of
the opposite foot, turning into a smooth sweep and
skating back to Ben.

"That was called a salchow," Kristin said. "Don't
worry, you're not required to do it on your first
skate. I'd hold your hand but that would only wreck
your balance. Let go of the wretched fence now."

"Quit bullying me," Ben snarled, but tried to
obey. He took a few tottering steps, staggered, and
grabbed for the fence again.

"Glide. Don't walk. Try it again."

By this time something deeply stubborn had woken in Ben, and he was determined that whatever happened, he would not give her the pleasure of watching him fall. He set his teeth, locked his knees, and let go of the fence again.

It took the better part of an hour for him to not only start to get the hang of things but, despite himself, to enjoy it.

"Hey," he called out triumphantly as he rounded a corner of the rink without slamming into the fence to make himself stop, "look—I can finally turn."

But Kristin was looking somewhere else, outside the rink. She came to a sudden stop, digging into the already deeply scored ice and spraying ice chips over Ben. He tried to turn his head, lost his precarious balance, and slammed into the fence again, jamming his knee painfully into the hard plastic. He stood there for a moment with his eyes closed, breathing fast, trying to control the sudden lancing pain in his leg, and then turned savagely on Kristin.

"What gives? I thought we—"

"*Look!*" she said, pointing. "There!"

He followed the line of her finger to the fifty-foot Christmas tree towering against the backdrop of the nine great arched windows in the back of the library that overlooked Bryant Park. It was true that the tree was spectacular, glowing with thousands of white lights enhanced with a layer of spell-spoken glow. But Kristin wasn't looking at the tree. It took Ben a few seconds to notice what had really caught her eye.

A single pigeon had landed softly on top of a street lamp not too far from the edge of the rink. To Ben the pigeon looked no different from any of the rest. But he noticed that Nikola Tesla's ghost had moved to that particular lamppost, and the expression on his face was a mix of disbelief and fierce joy.

"Is it one of ours?" Ben whispered.

"We'd better get out of here," Kristin said, skating jerkily past Ben, suddenly graceless again. "I have to get over there."

"Oh, *God*."

"What—" Kristin began, and then covered her mouth with her hands in shock as a flock of large black birds came down all around the pigeon on the lamppost, surrounding it. For a moment it seemed hopelessly outnumbered, but Tesla made a sudden sharp gesture with his hand, almost as though casting a spell of some kind, and the pigeon burst up and out, melting into the winter sky. And then there was no flock anymore, only one large raven. Then the raven, too, was gone, and in its place, standing practically nose-to-nose with Tesla but apparently unaware of it, was a man wearing a cowboy hat and tight jeans tucked into dusty snakeskin boots. He was looking up to the now unoccupied lamppost, frowning—and then he turned and looked straight at Ben and Kristin, gave them a wide smile as he tipped his hat in their direction, and turned away, vanishing almost as quickly as the pigeon.

"I've heard Thea describe him a dozen times," Ben said. "The raven. The hat. Those boots. That's Corey. Coyote. The Trickster. If he's here, the Alphiri are closing in."

"Come on," Kristin said, "we'd better get to Tesla. If there was one, the others might be somewhere near. And we don't want to make the same mistake again."

"I thought you wanted to shake our stalker," Ben said.

"I did, for a while, at least. But then I got caught up in the skating, and so did you, and I probably shouldn't have pointed. I shouldn't have identified it. This was my fault, and it was too close."

"We couldn't have gotten to it quickly anyway,

not with these things on," Ben said, glancing down at his skates. "But you're right, let's take the skates back and get our shoes."

Kristin had already stepped off the ice and was digging through her pockets for the shoe coupons.

Ben staggered to a bench and removed his skates, wriggling his toes in their woolen winter socks as Kristin waited impatiently for the attendant to locate their footwear.

The rink was slowly emptying now. It wasn't very late, but it was Christmas Eve and people were starting to wander off to warm homes. Ben watched people scurrying past, scanning the throng for any signs of the Alphiri or of Corey in his distinctive hat, but they all seemed to have melted away now that a certain objective had been achieved.

"Are they holed up somewhere and watching us?" Ben muttered, raking the shadows for lurking spies.

"We are running out of time," said Tesla's ghost, materializing beside him. "They have stopped hunting the pigeons. They are hunting *us* hunting the pigeons. This is not a good thing."

"Was that really one of yours?" Ben said curiously. "Which one? I couldn't see any difference. How can you tell?"

"You would know a part of yourself, if you were to lose it," Tesla said. "They have changed, which is not something that should surprise me—they have survived out here in the wild with their kind for a very long time. They have certainly lost the edge of being completely my own and have become almost . . . blurred, but that particular bird carries the Water Element."

Kristin, who had returned with the shoes, dropped Ben's boots by his feet.

"I'm sorry I pointed," she said to Tesla. "I might as well have hung a bell on him."

"Next time you will know better," Tesla said, a little frostily.

"It's late," Ben said, looking around. "Won't they go and sleep? Should we come back in the morning? We've been at this for a couple of days now; one more day won't make any—"

"This is the first time we have actually seen one," Tesla said.

Kristin was shaking her head. "No. Tonight. The real, mortal pigeons might sleep, but the ones we are looking for might come to us faster without being distracted by the flock."

"But we're losing the crowd," Ben pointed out.

"We can't hide in masses of people anymore."

"Neither can the Alphiri," Kristin said. "We'll see them coming."

Ben might have pointed out that there might be very little they could do if Corey the Trickster decided to turn into a flock of crows again, but logic seemed to be useless under the circumstances. He sighed.

"Fine," he said. "But I want something hot to drink first."

Kristin glanced back across the rink. "There's the café, right there. Or we could go grab a cup of hot chocolate; I saw a kiosk back at the other end."

Ben glanced back at Tesla, a look at once painfully honest, guilty, and apologetic.

"With all due respect, sir," he said, "we *have* been at this for days now. I'd really like to step outside of it for a moment and just go somewhere where I *don't* need to keep an eye out for pigeons. Only for a little while. I need a break."

Tesla furrowed his brows in silent disapproval.

Unexpectedly, Kristin laughed. "Okay, then. Lead on. What did you have in mind?"

The closest exit let them out near the Avenue of the Americas and Fortieth Street intersection. Tesla paused on the corner to stare, for the fourth time since they had arrived in New York, at the signpost on the corner, which held a sign bearing his own name: NIKOLA TESLA CORNER. The first time he had appeared astonished by the concept, and had merely raised his eyebrows without comment. Now, finally, it seemed that the idea had caught up with him. He stroked his mustache with one hand and tilted his head at the sign.

"They called me the New Wizard of the West when I came to this country," Tesla mused, apparently talking to himself. "And then . . . they all forgot about me, except to occasionally trot me out at special occasions. This . . . well, I am pleased, of course—pleased and flattered. Why would I not be? This was my city for so long, my park . . ." He turned away, began to drift east on Fortieth Street toward Fifth Avenue. "This was my street, even. There—my offices—the offices of the Nikola Tesla Company." He flung out an arm to point to a building on the opposite side of the road, straight into the path of a man talking animatedly into his cell phone. The man ploughed right through Tesla's outstretched arm without breaking stride.

A sudden clap of a pigeon's wings broke Tesla's

train of thought and he looked up, following the flight of a pair of birds who cleared the wrought iron fence and vanished somewhere into the park.

Ben turned to look at Tesla. "Were those . . . ?"

"No," Kristin said. "Just pigeons. Nothing extra-ordinary about them."

"See?" Ben said, shaking his head as they reached the library building and the noise and lights of Fifth Avenue rose to meet them. "We can't get *away* from them, back there. We watch every bird like it's one of Tesla's vanished Elemental angels. I want to turn my back on things feathered, just for a little while. I swear, I'm going to start counting pigeons in my sleep."

They found a coffee shop a little way down Fifth Avenue, just across from Lord & Taylor, a tiny hip-looking place called The New York Minute, tucked incongruously in between one of those ubiquitous NYC T-shirt and souvenir shops liberally scattered around the tourist-frequented parts of Manhattan and a shoe store in whose ostentatiously bespelled display window its wares—tiger-striped high-heeled boots and shiny pink vinyl ankle bootees fringed with fake baby-pink ostrich feathers—strutted up and down ramps and platforms, showing themselves off for the customers. Nikola Tesla sniffed with disapproval as he happened to catch sight of them.

"Women's fashions were always ridiculous," he opined. "Only the form of the absurdity has changed since my day, not the substance of it."

"There goes a man who spent a fortune on silk handkerchiefs," Ben muttered to Kristin as they pushed into the warm coffee shop, unwrapping scarves and unzipping coats. Tesla, wearing an expression of fastidious distaste, followed them, and stood hovering beside the table they commandeered as two other patrons got up to leave. Kristin caught the eye of a barista, who glanced over at the newly empty table and drew a tiny circle in the air with his forefinger, writing in the number 3 in the middle. The detritus left behind on the table by the newly departed customers—coffee cups and plates piled with dirty cutlery and crumpled paper napkins—gathered itself up into a precariously teetering pile and took itself off to the side counter where it all sorted itself out neatly into different bins. A damp rag appeared above the empty table and gave it a cursory wipe, leaving it dry and bare of stray crumbs but certainly a long way below Tesla's own high standards of hygiene.

"Back in my day," Tesla said, giving every impression that he wanted to run a white-gloved finger over surfaces and was certain beyond a shadow of a doubt that they would not pass the test, "it was the Palm Room at the Waldorf-Astoria. They never could polish their silver properly, though—it got so that they'd bring me eighteen linen napkins without my asking for them so I could polish the silverware. I do not think they even have linen napkins in this establishment."

"Nor silverware," Ben said. "Hey, you may not care, but it's cold and dark out there and I'm hungry."

"I always," said Tesla in a tone of mild reproof, "finish what I start before taking a break from the task at hand."

"We'll get them," Kristin murmured. She'd glanced at the display case as they had walked in and now she addressed the hovering rag that had cleared their table. "Two ham sandwiches, and a chocolate muffin. And two coffees. Cream." The rag vanished, and a few moments later their order materialized on the table before them. Kristin pulled a plate with a sandwich toward her. "We'll get them tonight," she said to Tesla.

"Are you sure we shouldn't just go back to the room and wait for them to come to us?" Ben said plaintively. Humphrey May had pulled a few strings, and they had been set up in the now rather tiny room that had once been Plaza Suite 3327 at the New Yorker Hotel, the very same room that had been Tesla's in the last months of his life. They had spent their first day in New York simply sitting in the room, waiting to see if any preternatural birds came back to a home roost—but although they had observed pigeons at the window, none of them were the ones that they were seeking. So they had left the hotel, and for the previous two days they had been combing Tesla's old haunts in the city, coming back again and again to Bryant Park behind the Central Library, the place where he had most often gone, where even the ghosts of pigeons long gone would remember him. And that evening had been the first time they had actually caught a glimpse of the possibility that what they sought was real, was there, waiting for them.

"The birds didn't come to the hotel before," Kristin said.

"But now they, uh, *know*," Ben said. "One of them came to him in the park. They might, well . . .

be able to *follow* him, now."

"We saw that one in the park," Kristin said obstinately. "We'll go back there first."

They nursed their drinks in silence; Kristin had polished off her sandwich, finding herself surprisingly hungry, and had started on the huge muffin before Ben was done. But Tesla was getting visibly more agitated, and finally Ben admitted defeat and shrugged back into his coat.

"All right," he said, "let's take another whack at it."

"I'll meet you there," Tesla said abruptly as they stepped outside again and gasped at the first cutting breath of cold air.

"Oh, right. Three times around the block," Ben said, sighing. One of Tesla's many idiosyncrasies, an obsession with the number three, somehow made it imperative for him to circle a given city block three times before he could actually go to his destination. The first couple of times Ben and Kristin had followed him, but they had given up on that and now waited for Tesla to join them at any given destination.

They hesitated on the sidewalk outside the coffee shop, looking around.

"Do you see any Alphiri?" Kristin whispered.

"No, but that doesn't mean there aren't any," Ben said. "Why don't we split up, and, um, meet in the park? If there's only one of them watching, they can follow only one of us." He hesitated. Something chivalrous in him stirred at the idea of letting Kristin trudge along by herself, but if they *were* being watched, and by only one entity, they might have just bought themselves a little time. "Watch your back," he said at length. "And don't do anything stupid. See you there."

"I can take care of myself," Kristin retorted, and flounced away in the direction of the Central Library building, whose iconic lions she could glimpse from where she stood.

Ben had the longer way to go—all Kristin had to do was walk down Fifth Avenue for a couple of short blocks, turn left onto Forty-second Street, and enter Bryant Park directly behind the library. She had every intention of doing that, but her Finder knack and her native impulsiveness turned on her. One of the first things she saw as she took her first couple of steps into the park was a pigeon sitting serenely on one of the statues. Not just any pigeon. A bird surrounded by a pale aura, a bird that turned its head to look directly at her.

Her breath caught for a moment, and then she expelled it carefully in a long slow sigh so as not to alarm the pigeon. She glanced around, but Ben was out of sight, and Tesla's ghost must still have been doing his laps around the block. She walked up to the statue where the bird rested, and slowly, very carefully, put out one gloved hand. The pigeon ducked a little, but allowed her to touch its head very lightly; it started to emit a low, guttural cooing, almost like purring.

Kristin reached out with the other hand, and cupped both around the pigeon. It did not object.

"Oh," she whispered, looking down at what she now held cradled between her palms. "Oh, my God. Oh . . ."

She was absorbed in her find; completely oblivious of her surroundings.

That was a mistake.

The hand that snaked around her from behind startled her into a recoil; she tightened her fingers reflexively around her prize, and the pigeon emitted a faint squawk of protest. But before she had a chance to do much more, another hand had followed the first, and somehow the pigeon was no longer in her grasp at all.

It was being held a step away from her by the smiling man in cowboy boots and the ten-gallon hat who had turned into a flock of crows only a couple of hours before: Corey the Trickster, Coyote, agent of the Alphiri.

"Thank you," Corey said, raising the now-struggling bird so that he effectively tipped his hat at Kristin with its head. "Much obliged. We were looking for this pretty thing."

"Give it back," Kristin said, outraged. "It isn't yours!"

Corey glanced down. "Possession has always been counted as nine tenths of the law, as I recall," he said.

"Finders keepers, if you insist on trotting out platitudes," Kristin retorted.

"Why, yes," Corey said agreeably. "You found it, and I'm keeping it. As I said, thanks."

"Give it *back*!" she said, launching herself at him.

But he was already gone. Someone was bending over her, asking if someone had attacked her; as she was being helped to her feet, she saw Corey place the pigeon into an ornate gilded cage held by a long-fingered Alphiri hand. The Trickster turned and tipped his hat to her, and then he and the Alphiri holding the cage melted away into the night.

"Wait," she sobbed, "*wait* . . ."

She heard, as if from a great distance, Ben calling her name repeatedly; heard a faint murmur of voices around her, a conversation that apparently established that she was all right and that no further assistance was required from outside sources; and then she shook her head and looked around, staring at Ben through tear-filled eyes.

"Where is Tesla?" Ben said, lifting his worried eyes from Kristin to spare a quick glance around the park.

"I'm here," Tesla said, from somewhere nearby. Ben could not see him. "There was nothing I could do. Nothing."

"I had him," Kristin whispered. "*I had him in my hands*. And he—Corey—*took* him. I let go, and then it was gone. *Gone*. The Alphiri have him."

"Or Corey does," Ben said. "He's been known to have his own agenda."

"No," said Tesla, stepping forward from the corona of light that surrounded the Christmas tree, where he had been effectively concealed from sight.

"There was an Alphiri waiting for him at the park gate with a cage. They took the pigeon."

Ben straightened and raked the park with his eyes, peering at every shadow and hiding place. "Well, they're gone now," he said. "Kristin . . . come on. Let's go back to the hotel. We can try again tomorrow, when there's more people. Maybe we can use the crowd . . ."

"But they have one," Kristin said.

"There are two more out here," Ben said. "If that one was here, then the others might be."

"But if the Alphiri already have one, and another was lost in Colorado . . . then we've already half failed," Kristin said mournfully.

"Even half," Tesla said, "is better than none."

"You don't believe that," Ben said abruptly. "You, who held the full Elemental range in your hands . . ."

"You're right," Tesla said, and his voice was edged with an odd bleakness. "Half of this whole will, of course, always remind me of the half that I no longer possess. But it will be something."

They walked the few blocks back to their hotel in mournful, doom-filled silence. Up in their room, Kristin was unable to settle, prowling like a caged

animal until Tesla informed her, in an impeccably
gentlemanly manner, that she was driving him crazy
and that she should please quit. She finally sat down
on the edge of the bed, reached out for the clock
radio, and fiddled with the stations; what came up,
predictably, was a program of Christmas carols.
The tail end of "Peace on Earth, Goodwill to Men"
came drifting out of the radio; Kristin's eyes filled
with tears.

"That one always makes me cry," she said, to
nobody in particular.

The choir switched to "Silent Night."

"We missed the Christmas Dance, back at school,
you know," Ben said.

Kristin turned to look at him. "Did you have a
date?"

"Not . . . quite," Ben said, avoiding her gaze.
"Oh well. No great loss, I suppose, seeing as I can't
dance."

"Not even waltz?" she asked.

"*Especially* not waltz," he said. "Wouldn't have
the first clue how to do it."

"I'll show you," Kristin said, getting up. "Come
here a sec."

"What, you're a professional dancer, too?" Ben

said, the memory of the skating still fresh in his mind. "Besides, waltz to what? 'Silent Night'?"

"It's a waltz," she said. "Count—*SI-two-three NIGHT-two-three HOLY-three NIGHT-two-three*. Come on, try it. It's the simplest dance there is. My dad taught me, when I was little. I used to stand on the tops of his feet, and he'd dance, and it just . . . stuck. C'mon."

"I'm far too stiff from your other bright idea," Ben said, but he was grinning. "You're odd, but you sure can do a whole heap of stuff nobody even suspected."

Kristin crossed to him and settled one of his hands on her waist, lifting up the other in a dance position. "You're supposed to be leading," she said, "but for the time being, follow my feet-two-three back-two-three. After a while your feet just take over; it becomes second nature."

Tesla watched from the far end of the room, a faint smile creasing his face. Ben blundered into Kristin several times, but he was doing a passable job of an elementary waltz when suddenly she lost the rhythm and stood stock still, staring at the window.

"What?" Ben said. He turned to follow her gaze and he, too, froze.

Two pigeons stood on the box of the air conditioner built into the window, just outside the glass. To Ben's eyes they might have been interchangeable with any other pigeon among New York's teeming millions, but obviously both Kristin and, now, Tesla saw something different.

"Earth," Tesla said softly. "And Air. They got Water, back at the park. These are the last two. I never thought . . . it was possible . . . to see them again."

*"That window doesn't open,"* Kristin said, suddenly tense in Ben's arms. "How do we get them inside?"

"There was a time it did," Tesla said. "I had a coop there, on the ledge, right where the air conditioner is now. They knew it. They knew where to come. But when I came back to New York, after the fiasco in Colorado, they never came to me. They never came back."

"They're here now," Ben said. He fished out the dream catcher in which Tesla had traveled here, and turned to face their ghostly companion. "Mr. Tesla, make sure you're ready to get back in here, fast. We may have to leave in a hurry. Now both of you, don't let *go* of them. Keep thinking about them, keep them here—they *will* flee, but you have to call them back."

"What are you doing?" Kristin said as Ben, who had been looking around for a bludgeon, picked up the chair by the hotel room's desk and hefted it experimentally.

"In case of fire, break glass," Ben muttered. "In case of Earth and Air, then, Humphrey May and the FBM will just have to cough up for the damages."

The pigeons exploded from the windowsill as he brought the chair down on the glass. It took two more smashes to shatter the window, and Ben closed his eyes and prayed that the pieces of broken glass were being caught by the lower ledges of the New Yorker Hotel's ziggurat terraces and not raining like shrapnel onto unsuspecting pedestrians. But the window was open, now, with cold winter air and a few flakes of snow drifting inside.

"Call them back," Ben said breathlessly. "Call them back, now."

"I have no idea how to even begin," Kristin said, but Tesla, half-translucent, stepped up to the broken window, put an arm through the hole that Ben had made, and just stood there, still and silent, eyes closed.

They came, the Elemental pigeons. First one, then the other—gently, fluttering warily down, settling on incorporeal flesh, cooing softly as Tesla slowly, slowly, drew his arm and both pigeons inside the room. He seemed to have a hypnotic effect on them, because the one that had landed first simply tucked its head under one wing and appeared to go to sleep. The second one sat quiescent, its chest vibrating gently from the cooing.

"Get them," Ben whispered.

They had been furnished with a birdcage in case they met with success. Kristin reached for it and then folded her hands around the second, more awake pigeon. It roused for a moment, its coos never quite stopping, and allowed itself to be transported into the cage without further protest. The sleeping bird did not stir at all. Kristin expelled a deep sigh and latched the cage door.

Ben was already peering at the Tesla wraith through the eye of the dream catcher, setting it spinning as he had been instructed to do.

"We don't have much time," Ben said, glancing back toward the door. There was no sign of movement or noise yet out in the corridor, but he was certain there would be very soon. With the dream catcher spinning rapidly in one hand, he rooted around in his pocket for a cell phone and tossed it back to Kristin. "Call Tess. Whatever emergency contact they've set up with Thea, they'd better invoke it. She needs to get us *out* of here. Right now."

## 12

"IT FEELS," A YOUNG, dark-haired Nikola Tesla said in a voice that was tightly controlled, "as though there's one too many of me here."

"The other Tesla can't see you. He has no way of knowing about or even suspecting your presence," Thea said.

"I can see *him*," her ghostly companion said. "I can see him, and I know what he is about to do."

He lifted his hand and laid it across his chest, as though trying to prevent a racing heart from leaping out of it. The three of them—Magpie, Thea, and the young Tesla ghost—were alone in the wooden building that had housed Tesla's Colorado Springs laboratory a hundred years before. Thea had arranged it so that they could be either participants or observers in this particular universe, but they were invisible to the other, *real* Tesla who was working here at this time. However, the Tesla ghost always succumbed to what was almost a panic attack whenever his alter ego was approaching, and sure enough the door to the laboratory opened before the ghost Tesla had finished speaking.

"It is to be today," the ghost said. "The mail arrived two days ago. It was that mail that finally pushed me into attempting this."

"You never mentioned that before," Thea said.

"Did I not?" Tesla murmured, his mouth slightly open as he stared at his other self moving around the room, checking, adjusting. "It must have slipped my mind. Many things slipped my mind, after."

"But what was in the . . ." Magpie began, turning to stare at him with sudden curiosity.

Tesla hushed her with a peremptory gesture, and then rubbed his temples with both hands as though warding off a headache.

"I am not certain if I can watch myself doing this," he said faintly.

"We are here to try and change the outcome, if we can," Thea said. "But first you need to tell us exactly what happened."

Tesla, watching his other self busy with preparations for the experiment to follow, began what was almost a running commentary, delivered for the most part in a flat, inflectionless voice. Two spots of hectic color burned on his usually pale cheeks.

"Two letters," he said. "One, letting me know that a loan had been denied—a loan I desperately needed to continue working. And another, without a signature, merely asking if I realized what would happen to me if I lost everything again, as I had done in New York, in that fire. That if anything more of that sort happened to me, I would *die*. That unless I took steps to protect my gifts, and keep them somehow safe, and perhaps in a different place than I bestowed myself . . ."

"Sounds like a trick Corey would pull," Thea muttered.

"It was that last that brought Kaschei to my mind," Tesla said, ignoring the interruption. "I had been brought low; this place, and all the tools I had assembled here against all odds—this was a new hope, almost a last hope. I needed to come up with a way to channel the power that was in me, to keep it safe—to keep it immortal."

"What is he doing?" Magpie said, craning her neck; the other Tesla had stopped with his back to them, busy with something on a bench in front of him, out of their sight.

"He . . . I . . . the warding mechanism needs to be reset every time." Tesla shook his head. "It is hard to explain. Elemental magic, especially at the scale on which I was planning to unleash it here, needs to be warded carefully; it is possible to achieve this in the mind of the mage, but when you are juggling all four Elements at once you are best doing it with all of your faculties. The warding mechanism sets an outer circle that will bounce back any stray shafts. We do not want local inhabitants getting caught up in the backwash—at best there would probably be physical repercussions that would have been diffi-cult to explain."

"Like what?" Magpie asked, fascinated.

"Does it matter?" Tesla said sharply. "What if I told you that it would be quite possible, for instance, for an escaped pod of Water Elemental out here in the mountains to result in the birth of children with gills—children who were born on a mountaintop a thousand miles away from the sea?"

"And that would be the *best* case scenario?"

Tesla was silent for so long that Magpie thought he had decided to deliberately ignore her, but then he sighed, raising one hand to smooth his mustache, keeping his eyes down.

"At worst . . . well, magic can kill," he said. "And wild Elemental magic can be more murderous than anything you can imagine."

Magpie took a step away from Tesla, as though the wild magic he spoke of might unexpectedly burst forth from his fingertips.

"I think he is ready," Thea said.

The real Tesla had turned now to the platform on which Thea and her friends had, during their first visit, seen his Elemental magic splinter into its component parts. He looked a little wild-eyed, his long-fingered hands clenching and unclenching as he hesitated, staring for a long moment at the empty platform, a wooden cylinder that resembled an upside-down barrel. As he seemed to come to a decision, he raised his arms and raked his hands through his hair, leaving it standing on end in a riotous and very un-Tesla-like disarray.

The ghost Tesla closed his own eyes.

"What will come," he whispered. "If you have never seen Elemental magic at work, this was such a moment. Perhaps it is worth seeing. But I was once inside of it. I cannot bear to watch."

The roof above the platform was open, rising in

a gabled pyramid into the tower rearing above the building, the tower with its strange bulbous onion-shaped top. Even as the ghost Tesla closed his eyes and turned away, there was a sound like thunder; twin sparks from the real Tesla's hands met upon the platform, twined together like two snakes of fire, and then flowed together into a solid column of flame that went straight up, through the open roof and into the tower, wreathing the mushroom bulb at the top of the tower's antenna in a blue-white glow before rejoining into a single column and continuing straight up into the sky. The air smelled of ozone and smoke.

A pigeon appeared just over the edge of the open roof; it hovered for a moment, and then circled down into the laboratory. At first, it slipped through the narrow gap between the column of flame and the roof, but then, apparently glimpsing Tesla standing there with one hand thrust straight into the fire, it plunged directly down, into the heart of Tesla's fiery pillar.

And vanished.

Both Teslas flinched, the one in the laboratory with his hand in the fire, lifting his free hand slowly as though reaching for a switch or trying to make a gesture of power; the other, the ghost, shuddered without opening his eyes.

Then the bird reappeared.

*Two* birds.

The pair of pigeons hung suspended in the flame for a long moment . . . and then they both disappeared.

"Wait," they heard the real Tesla say. "Wait, this isn't . . ."

The birds reappeared. Three of them.

And vanished again, even as the real Tesla's hand strained to rise, as though some great force was keeping it down.

Four birds reappeared.

Tesla touched a piece of his apparatus with a superhuman effort.

The pillar of fire died instantly.

In its place, in the center of where it had been, a bird lay with its wings splayed out awkwardly, its coral feet in the air.

"It's dead," Magpie said, her hand at her throat.

The ghost Tesla flinched, covering his face with his fingers.

They saw the real Tesla, as they had seen him once before, gather up the bird into his cupped hands, very gently. They heard him whisper, as though he were offering up a prayer, "Please . . . oh, please . . ."

And then he lifted his head, his face a raw mask of pain and anguish, and screamed.

Thea had steeled herself for this, but still could not help shuddering as she reached for her keypad and typed a few key phrases. The scene winked out; they were back, once again, to a time just before the pigeon's immolation.

The ghost Tesla was still standing with his face buried in his hands. Magpie was breathing in shallow gasps. Thea closed her eyes.

"All right," she said, her voice coming out more faintly than she had intended. She cleared her throat. "All right," she said again, more forcefully. "I'm sorry. It had to be done. We had to see. Before, it was all too fast, and we didn't understand. We were too far away, and we didn't have you with us. Talk to me, please; tell me what I need to do. Is there any way of making it unhappen?"

Tesla heaved a huge sigh and allowed his long fingers to drop from where they had been pressing into his temples.

"I know what he—I—did, and how it was done,"

he said, fighting to keep his own voice level. "As far as I know now, which is as much as I knew then, there was every reason for this to work exactly the way I had projected. When *this* happened . . . it was a shock to me, a deep and hard blow, and that was before I realized all the ramifications of what I had just done. I had meant to take the Elemental out of myself and keep that precious part of me safe from harm, in a place where it could come to my aid if my physical shell was ever in need. But what I did instead . . . when that bird died . . . was to sever my connection with it. I was left with only a thin and oily slick of magic that clung to the surface of my core; I would never, in my lifetime, touch it again, that thing that I had sought so hard to protect. I looked for them, after, the pigeons. I spent my life looking for them. I would feed and minister to thousands of their fellows in the years that were to come. But if these particular birds ever came close to me again . . . I do not remember it."

"But if the others find the rest of them, in New York, and if we achieve anything at all here in Colorado . . ." Thea frowned, shaking her head. "There isn't just one paradox; there are a dozen. What else might we be changing?"

Tesla glanced at her with the faintest of smiles curving under his black mustache. "Elemental magic," he said, "does not play by the rules. A true Elemental mage changes the world a little every day, every minute, with every breath that he takes. It might be that doing nothing would be the thing that changed the flow of history and time. With Elemental magic . . . you do what it tells you, and you worry about consequences later. It's a touch of raw chaos matter, my dear. You can predict nothing ahead of time. Elemental magic has been described as deliberately acting to confound the expectations placed upon it." He saw the shocked expression on Thea's face, and added, "Did they tell you this would be easy?"

"She's trying to help you," Magpie said.

Tesla's face crumpled again, the smile fading into pain. "I know," he said. "I apologize. What is it that you need me to do?"

"We can watch," Thea said, taking a few breaths to pull herself together. "We can observe, and up to a point we can interact with what's going on back there, but the only one who can *control* it . . . is you." She lifted her eyes to meet Tesla's pale blue gaze. "You were in charge out there. You know what went wrong. Maybe there's a chance, the faintest of chances, that if you were to do it again, you would do it right—that the Elemental magic would behave in the way that you wanted it to."

"What are you saying?" Tesla said, frowning.

"I need you to . . . to be him," Thea said faintly. "The other you. I need you to merge into him, to possess him, if you want to think of it that way. I want *you* inside that body, I want *you* controlling what's going on, I want *you* to hold your hand in that flame. Again." She drew a deep breath as she watched his stricken expression. "Did they tell you this would be easy?" she whispered, returning the barb that he had flung at her. She regretted it almost instantly, seeing the way he flinched as the words connected, but before she had a chance to apologize, Tesla turned his head away in a small, sharp motion, holding up a hand to silence any further commentary.

Magpie and Thea waited.

When he looked back at the two of them again, his eyes were terrible—full of pain, and power, and regret.

"It is," he said, "what I came here to do. I will do it. But, oh, you have no idea what you ask."

"*I* do," Magpie said, reaching out to touch his wrist with her fingers. He twitched it away instinctively, and then he turned to smile down at her.

"I am sorry, please forgive me," he murmured. "I did not mean to reject a kind heart. I . . . am grateful." He drew a deep ragged breath. "I am as ready as I can be to do a thing like this," he said. "Let it begin."

It was as though they had simply rewound time on a spool. Things started happening again exactly as they had happened before—except this time, when the real Tesla entered the room, the ghost Tesla clenched his hands into fists, took another deep breath, and stepped out into the room.

As the real Tesla busied himself with the thing on the bench that they could not see, calibrating the warding mechanism, the ghost Tesla walked up behind him until he seemed to stand with his chest pressed against the other's back. Then, slowly, almost unwillingly, he brought his arms up and around, sliding them on the outside of the other's, and then his essence simply seemed to fade, or flow, into the other body until there was only one Tesla standing there. He paused in his work and shook his head, as though he had been momentarily distracted. He cast an eye up to where the gap in the roof showed a ribbon of sky, and then bent over his task again.

Events unfolded as they had before. When the pillar of flame was born, the bird came; then two; then three; then four . . . and then Tesla shut off the fire.

Thea held her breath. At first, things seemed all right. The platform, at least for a fraction of a second, was empty—empty of life, empty of death, empty of anything at all to indicate that it had held a tower of fire only moments ago.

And then a dead bird lay on the platform, just as before. Exactly like before.

Thea heard Tesla's cry as he picked it up, and it tore her up inside because she knew now that two men were making that howl of pain, that it was twice as real, twice as heartbreaking.

She saw the two Teslas come apart, the ghost ripping itself out of the other body, stumbling away, wavering, weak, almost shredding itself. Thea frantically typed a reset on her keypad, wrenching them all away.

They were back again at the moment before the experiment. Tesla was shaking, his eyes wild.

"I had forgotten," he said, "how badly this had hurt."

"Something felt different," Magpie said. "There was . . . an energy. And then, for a moment, there was . . . a possibility. I could feel it. It changed back in less time than it takes to blink—but there was a difference. And there was no bird there, when you broke things off. Just for a moment, there wasn't."

"What do you think?" Thea said, looking back at Tesla.

"I do not know. I do not know." He was still shaking, trying to calm himself. "There . . . may have been. I cannot tell. I only know I felt it all again. Felt it . . . just like it was the first time. Except that this time it is worse, because back then he . . . I . . . never even knew just what it was that had been lost, squandered, thrown away. Now I know. And knowing makes it worse. I did not know that it would be possible for this to be worse, but it is."

"Can you," Thea said faintly, "do it again?"

Tesla skewered her with a gaze that was a bolt of blue lightning.

"Child, you have no idea what you ask of me."

"All I know is this: If *we* sensed a difference . . . if *you* thought you did . . . one more time and the pain could be only a bad memory. You could have it back. All of it."

Tesla stared at her. "*You* would do this? If it were you?"

"I have no idea," Thea said. "Would I allow my soul to be shredded as I am asking you to let yours be shredded? How could I know? I never had to choose."

"You have spirit, and courage, and integrity," Tesla said. "Many would have given the easy answer, and lied. Very well. I will try it again."

Thea flushed, using the pretext of fiddling with her keypad to avoid looking up at Tesla in the wake of the compliment. "Ready," she said faintly. "Here we go again. Magpie, we need to know *exactly* when . . ."

The real Tesla entered; the ghost Tesla tensed his shoulders and approached his other body again. The events unrolled inexorably, as they had already done before—the flame, the bird appearing at the edge of the roof, the vanishing and the multiplying of the pigeons, and then it was over once more, and the two girls strained forward to see the platform.

For a fraction of a second it remained empty, as it had done the previous time—and then the bird appeared on it again, the pigeon that had been given Tesla's Fire Element.

Except this time it was not on its back, its legs up in the air, dead. The pigeon was on its feet, staggering weakly, wings spread out for balance and support, emitting small, wounded noises.

"*It's alive,*" Thea breathed.

"But it looks in bad shape," Magpie said. She ran over to where Tesla had gently gathered up the pigeon into his cupped hands, and reached out with her own. She touched the pigeon's small head, an improbable shade of lilac-tinged gray, and stroked it gently. "Let me see," she whispered to Tesla. "Let me hold him."

He hesitated—the ghost could hear her, see her, but the real Tesla could not, and it was hard to say which of the two controlled the man's body.

"His heart," Tesla said, through lips that barely opened. "His heart is beating so fast . . . so slow . . . the heartbeat is not right . . ."

Even as he spoke, the pigeon freed one of its wings from his fingers, and Tesla loosened his hold a little so that the other wing would be free too. The pigeon roused, and its wings beat an astonishingly strong tattoo against both Tesla's hands and Magpie's. It turned its head, meeting Tesla's eyes and then Magpie's. The bird and the girl gazed at each other, and

Magpie almost sobbed as she reached out for it, her fingers on the sides of the pigeon's head.

And then the bird simply folded, its wings fluttering down without any further control to splay at an awkward angle over human wrists and fingers; its head lolled on a neck suddenly boneless, coming to rest gently on the web between Tesla's left thumb and forefinger, and it was still. A couple of small feathers floated slowly down to the floor at Tesla's feet.

"Wait," Magpie said, unconsciously echoing Tesla's own words. "Please . . . oh, please . . ."

It all seemed to take a very long time, but in reality only a few seconds had passed before Thea came thumping down on her knees beside the two of them and the dead bird.

"Is it—" she began breathlessly, and then broke off as she looked at Magpie's stricken face. "Oh, God. Was there nothing you could do?"

Magpie shook her head mutely, her index finger gently stroking the curve of the pigeon's neck where it lay cradled in Tesla's hands.

"Was there even a chance . . . ?"

"I don't know," Magpie whispered. "I felt it go. I'm not even entirely sure what killed it. It was just . . . gone. As though . . . as though it was not meant to live in this world at all."

Tesla stirred, gathering the pigeon a little closer, but he remained silent.

Thea, torn between a terrible pity and a need to understand, to *know*, hesitated to intrude on a grief that he was wearing like armor. After a moment she, too, reached out and touched the still-warm body of the bird.

"But it was alive this time," she whispered. "*Alive. We made it that far. Maybe . . .*"

There was a disconcerting wrench in perspective; the real Tesla did not move, bent protectively over the pigeon, his hands frozen in position with the bird's head pillowed on his thumb, but the ghost Tesla, still contained in the same body, lifted his head to meet Thea's eyes, and one ghostly hand appeared to leave the pigeon's body and came up in a gesture intended to silence her.

"No," the ghost Tesla said, in a voice that sliced into Thea like a knife. "I cannot do this again. I cannot hold him and feel his life going from him, feel his heart beating inside of him as though it was bursting. This, too, was part of me. It hurts in too many ways. Not again. I cannot."

"But you lived for forty years or more after this day," Thea whispered, tears standing in her eyes. "If we can bring back light and life to the rest of your days . . ."

"I did this," Tesla said. "I have already lived with it. I will have to continue to live with it. It was a grievous mistake on my part, and as long as I am here that death is with me. Every time we have repeated this a little bit more of me has died. No, Thea." It was the first time he had addressed her by name. The ghost Tesla bent his head again, let his hand drop, folding back into the real Tesla body holding the bird in his hands. "What is, is. I will pay the price of my folly."

Magpie stumbled to her feet. "Give him some space," she murmured. "It's hard enough to say good-bye to the simple creatures who cross your life like shooting stars—here one day, gone the next. That thing that he is holding is so much more than that."

Thea became aware, as she accepted the pull of Magpie's hand, that Tesla was humming a quiet, simple tune over the pigeon he held in his lap; the hum turned into words, but they were strange words, in a language she did not know, perhaps the language that Tesla had spoken from the cradle.

He seemed to be oblivious of the two of them, to the room that surrounded them, to the smell of Elemental fires that still lingered in the air. He was alone with that part of him that was gone, singing a part of his soul to a sleep from which it would never wake again.

"This might have been a very bad idea," Thea said, her throat tight with tears.

Magpie stroked her arm gently a few times. "You tried your best," she said. "It wasn't your fault."

Thea gave her a small smile. "I had hoped that with *you* here . . . You have helped so many creatures before, I hoped having *you* here would make a difference."

"Against Elemental magic?" Magpie said. "You heard him speak of it. What chance would I and the small things that I can do have against a force like that?"

"They're not small. Even if they were, it's the smaller things that get past the great blundering forces, slip through the cracks that something grander and flashier might never even see."

"That was before we came here," Magpie murmured. "Before we saw him do that. I think maybe I could have done something if I had been stronger, or more experienced. You saw the way that bird looked at me. It knew me. We could have come to an understanding, the pigeon and I—but on the other side of that . . . was Elemental magic."

They heard a noise and turned to see Tesla getting to his feet. He still held the pigeon in his hands, but awkwardly now, as though he didn't quite know what to do with it. Without a word, Magpie unwrapped the black silk shawl tied around her shoulders and folded it into a smaller triangle, stepping up to Tesla and offering it as a cradle. He appeared to look straight through Magpie, as though she were not there—which, in a sense, she was not; the real Tesla's body was not aware of her at all. But the ghost Tesla was still partly in charge of that body, and to him Magpie was a real and solid presence. It was the ghost Tesla who finally took control and gently placed the pigeon in the shawl, nodding mute thanks as Magpie threw a corner of the fabric over the bird. Empty-handed, with his arms now hanging at his sides, Tesla looked lost, dazed.

"I'm sorry," Thea said. "I'm so sorry. I really thought that we might turn it . . ."

"I appreciate the attempt," he said.

He stepped *out* of the real Tesla's body, and the real Tesla stumbled away toward his workbench, catching himself on it as though it was the only thing holding him upright. The ghost Tesla remained where the real man had been.

"What was that tune you were singing? . . . It was quite lovely."

"When they asked me to show my magic tricks at the Chicago fair," Tesla said, apparently arbitrarily, "I chose to twist fire into letters, make a name glow in the dark. What name did I choose? There might have been many—but I picked one, the name of a different kind of wizard, a poet who brought many lovely dreams into my head when I was young. His name was Zmaj, and that means 'dragon' in your language. It is his name I put up in lights in Chicago, a city he had never heard of, had no idea even existed." He paused. "One of his poems was set to music, as a lullaby. It was sung to me and my brother and my sisters in our cribs. *Tiho, noći, moje sunce spava.* 'Quiet, night, for my sunshine is asleep'—my sunshine, my child, the one that I love. The poem speaks of nightingales weaving a coverlet out of their song, to tuck around the sleeping child so that she sleeps safe, and doesn't wake." He turned his head, to where Magpie stood with the pigeon bundled up in black silk. "It seemed appropriate."

A faint ping from Thea's keypad claimed her attention, and she glanced down almost unwillingly. Skimming the message on her screen, she brought her head up again with a sudden hope.

"It's Tess," she said. "She's heard from the others. They sent a message that they need snatching out of New York—it's urgent, like they're in danger or something, but she says it sounds as though they've done it. Give me a minute, I need to get them out of there."

"Good," said Magpie faintly, her arms folded protectively around a dead bird draped in black silk. "I could use some good news."

13.

"I HAVE GOOD NEWS AND bad news," Ben said.

Thea had gathered them all together—Tess and Terry from the Nexus room at the school, Ben and Kristin snatched from the shattered hotel room in contemporary New York, herself and Magpie from the wreckage of Colorado—and brought them back to Tesla's world, to the New Yorker hotel room as it was in his time, a bank of old-fashioned filing cabinets against one wall and the pigeon coop in the window.

Tesla himself presided over the meeting, sitting in his favorite leather armchair, gazing at the six of them with stern blue eyes.

Kristin stepped out from behind Ben with the birdcage held in both hands. The two pigeons inside were awake, and fluttering about.

"Great! You got them!" Tess exclaimed, and then

did a double take. "Two—there's two—shouldn't there be—?"

"That's the bad news," Ben said.

"Is that one dead too?" Magpie gasped.

"Worse," Kristin said, hanging her head. "And it's all my fault."

"No, it isn't," Ben said. "I had my share of stupid ideas. You were just doing what you were there for."

Thea gave a small exasperated sigh. "What *happened?!*"

Kristin and Ben exchanged a troubled look, and Terry frowned at them. "That bad, was it?"

"Corey has the Water pigeon," Ben said.

But Kristin was shaking her head. "No, he doesn't. Corey *took* the Water pigeon. The Alphiri *have* it."

In his armchair, Tesla roused. "Have it. How do you mean, have it?"

"Your other self knows," Ben said. "You were—*he* was—right there."

Tesla was gazing at the pigeons in the cage. "Air . . . and Earth," he said. "I could barely believe that they still existed. That you would find them. That they would come to *you*, and that they never, in forty long years, came back to me at all. Not even to glimpse them. That which I did must have been ill done indeed, if pieces of my own soul chose to stay away from me for so long . . . and come to you, when you went to seek them."

"You're wrong," Ben said. "They came to you— they *all* came to you. When we were in the park, you were covered with birds, as though they were celebrating your return. And when these came, it was you who took them, your hand that they came to. They did not desert you, in the end."

"Forty lonely years," Tesla murmured, reaching out to the cage and pushing a couple of long fingers through the wire. One of the pigeons sidled closer, cooing louder, and rubbed his head on Tesla's hand.

"Yes," he said to it, his voice suddenly very soft and gentle, his index finger ruffling the feathers at the back of the bird's neck, "I am very happy to see you, too."

Thea suddenly flashed back to Tesla's last lullaby to another bird, lying still in his hands; she met Magpie's eyes, briefly, and could see the same thought reflected there. She cleared her throat, but before she could speak Terry stirred.

"Humphrey won't be happy," he said. "Have you

been in touch with him, Thea? He wants to know what's going on. He's been bugging me several times a day—e-mail, phone, once even a personal visit."

"He phoned us in New York. Twice. And I know he had an FBM shadow on us—it wasn't just the Alphiri that were following us around," said Ben. "For all I know, he might already know about the results of the New York expedition."

"This Humphrey May," Tesla said. "What exactly is his own role in all of this? In my own experience with the Federal Bureau of Magic, whenever they did something it was for their own reasons, not anyone's well-being. I am a little disturbed that he is involved so deeply in all of this."

"He thought it might be possible to get you back," Thea said. "To give back what you'd lost. To *reclaim* you. I know he was doing it for his own reasons, but when I said I would help find those pigeons of yours, I told him I was doing it for *you*, not for him. All I wanted to do was try and set you free; I don't know what he wanted, exactly, or what he would take instead of that if he didn't get it."

"He would have taken you," Tesla said shrewdly. "He was betting on one of us. I would be very careful around the FBM, my dear."

"I wouldn't say you were far wrong," Terry said, "even though my uncle runs the place. But Thea, we need to do *something*. He's been a confounded nuisance, and I can't tell him to bug off; he's technically my boss."

"What would the Alphiri want with that pigeon they stole?" Tess asked.

"Hold it for ransom, maybe, or hold it over our heads as a threat. They will find a way to make a profit on the situation," Terry said grimly. "They'll threaten to wring its neck if we don't produce its fellows, or Tesla."

"I thought they did not steal," Kristin said, clutching her cage as though her mere touch would protect the precious birds inside it. "But Corey . . ."

"Exactly. Corey." Thea tossed her hair back in a small frustrated gesture. "They stole nothing. They *bought* the pigeon from Corey. And Corey had no compunction about stealing. None at all. Well, two can play at that game."

"Oh?" Ben said sharply.

"Who knows someone who's got Tersii in the house?" Thea said, turning to her friends.

She was greeted with five sets of blank stares.

"The Faele Cleaner Clan?" Tess echoed. "The

imps that do the housework when nobody's looking, and as long as everybody pretends not to notice?"

"Those," Thea said, beginning to grin.

"But they're the lowest Faele rank there is—they have no power at all. What do you want with the Tersii?"

"Uh," Ben said, hesitating. "I don't know, not for sure, but my father's lab is always immaculate, and I never see *him* tidying up. It *could* be one of the Tersii, but I don't know for sure."

"Worth a try," Thea said. "I hope it's the helpful kind and not the malicious tribe. Getting tangled up with those would be all we need right now."

"*Tersii*, for heaven's sake? Why do you want to get tangled up with the Faele anyway? Don't we have enough trouble on our plate?" Tess said.

But Tesla was wearing a wolfish smile. "I think I understand," he said. "Good luck."

"Wait for me here," Thea said. "Ben, can you describe your father's lab for me?"

"I can do better than that. Take me with you, and I'll get you there directly," Ben said.

"All right, then. The sooner we—"

"Wait."

They turned to see Magpie standing a little apart

from them, laying down a small silk-wrapped bundle.

"Take me with you too," she said.

Thea stared at her and then nodded.

"Okay," she said. "The rest of you, wait here. Come on, Ben."

She typed something on her wrist pad, showed it to Ben, who murmured assent, and hit ENTER.

The three of them found themselves in an empty laboratory, just at the instant that someone had switched off the overhead lights and was softly closing the door behind them. They heard the snick of a lock, and then they were alone in a large room, with a couple of safety lights over two of the benches and the muted glow of the light in the fume cupboard. It glinted on glassware—some rinsed and left out to dry on one of the benches, the rest piled into the scarred and pitted sink.

"It's promising," Ben said. "It never looks like this in the morning."

"Shhh," Thea said, straining forward to see.

They waited in silence, without moving, until they heard a sound, very faint, of glass clinking against glass. Thea hid a smile as she typed something else into the wrist pad, hiding the small screen's glow

under her sleeve; in the next instant, she was standing beside the sink without ever having actually
physically moved, and a smothered squawk from her
closed hand betrayed the presence of an astonished
and furious little man less than a foot tall. Ben and
Magpie hurried over. At first, all they could see were
two angrily waving arms below a peaked brown hat
that seemed two sizes too large for its owner.

"Put me down! Put me down this instant! Put me
*down*, you great human elephant! We had a deal!
You weren't even supposed to know I was here!"

"It's hard not to know, when you do what you
do," Ben said, unable to help himself.

The Tersii's hat turned around, revealing a small,
pointed face with dark eyes and a broad, bulbous
nose. The gnome stared at Ben, his lips pursed in an
annoyed grimace of recognition.

"You," he said peevishly. "I should've known. It
was an inside job."

"Hush," Thea said. "I have another deal for you—
you, or someone else of your kindred. I mean you no
harm, and will not reveal your presence to anybody.
Nor will anyone else here. Your secret is safe with us
if you will lead us to those we need to speak to."

"What do you want?" the Tersii said suspiciously,

squinting up at Thea.

"I need a changeling."

The Tersii stared at her. "That will cost you."

"That's my problem. Mine, and whoever it is I bargain with. Do we have a deal with you?"

"Uh, sure. But I can't get you a changeling. You'd need to go much further up the hierarchy for that. The Court, even."

"How do I get there?"

"They don't let just *anyone* . . ." the Tersii said, outraged.

"Yes, but it was the Faele themselves who labeled me a seeker in my cradle," Thea said. "I'm not just anyone. How do I get there?"

"Let me get my boss," the Tersii said, after a pause. "I can't do any of this. I'm just clean-up crew. I earn my keep; I'm a working-class body, not like some mucky mucks up above me."

"Like your boss?" Magpie said, unable to help herself.

The Tersii blinked. "Tricksy. I didn't say that. Let me go, and I'll get—"

Thea shook her head. "No. You can call him. I'll let you go when he gets here. The boss."

The Tersii, looking sulky, straightened his hat with

both hands. "Fine," he said sullenly. "Oh, *fine.*"

He tilted his head and closed his eyes for a moment, and then opened them again. "Coming," he said. "Can I get on with my work now? You sure nobody will know?"

"Oh everybody *knows*," Ben said. "But nobody will have seen you. Cross my heart."

Thea opened her hand and the little man stepped smartly out of her reach, straightening his clothes as he did so. "Caught like a nipper," he muttered to himself. "As though I haven't been doing this for a hundred and fifty years."

"Do they really live that long?" Magpie said, astonished, turning to Thea.

"How do you know how long their year is?" Thea said, grinning.

A small, theatrical flash of white light announced the arrival of the Tersii worker's boss. He stood just a smidge taller than his underling, and his hat was more gold than brown, but other than that, he didn't look much different from the original Tersii, who had vanished somewhere into the pile of dirty glassware and by the sound of things was hard at work.

"Well, who wants me?" the boss Tersii asked

with some asperity.

"Lay off my father's phosphorus," Ben muttered. "I recognize that flash."

"I come bargaining," Thea said, ignoring the interruption. "I need a changeling."

Boss Tersii stood up a little straighter. "A changeling," he said. "You don't say. And what might this changeling be for?"

"That's for the one who can provide me one to know," Thea said.

"Well, *I* can't," the little man said, throwing his arms wide. "Did that doofus over there tell you this was something I could accomplish? I'll flay him. . . ."

"No," Thea said. "What he said, I believe, is that you can give us access to a higher level. To the Court."

"The Court isn't in session," Boss Tersii said, crossing his arms.

"They will be," Thea said. "For this. Get the message out."

"You would summon the Court here? To this filthy place?"

"I'm working as fast as I can!" the original Tersii grumbled from the sink.

Thea shrugged. "Here, or wherever they choose."

"A changeling. What would a human want with a changeling?"

"Not a human changeling. A pigeon change-ling."

Ben whipped his head around to stare at Thea, his mouth hanging open. He looked like he was about to say something, but Magpie touched his arm gently, giving him a light shake of her head.

Boss Tersii didn't entirely miss all of that, but he was far too busy trying to make sense of Thea's words to pay all that much attention.

"A *pigeon* changeling?" he echoed, not bother-ing to conceal his astonishment. "What possible use would there be in a Faele pigeon changeling?"

"Court," Thea said sweetly. "Call them and find out."

The Boss Tersii looked the three of them up and down. "Great galumphing humans," he muttered. "You'd stomp on the Court with those clodhoppers and that would be the end of that. I will get the Queen's Chancellor."

"The Queen," Thea said, gently but insistently. "Or else the Chancellor will just have to go and get her himself. What I ask is not for the common official."

"The Chancellor is a Royal Paladin, I will have you know," Boss Tersii said.

"The Queen," Thea said.

"Oh, fine," Boss Tersii said. "On your own head be it. I can tell you now she is not used to being summoned by the likes of you. She will not be happy." He winked out.

Ben shook off Magpie's hand and turned to Thea. "Are you sure you know what you are doing?" he whispered.

Thea smiled and shook her head. "Nope," she said. "I'm figuring things out as I go along. I've got the Feds behind me—for now—and Humphrey's still backing me."

"But *he* doesn't know what you're doing, either," Ben said doggedly.

"He never did," Thea said. "But even if all that fails, I have Tesla. I have me."

"You might be putting too much in that basket. Even Elemental magic can't take on two other polities at once."

Further conversation was prevented by an odd distortion of the air above one of the benches. It slowly resolved into a window that looked into what appeared to be a forest glade wreathed in amethyst twilight. Lanterns filled with fireflies hung from twigs and branches, most of them in an arch above a bower thick with rose petals on which reclined the tiny, delicate form of an exquisite silver-haired woman with a single white gem on her brow. She held what looked like a large jeweled hatpin as a scepter. Her arms were weighed down with silver bracelets from wrist to elbow, and she wore a fragile-looking silver gown that glittered with tiny crystals over an undergarment of a shimmering royal purple.

"This," said the Queen of the Faele Court, "had better be good."

Thea bobbed a small curtsy. "Your Majesty," she said. "I come for help only you can give."

"Sounds promising already," the Queen said, with just a touch of irony. "What did you have in mind?"

"Something important to me has been stolen. I want it replaced with a Faele changeling. This does not have to be a permanent thing at all—just long enough so that the thief doesn't notice the switch. And I want the original restored to me."

"A living something. Else you would not be asking for a changeling at all."

"Yes, Your Majesty. A bird."

"It sounds elaborate," the Queen said, after a pause. "Perhaps a shade too elaborate. If stolen, why can it not be recovered by more straightforward means? And perhaps more to the point, who holds it?"

"Well, this is why I need your people and their skills," Thea murmured. "It is being held by the Alphiri."

The Queen sat up, throwing her scepter down on her bower. "Then it wasn't stolen," she said. "The Alphiri do not steal. This is known. They make a bargain, and they hold to it."

"It was stolen from one of the Human Polity by one whom your polity knows well, and has done many deals with: the Trickster. If the Alphiri bargained with him, then that is between them and the Trickster, but the bird of which I speak *was* stolen, from us."

"You seriously expect my people to bring the wrath of the Alphiri on our heads?" the Queen asked. "Why would I do such a thing? And if you are right and the Trickster is involved, he is not part

of this Court, but is an Elder Spirit of a fellow polity ratified by formal law. His word easily carries
the weight of my own within the hierarchy, and I
have no say over what he does or does not do. I owe
you nothing. Nothing that I want to get the Alphiri
angry at me over, anyway."

"What if there is nothing they can do to you?"

"They would know it was me," the Queen said.
"A Faele changeling pigeon? Who else would sanction or make possible such a thing?"

"But you yourself said it—the Alphiri understand
a bargain," Thea said. "And you would be making
one, with us. We—the Human Polity—would stand
surety for this one. If they wish to challenge that,
they will have to take it to the Polity Court for arbi-
tration. And our lawyers are just as well versed in
cross-polity law as the Alphiri are."

"You are a younger polity," the Faele Queen said
slowly. "You haven't felt Alphiri fury. Not yet. Not
completely."

"Neither would you. Immunity."

"No," the Queen said, shaking her head slowly.
"It goes a long way, but it doesn't go far enough. I
will not risk—"

"Wait," Magpie said, stepping forward.

Thea turned, astonished.

Magpie already held all the earrings from both her ears and half a dozen rings cupped in one hand. With the other, she was in the process of undoing the clasp of a chain bearing a large prismatic crystal that hung around her neck. It came loose even as she spoke and she poured it into the hand with the rest of the loot. Then she held it all out to the Queen.

"There is more," she said, "where these came from. It may be more or less valuable than the chance to actually pull one over on the Alphiri with absolute impunity. Everything I own that is shiny and that sparkles—and I can see that there is a love of such things in your court, Your Majesty—I pledge it all."

"Magpie," Thea began, strangely moved.

But the Queen leaned forward. "Bring it closer," she instructed, waving Magpie to approach with one imperious hand. "I wish to see."

"Magpie, wait," Thea said, putting out a hand to restrain her friend, but Magpie shook her off.

"I owe it," she said. "For the other life I couldn't touch."

"Bring it," the Queen said. "Now."

Magpie stepped forward, holding out her hand.

The Queen reached out with both her exquisite hands and rummaged around in the stash in Magpie's palm. She lifted her head, and a winged minion stepped up to her from the shadows beyond the firefly lights; she said something into its pointed ear, and the minion nodded and vanished in a bright spark of light. When the messenger returned a few minutes later, he made his report—quite a lengthy one—into the Queen's ear, again out of earshot. When he was done, the Queen dismissed him with another wave of her hand.

"Your offer pleases me," the Queen said. "It would be satisfactory . . . to liberate the pigeon from Alphiri captivity."

"And restore it to us," Thea said.

The Queen shook her head. "The price for that is still too high," she said. "Even with your promised immunity. Even with all of this. I cannot put myself or my people at such risk."

Thea bit her lip, and then lifted her head to speak again, but once more Magpie spoke first.

"Then I will offer more," she said faintly. "Your kindred has always known the power of true-names, better than any other."

"This is true," the Queen said. "I am listening."

Magpie swallowed hard.

"I am called Magpie," she said. "That is the name by which everyone knows me, everyone calls me. It is my true-name, always has been, even though it is not the name given to me in the cradle—but it is the name that makes me who I am, what I am. I have already offered you everything that makes that name fit me, for I no longer own any shiny thing that a magpie might covet. But I will lay the name, too, at your feet tonight. For the rest. For the pigeon's safe return."

Her words fell into a stillness so profound that time seemed to have stopped.

Thea found herself staring at Magpie, her eyes filled with tears. Ben had locked his hand around Thea's free wrist with a white-knuckled grip, his attention wholly focused on Magpie.

"It is acceptable," the Queen said at last, after a long moment of silence. "It is done. When the changeling bird has been left in place of your own, and the real one procured, I will send word. So let it be."

The girl once known as Magpie allowed the silver and crystal in her hand to fall at the Queen's feet, and stepped back, her head bowed, veiled in her own dark hair, her hands empty of rings, her throat empty of necklace and crystal and charm, a stranger without a name. The Queen made a sharp gesture with her hand, and the air closed over the rose-petal bower under firefly lanterns. They were back in the laboratory, with only the safety lights and the dim glow of the fume cupboard to light them. Even the Tersii were gone; they were quite alone.

"Mag . . ." Ben began, his throat tight, but the name really didn't fit anymore. It had been given away, freely, the last jewel in a dragon hoard of gems. He fell silent.

"What do we call you now?" Thea said quietly. "I did not mean for this to happen."

"*You gave it away*," Ben said. "It's theirs now, and it's your true-name—you gave them yourself. If they call you by that name, you have to come—you have to do whatever they . . . You took on *chains*, do you realize that?"

"It was my choice," said the dark-haired girl, lifting her pale face into the glint of the cupboard light. "It isn't as though I am now nameless—I *have* a name. Catherine. That is the name my parents gave me when I was born. I've never owned it, lived by it; I think I answered to it for my first five or six years, and then I gathered up my first shiny thing, and I became . . . what I became. But I am . . . I am Catherine."

"No, you're not," Ben said. "How am I supposed to get used to this? It's *wrong*. . . ."

"You're right, she's not. She's not a Catherine." Thea stepped forward and wrapped her friend in a fierce hug. "You're Cat. I rechristen you Cat."

"Cat. It's an animal name."

"Is that going to be . . ."

"No, you don't understand," Cat said, shaking her head, tears standing in her eyes. "Do you remember when I told you, a long, *long* time ago, that I had gone into the woods looking for the animal that was going to be my own spirit guide? And failed to find one?"

"That was back when we first met," Thea said.

"Looks like I found it," Cat said. "Or at least, it found me. I give up the only identity I've ever known and another steps up to claim me. An *animal* name. A spirit guide name. Maybe I was meant to find out this way."

"Cat," Ben said. "But you were so much of a mag—" He shook his head. "It's *weird*," he said. "I can't even say it anymore. I can't look at you and think it."

"It's gone," Thea said. "The Faele own it now. It's theirs, not hers."

"Do you think the others will notice?" Cat said, staring at her ringless hands.

"I don't know," Thea said. "You don't look anything like I think you should look, but I recognize you anyway. I would know you anywhere."

"Do you miss it? All the stuff?" Ben waved at his own ear, throat, arm. "I've never seen you without it."

Cat lifted her head. "Miss it? Miss what?" she inquired softly. "It's as though . . . it never was. Like I sloughed off a skin. It's still me, but I'm not sure . . ." She swallowed, glanced at Thea. "Frankly, I'm terrified," she said. "I suppose it has to happen sooner or later, and I'd rather just get it over with. Let's get back to the others."

### 14.

"IHAVE GOOD NEWS AND bad news," Thea said as she and her two companions returned to Tesla's room, echoing Ben's earlier words. "I spoke to the Faele Queen. They'll get the missing pigeon for us."

"Is that the good news or the bad news?" Terry asked pragmatically.

"Something's . . . different," Tess said. "M-Mag . . ."

The girl who used to be Magpie shook her head. "No longer," she said quietly. "We will get the pigeon back. But the name . . . was part of the price."

"Cat," Ben said. "Her name is Cat. For Catherine."

"What have you *done*?" Tess said, aghast. "If they accepted this kind of bargain, they must have thought . . . and I can't even think of you anymore as . . ."

"It was a true-name," Cat said. "It had value. I

gave it together with the rest—all the jewelry, every-thing."

"But now they own you," Tess said. "They *own* you."

"But I am no longer the person to whom that name belonged," Cat said quietly. "They own . . . a memory of who I used to be."

"They can make it real. They *can*, uh, Cat. They have a knack with things like this. Sometime in the future, when you least expect it, you'll have the Faele knocking on your door and asking you for things you don't want to give them, calling you by your own true-name, making it impossible to refuse."

"I am so selfish," Kristin said unexpectedly.

She had hung back a little at first, because the others had known Cat for far longer, and had the right to respond first, to react, to mourn. But now they all turned. Kristin was clutching her elbows with her hands, her arms crossed, her face flushed, and her expression stricken.

"What are you talking about?" Thea said.

"If you had lingered here one moment longer I might even have asked it out loud," Kristin said. "You were going to speak to the Faele. I know why; I know what's at stake and I know that I am partially to blame for the situation."

"It was hardly your fault . . ." Ben began, but Kristin shook her head.

"But it's true. And yet, when you were on the point of leaving here to go and find the Faele . . . all I could think of was the absolute *need* to ask, to beg, that you talk to them about this." One of her hands lifted and her fingers fluttered over her unfortunate teeth. "You'd think I'd have learned, after the spell-spam three-wishes fiasco. But it's just that it's the first thing that anyone sees, ever, and it will always make people want to run and hide."

Ben stared at her. "I had stopped noticing," he said, "some time ago, actually."

Kristin gave him a smile, and then looked back at Cat.

"I'm sorry," she said. "You went in there willing to give something up. And all I could think about was what might be in it for me."

Tesla had risen from his chair and had come to stand at the back of the group, looming over them. Now he cleared his throat and they all turned their attention to him.

"Hardly selfish," he said, "under the circumstances. But as I understand things, it is thanks to you and your gift that we have the two Elementals that we do. Perhaps it is time you began to look at your identity in terms of your accomplishments and your abilities rather than the superficial impressions others might get from a first glance."

It was pure Tesla, managing to be a compliment and a rebuke at the same time, but he didn't leave them much time to ponder it, turning instead to Cat and Thea. "As for the rest . . . speaking as one who has made my own deals with the Faele, it was a good idea, and a brave attempt, and I must offer both my congratulations at your perceptiveness and my grateful thanks for your willingness to carry it out. And I think I owe far more than that . . . to *you*, my dear."

He reached out to Cat, and lifted her hand to his lips in a gallant continental gesture that made her blush and drop her eyes. Tesla lifted his head, wrapped both his long-fingered hands around hers, and gazed at her with an expression at once kind and very serious.

"I make you a promise," he said. "As you have put me in your debt, I stand in yours. Should any of this come back to haunt you, please know that I will stand surety for you in any way that I am able—and that you will never take harm from this if it lies in my power to put myself in that harm's way for your sake."

He might have been on the ebb of his powers, but he stood on the reputation of one who had been and might again be an Elemental mage.

Cat, when she lifted her head again, had tears sparkling in her eyes.

"I failed you, in Colorado," Cat said. "You—the you here, now—might not remember, but I . . ."

"I reconstituted him," Terry murmured. "He knows all that the other avatars learned."

"*I* failed me in Colorado," Tesla said. "Not you. There is no way you can bear the responsibility for decisions I made before your generation was born. But remember what I have just said to you." He squeezed her hand, then dropped it and turned back to Thea. "Now," he said, "this FBM agent."

"Oh, yes, please, someone deal with Humphrey May," Terry said.

"It's probably about time I gave him an update," Thea said, lifting her left wrist and gazing at her keypad thoughtfully.

"Are you going to tell him about the cube?" Kristin asked. "That you took it?"

"Before or after you tell him that the Alphiri have one of those precious pigeons he coveted?" Tess added.

"Or that you've committed him to giving the Faele immunity for breaking cross-polity laws?" Ben said.

"You did *what*?" Terry said sharply.

"Well, there is a logic to it," Thea said, shrugging her shoulders. "He'll probably see the situation for what it is, if I explain it properly. He doesn't want that pigeon in Alphiri hands any more than we do."

"Perhaps I should come along to this meeting," Tesla suggested. "Quite aside from any other considerations, I would very much appreciate another demonstration of this thing that I have now seen you do several times with the device on your wrist."

Terry held up one of Grandmother Spider's dream catchers. "I reconstituted him. *All* of him is now in here—you could take him across just as you took the other Tesla into Colorado, and release him whenever you get to wherever you're going." He tossed the dream catcher across to Thea, who caught it reflexively.

"What *are* you going to tell Humphrey?" Ben asked.

"Don't let him bully you," Terry said. "Do you want me to come with you?"

"You've been trying to avoid him, by all accounts," Thea said, grinning at him. "Thanks, but I'll be fine."

"I know *I* wouldn't be exactly keen to face him alone at this point," Terry said.

"You won't have to tell him you have the cube," Kristin said, glancing at Tesla. "He'll kind of . . . get the idea."

"I suppose he's going to find out sooner or later," Thea said. "Very well. If you'll step into the web, sir . . ."

Tesla gave her a small, formal bow. She lifted the dream catcher and peered at him until she could hold his entire image within the circle; then she spun it. Tesla vanished, and the dream catcher began to glow once again with a pale blue light as it dangled from Thea's fingers.

"That will do it," Thea said, "except it's hardly what he had in mind when he wanted me to show him what I was doing."

Ben looked around. "What about the rest of us?" he said. "You might not want an entourage when you get to see Humphrey, but we're kind of done here, aren't we?"

"I don't want to take the pigeons back to the school," Thea said. "Not until some sort of arrangements have been made. Particularly not given that I'll have Tesla himself with me."

"Cheveyo's," Cat said. "Everything will be safe there. And you aren't going to be gone for that long."

Ben sniffed. "It's a lot less *comfortable* than this place," he said.

"Yes, but I'm not sure I want to abandon you guys inside an Elemental cube, without even its wizard in residence. Cat's right. Cheveyo's house is safe enough for the time being, and when I get back from seeing Humphrey, we'll figure out the rest. Got everything?"

She typed in two lines of instructions on her keypad—one sending herself back to the Academy with the dream catcher, the other sending everyone else with the pigeons to Cheveyo's house—and pressed ENTER. The walls of Tesla's room vanished around them.

Thea found herself in the cedar woods just behind her residence hall at the school—the same place where she had overheard Humphrey May talking to

Mrs. Chen about her own possible fate. She looked around, but the woods appeared to be deserted; she fished out the dream catcher that housed Tesla, and spun it to release him.

Tesla, his formal dress incongruous under the trees, nodded his thanks to Thea as she retrieved her cell phone from her pocket and punched in Humphrey May's number. She was expecting voice mail, but Humphrey picked up on the second ring.

"Where are you?" Humphrey said without pre-amble.

"School. The woods behind the res hall, where you met Mrs. Chen. I've got news."

"Don't move. I'll be right there."

Thea flipped the phone closed as the connection went dead. Tesla, substantial enough in this world to be able to interact with it by touch, held out his hand.

"May I see?" he said, indicating the phone. "The people on New York streets seemed to have those things glued to their ears." He turned the phone over in his hands, peering at it from every angle. "Fascinating."

"Humphrey May said he'd be here any minute," Thea said.

"Your FBM man," Tesla said. "I had my share of run-ins with the FBM. I will be interested to hear what this one has to say—to see if they have changed at all in the last half a century."

He handed the cell phone back to Thea, who sighed.

"Did you win?" she asked.

"Win?" Tesla frowned a little, puzzled.

"You and the FBM. The run-ins. Did you win?"

"Not all the time. Juggernauts are hard to stop once they get going. But I held my own," Tesla said.

"I'm not sure I'll be able to," Thea said. "There are times I wish I had a champion—like you promised Cat you'd be for her."

Tesla inclined his head a little. "But, my dear, I could not be such a thing for you," he said. "Elemental magic is the stuff from which the world is made. If called to do battle, two Elemental mages would fight side by side and not as each other's champions or shields. You may be very young still in years and in your understanding of your gifts—but you and I, we are equals."

A quiet crack of a twig broke the moment. Thea fought down her astonishment and unexpected exhilaration at Tesla's words, and peered into the trees.

"I think he's coming," she said in a low voice. "Perhaps you'd better . . . keep out of sight. Let me speak to him alone first."

"As you wish," Tesla said, stepping back and blending into the shadows underneath a large cedar tree.

"Where have you *been*?" Humphrey said, as soon as he caught sight of Thea. "You were supposed to check in. I've been going out of my mind."

"Yes, Terry said something about that," Thea said. "And so did Ben. Sorry. Things got a bit busy. We were a little stretched, trying to get something done on two fronts, and we've had . . . mixed success."

"Thea," Humphrey said, a warning in his voice, "I need to know what's going on."

"Well," Thea said, reaching for the same words that had already been used so often, "I have bad news and good news. And you might not entirely agree which is which."

Humphrey sighed. "Spill it," he said.

"On the pigeon front," Thea said, "I'm afraid that the Colorado situation might be . . . beyond salvaging. One of them is dead. There doesn't seem to be much we can do about it—we tried a few things, but they didn't work. As for the others—two of the remaining pigeons, we've got."

"When? How?" Humphrey said. "I had an agent in the city keeping an eye on Kristin and Ben—they didn't seem to be meeting with much success. The Alphiri were out there, though."

"Ben said you had a tail on them," Thea said.

"Hardly a *tail*. Just a backup, in case something went wrong. But somehow they kept slipping out of his . . ." He frowned. "Never mind that, now. We have two, but only one died in Colorado. Shouldn't there be three?"

"One is gone," Thea said, ticking it off on her fingers. "Two we have in hand. The last one . . . the Alphiri got."

Humphrey reached out a hand and leaned heavily on the nearest tree. He said something under his breath, too softly for Thea to hear.

"I knew I should have sent in a stronger force," he said. "How did it happen?"

"Your spy didn't tell you that?" Thea asked.

Humphrey glared at her. "I told you, it wasn't like that. But no, I heard nothing of the sort."

"That's because the Trickster was involved again," Thea said. "It's entirely possible your guy witnessed the entire incident and had no idea what he saw. But we have . . . a line on it."

"A line on what?" Humphrey shook his head, confused.

"That last pigeon. The one that's missing. I've made arrangements, and I'm waiting for word on that. I'm afraid I had to make a promise on your behalf."

"What did you do?" Humphrey said in a low voice, suddenly sounding afraid.

"You'll owe immunity to the Faele," Thea said. "They're about to go snatch the Water Pigeon from the Alphiri, and leave them a changeling."

Humphrey opened and closed his mouth several times, like a fish out of water, before he could speak.

"Immunity? To the *Faele*? I owe . . . immunity . . . a *pigeon changeling*? The Water . . ." He stopped, suddenly struck by the precision of that description. "Wait. You can tell the Elements apart? In the pigeons? How can you tell?"

"We couldn't. We didn't know, of course. But Nikola Tesla knew."

"Nikola Tesla knew." Humphrey May repeated Thea's words, as though uttering a foreign language that he completely failed to understand. "The cube," he finally said. "You've still got access to the cube. How could you keep this from me? Do you realize what's been going on back at the office since that thing disappeared?"

He still hadn't completely understood, though, because when Tesla suddenly stepped out from the shadows Humphrey could only stare in frozen shock.

"The Alphiri do not have the cube," Tesla said. "Which is a good thing, as I gather. But I never intended for it to be in the possession of the FBM, either."

"I have it," Thea said quietly.

"*Why?*" It was the only word Humphrey seemed able to muster.

"How did you know where to find me?" she asked him, apparently changing the subject completely. "I said on the phone that I was in the woods where you met Mrs. Chen . . . and you came straight to me."

Humphrey searched her eyes with his own. "I completely missed that," he said quietly. "You should not have known about that meeting, should you? I had it shielded. But I forgot I had a fledgling Elemental on the grounds. What did you hear?"

"Enough," Thea said, glancing back at Tesla. "I wanted the cube because I couldn't handle the possibility of another Diego de los Reyes—not again. The last time, it was the Alphiri; this time, it sounded like it might be you guys."

"That we might be what?" Humphrey asked, after a beat.

"Take him. Use him. Control him." She paused, and met Humphrey's eyes squarely. "Use *me* to control him."

"So you set out to save him," Humphrey said a little bitterly, crossing his arms across his chest. "You overhear part of a conversation, take it out of context, and decide that we are the bad guys this time around?"

"You said I was a weapon you would use if you had to," Thea said.

"I believe I also said I was sworn to protect, and that is what I would do, whatever it takes," Humphrey said.

"Whatever it takes," Thea said, nodding. "That's exactly what freaked me out. Protect what? Against whom?"

"The preservation of the safety and security of the world as you know it is my job," Humphrey said. "It's what I *do*, Thea. You've helped save the world a couple of times, and it was a tough thing for you to do—but I save the world on a daily basis from threats you haven't even heard of." This time it was Tesla's turn to react, and he gathered his brows together in a delicate frown at the sweeping statement. But Humphrey was concentrating on Thea. "You decided unilaterally that saving one man— whether or not he needed saving from *me*—was far more important than perhaps using that man to save the world."

"Sometimes," Thea said, "saving a single man *is* saving the world."

"I had made my own plans," Tesla said. "If they had all gone according to my wishes, you would never have had the cube in your possession in the first place. Your young mage reacted on pure instinct—but the instinct was completely correct. I, too, made a bargain with the Faele, back in the days when my body was failing me and I knew it was time to transfer myself to the world I had set up inside the Elemental cube. I knew the FBM would be all over my room and the things I had left behind. So I bargained with the Faele to come and take the cube as soon as I was gone. I had no doubt it would surface when circumstances were correct for it to be found, but I did not want to wait for that day in the vaults of the FBM, where I would be subject, every day, to misguided and incompetent attempts to open my cube by mages who had no idea what they were doing or how to go about it, who saw only the end and did not care about the means, who could not possibly understand the way another Elemental could understand."

Humphrey was shaking his head a little. "You make us sound like malevolent idiots," he said. "It's been a long time since we've had a true Elemental to deal with. The ones who are left are all too low-level or too old, their powers failing, to be useful. I'd forgotten just how intransigent an Elemental could be. Your kind has no respect, no understanding, for society's laws—and you forget that laws are made to protect people."

"From whom? From us?" Tesla raised an eyebrow at Humphrey. "Just what is it that you think I might do—split the planet like an apple?"

"According to some of the notes we *did* inherit from you," Humphrey said, "you had means to do such a thing."

"If the notes gave you any idea that I ever intended to put such a possibility into practice, you understand even less than I gave you credit for," Tesla snapped. "Or is it that, if any planet-splitting is to be done, you would prefer it to be on your terms and with you giving the orders?"

Humphrey flushed. "It isn't like that at all. And if we're going to talk motives, what made you sequester yourself away in the first place? You couldn't have possibly known what the future would bring. You were locking yourself away, perhaps for all eternity, and *after* you had ripped out your Elemental gifts. Why would you do that, if you didn't have your own agenda?"

"The future would evaluate each one according to his work and accomplishments," Tesla said. "The present, my then-present, belonged to the humanity living in that moment of time; the future, for which I had always worked, was mine. It would bring me what I needed. That much, I knew. The form it would take . . . I had no way of predicting. Elementals are as inevitable as they are rare—I knew that someday, you would have one again. And what's more, from observing Thea's work, I have come to believe that you have an entirely new kind of Elemental on your hands."

Thea's heart lurched. "What do you mean?"

"Did they tell you that it was I who cobbled together the first real Nexus?" Tesla said, turning his full attention to her. "At that time, in that place, the thing you know as a computer was only a vision, a pipe dream. But there was a first version of a computerlike device that used tapes to store information."

"The tapes they found with the cube," Thea said.

"Precisely. Those were an accessory to the prototype I created. I did not have time to do much more than that. When the Faele came to retrieve the cube, as was our arrangement, they took those tapes as well, and because they had no idea how fragile and vulnerable they were, most of the information on them was lost, as I discovered when I was assisting your friend Terry at the current Nexus. It is so much more than even I envisioned it could be; he knows his way around it, but you . . ." Tesla touched Thea's shoulder lightly. "You have harnessed this thing with as much control and raw intuition as I once harnessed the power of Water or Fire in my time. I heard Terry refer to that world by the prefix 'cyber,'

and in as much as I am—as I had been—a quad-
Elemental mage who could rule Water, Fire, Air,
and Earth, it is your gift to rule the Cyber-Element,
which is as much a basic building block of your
world as the rest have ever been." He paused. "You
are a new thing, Thea Winthrop," he said. "You are
a Cyber-Elemental. A Cybermage."

"That makes you a tri-Elemental." Humphrey
said, staring at Thea.

The shadows in the cool, damp, cedar glade
brightened for a moment as a flash of light made
all three of them throw up arms to shade narrowed
eyes, and then a small winged creature hovered over
Thea's head before coming to rest on her shoulder.
It crouched for balance and whispered something
directly into her ear with its hands cupped around
its mouth for secrecy. Thea listened, then nodded,
and the winged imp launched itself and vanished in
another shower of sparks.

"Our lost pigeon is home to roost," Thea said.
"It's with the others. I think we'd better get back
there."

"Wait. Where? Where is everyone? Thea, I am
not the enemy! Let me in."

"Back with Cheveyo," Thea said.

Humphrey's eyes narrowed a little. "You owe me that," he said, his voice tightly controlled.

She sighed. "You're right. I do. Mr. Tesla, you need to get back into the catcher again."

"I am at your disposal," said Tesla, with a small bow.

Thea lifted the dream catcher again and sighted Tesla through it.

"What are you doing? Aren't those the same dream catchers that you had when the spellspam . . . Where did he go?" Humphrey looked around wildly as Tesla winked out.

Thea shook the dream catcher lightly to focus his attention back on it. "In here," she said. "It's a way of carrying him around. Well? Are you coming?"

Humphrey began to step forward while still in the shadow of the cedars, but the foot that had left damp earth covered with soggy brown cedar fronds dropped from the trees came back down in the soft red dust of Cheveyo's country.

Thea released Tesla from his dream catcher, and he gave everyone a nod of greeting before striding off to crouch like some large spider before Kristin's birdcage, where now three birds fussed and cooed. Away to one side a trio of winged Faele waited, squirming, in an obvious agony of impatience. Cheveyo himself presided over the whole scene with poise and serenity.

The Faele scurried forward as soon as they realized they had Thea's attention.

"We lingered on our Queen's command until you were here," one of the Faele said. "We just wished to make certain that the bird was conveyed. The bargain is done, and our obligations are concluded. Yes?"

"My thanks to your Queen," Thea said.

The Faele glanced over at Humphrey, briefly. "The immunity?"

Humphrey glared at Thea, and then back at the Faele who stood awaiting his answer. Finally he gave a curt nod. "I will see to it," he said. "Immunity."

The Faele inclined his head in acknowledgment of the compact that had just been entered into, and then trilled something at his companions in a language too high and fast for the humans to understand. They all launched themselves into the air, vanishing instantly.

"Now what?" Ben said, staring at the cage where Tesla was still communing with the pigeons.

"Terry, you simply . . . spun them all together, back

in the room," Tess said. "And you reconstituted all of Tesla's component parts that we had taken off in different directions. Can you do the same thing with him and those pigeons? Just spin them all together in the dream catcher and make him whole again?"

"As whole as he can be, with only three," Cat murmured. She still carried her bundle—the last pigeon, wrapped in its shroud of black silk—as though expecting a miracle.

"No, I am afraid that would not quite work," said a new voice, and they all turned to see Grandmother Spider smiling at them from beside Cheveyo. She wore her hair in two dark braids that fell to her waist, her eyes were slanted and dark, and her skin was a burnished bronze.

"Who's *that*? Where did she come from?" Humphrey demanded, looking around.

"Grandmother Spider," Thea said, leaning a little closer to whisper the name.

"She's someone's grandmother?" he said, staring.

Grandmother Spider caught his eye, smiling a little, and Humphrey dropped his gaze.

"Should you try that with the catcher that I gave you, all you will accomplish is to integrate three pigeons into a human being," Grandmother Spider said, graciously passing over Humphrey's discomfort. "Not their essences, themselves. The reason you were able to bring Tesla himself back together the way you did was simply because *all* the pieces you were playing with were part of the same puzzle. But the pigeons would have to be rendered less pigeonlike if that were to work with the dream catchers."

"I . . . uh, I think I have a way," Terry said, glancing at Humphrey. He wore a laptop satchel slung diagonally across his body, shoulder to hip. "Tesla and Twitterpat helped me work it out. I need to set up the program, but I think I can digitize the pigeons, sort of, and get them into a form that Tesla can—"

Kristin suddenly sucked in her breath. "I think it might have to wait," she said, nodding at something back toward Cheveyo's outside hearth. "We might have a problem."

Everyone spun around to look.

Beside the fire pit an Alphiri portal had opened, and through that stepped two tall male Alphiri, dressed in unusually simple and appropriate attire of dark, ankle-length robes, followed by a woman whose loose dark-gold hair was held back by a burnished jeweled circlet. She wore little more by way of ornament except one signet ring that looked like it was weighing down her left hand.

Humphrey winced, closing his eyes.

"It's the Alphiri Queen," he said in a low voice. "That's *all* we need."

## 15.

ERRY, WHO HAD ALREADY half pulled his laptop out of its case, froze in midmotion as the Alphiri Queen stepped out of the portal. Thea nudged him; he turned his head to glance back at her, and she nodded at him and at the computer as if to say, *Keep going; this might need to be done in a hurry.*

"We come in pursuit of something that belongs to us," the Queen said regally.

Terry opened up the laptop screen and waited, his hand poised on the POWER button.

"Something we had bargained for," one of the other Alphiri said.

"Fair price for fair trade," the third added.

Terry punched the button as they spoke; the Alphiri always spoke in threes, and the sound of their voices masked the noises of the computer's waking-up routine.

Thea had never managed to get over her fear of the Alphiri, but she bit down on it, tasting its harsh and bitter residue in her mouth, and stepped forward.

"Your Majesty," Thea said with great formality, "there is nothing here that lawfully belongs to the Alphiri, or may be bargained for with intent to purchase."

*The Human Polity does not sell its people.*

"We do not seek a person," the Alphiri Queen said, her eyes flickering briefly over Thea and then regally dismissing her.

"We seek a bird," the second Alphiri said. "A creature."

"We have bought creatures before from the Human Polity," said the third, in a tone of triumphant reason.

"The bird is not a bird," Thea said. "The bird carries a part of a human being, so it belongs to that human being, and to nobody else. If you bought and paid for it, then you must take up that contract with whomever you bargained with. You already know that the one who offered it for sale had no right to sell. And we know that you know it."

"Oh, *now,*" said Corey the Trickster, stepping out

from behind one of the two Alphiri escorts. "It was a pigeon. Humans buy and sell kittens and puppies and birds every day. I broke no laws—I only sold a dumb beast that someone else had a use for, and wanted, and I could provide."

"I was wondering how they got here so fast," Thea muttered. "Why am I not surprised that you are here, *Miss Kay Otis*?"

There was a snort of disbelief behind her, and Thea spared a quick glance back at Humphrey, whose hands were clenched into fists, his expression a mixture of astonishment and fury. Terry, just off to Humphrey's left, caught Thea's eye and shook his head minutely, hands still flying over his keyboard.

Tesla had risen from his crouch beside the pigeon cage and stood beside Cheveyo. The two men looked at the Alphiri Queen in a strangely serene manner, as though she concerned neither of them.

"We buy from the one who sells," the Queen said.

"We are not responsible for what went before."

"We cannot be expected to trace the origin of every purchase."

"And yet, you must, when you deal with us, who

hold history to be important," Thea said. "How would you lay claim to what you call your property? How was it marked?"

"It was a bird," the Queen said.

"One that you call a pigeon," said the second Alphiri.

"A gray and white bird," the third Alphiri added helpfully.

"One of those?" Thea said, indicating the cage.

The Queen deigned to turn her head, just a little.

"It may be," she said.

"Could be."

"Perhaps."

"Which one?" Thea asked politely.

The Queen turned back to her, her face set in an expression of an unspoken royal affront. But Tesla, who saw where Thea was heading, gave a small approving nod.

"There are three," Thea said, somehow managing to keep her voice cool and level, "in the cage. Can you tell—without a trace of doubt—which is the one you claim to have lost?"

All the Alphiri stared at the cage.

"The middle one," the Queen said, after a small hesitation.

The other two spoke at once, stepping on each other's words.

"The one on the left."

"The one on the right."

"Oh, *great*," Corey muttered, rolling his eyes.

The Queen raised an eyebrow in the direction of her escorts with a distinctly frosty expression. She did not even bother to look at Corey. Thea saw him rouse at that, annoyed at being sidelined by the very people he had plotted and connived for. A stray raven feather suddenly popped out from under his left sleeve, and he plucked at it with his right hand, emitting a low growl.

But Thea couldn't afford to allow her attention to linger on Corey.

"If you had brought the changeling," Thea said quietly to the Alphiri Queen, "you might have had a basis for comparison, but the people you sent to New York, Your Majesty, will already have told you that pigeons look very much alike."

The Queen's head came around sharply.

"You know about this. The changeling bird that was left in place of the one we had purchased."

"You know it was stolen."

"You know it was stolen from us."

"Well, *I* could tell," Corey muttered, still ignored by everybody.

"No. It was recovered from you, restored to the one to whom it truly belongs, the man who stands beside that cage. *You* can't tell which one it is, but he can—he knows precisely which bird is which. That alone proves that it is his property and not yours, however you claim to have obtained it. Everyone knows that the Alphiri pay for what they take, that the Alphiri do not steal—your polity was built on that reputation. You are close to breaking your own fundamental law. Representatives of the Alphiri were there when the pigeon was found, taken from a human being's hands, without that human being's permission. That's stealing. If the Alphiri did not take this bird with their own hands, they certainly sanctioned its taking, and even stood back and watched it happen."

The Queen lifted her chin. *"The Alphiri do not steal,"* she said, her words dripping with outrage.

"Fair price for fair service," said one of her henchmen.

"We do not cheat," said the other.

Thea looked sideways again; Terry nodded at her—*I'm ready when you are.*

"The Faele stole from *us*," the Queen said.

"The Faele will be chastised," the first escort said sonorously.

"The Faele will be punished," added the second, with a slow nod of judgment.

Thea turned to Humphrey. *Now.*

He stepped forward swiftly, as though released from a bow. "I speak for the government of the Human Polity," he said. "The Faele changeling was left with you on our behest. They were merely agents acting on our behalf; if you have a grievance, it is with the Human Polity. The Faele have been granted immunity in this matter."

The Queen stared at him. "You cannot do this," she said.

"It is not your place."

"It is not your right."

"Then it will fall squarely in the jurisdiction of the Polity Court, and we can take it as high as it needs to go," Humphrey said.

He stood beside Thea, his feet a little apart, his arms at his sides, his back straight. In this moment he was a towering ally, a presence of strength and power. He stood for the Human Polity in a battle of wits with the Alphiri; Thea wondered if he was even aware that he was doing exactly what he had accused her of doing—standing up to save one man, the man who stood grave and silent beside a cage full of fluttering birds, waiting for the verdict of this confrontation.

Thea lowered her eyes and turned her head just far enough to give Terry a small nod.

He punched a key sequence on his laptop.

At first, nothing happened. But when the Alphiri Queen opened her mouth to speak again, the three pigeons in the cage somehow became two-dimensional and glossy, as though they had turned into photographs of themselves. Then those disintegrated into a pigeon-shaped patch of air, glowing pale blue, watery pale green, and milky ivory, only barely constrained by the bars of the birdcage.

The Queen took a step back, betraying surprise.

Humphrey's head had whipped around to where Terry crouched over his computer.

Tesla's shoulders went rigid under the elegant lines of his dark suit.

Terry stood up, balancing the computer in the palm of his left hand.

"They're digitized," he said. "To what they really were. Are. The pigeon shapes were merely a disguise, a form that permitted them to exist in our own world—but *that* is what they are. Energy."

"Pure Elemental magic," Humphrey breathed, unable to hide his own astonishment.

"Water, Air, Earth," Tesla said in a low voice. He reached out one hand and the three shapes in the birdcage streamed toward him, almost losing cohesion.

"Sir . . ." Terry said warningly, and Tesla, with a small sigh, withdrew his hand—but not his hot, yearning gaze, looking at what he had lost and lived without for so many years.

Thea seized the moment, her heart thumping painfully, and turned to the Alphiri Queen once more. "Your bargain is twice void," she said. "You said you bought a pigeon, but you couldn't even pick it out from among three of its kind, and now you see that you never had a bird at all. You never bought or paid for *that*." She indicated the three coruscating Elemental clouds with a sweeping gesture of one hand. "One keystroke, and we will restore these things to the man to whom they have always belonged. And once it is done and all these parts that make up one whole have been reunited in a single entity, you can make no further demands—because it will be part of a living entity."

The Queen turned with a triumphant air. "But that is not true."

"There is no living entity."

"Not as you define it."

Thea pointed at Tesla. "There he stands."

"Not alive," the Queen said. "Not as you have defined life."

"An automaton."

"A dream."

"An incomplete entity, at that," the Queen added.

"There should be four."

"Four Elements, not three."

"But the fourth one is gone," Cat said in a small voice, clutching her black silk bundle convulsively.

"That may not be completely true," said a new voice, rich and warm.

Thea closed her eyes for a moment. She felt a surge of warmth pass her as Tawaha rounded her side to stand between her and the Alphiri Queen, and remembered his words: *Where you are, and where light is, I will be with you.*

"Who is *that*?" Humphrey said, staring.

"Tawaha," Thea said. "The Sun God."

Grandmother Spider, now a golden-haired woman, had stepped up to Tawaha's side.

"Bring the bird, child," Tawaha said, beckoning to Cat with one golden hand.

Cat stepped forward, carrying the silk-wrapped body of the Fire Element pigeon in both her hands, and laid it at Tawaha's feet with reverence, like an offering. Tawaha glanced at Grandmother Spider, who went down on one knee, gently folding the silk back until the small body was revealed, its wings neatly tucked against its sides. Tawaha gazed at it thoughtfully.

"It is a Fire bird," he said. "One of my own Element. It is quenched, but as with every fire, there is still an ember, even when it looks like there is nothing left except a dead piece of coal. There is, however, a price."

He looked up, beckoned Tesla forward, and then turned to Thea as Grandmother Spider rose to her feet.

"This fire can be brought back," Tawaha said, his eyes resting on Thea, enveloping her in light and warmth. "But it needs a spark. If one who carries the Fire Element offers that spark freely, a spark that only another keeper of the Fire can provide, then this Elemental may take new life from it. Another keeper . . . like yourself, child."

"We can reboot it," Grandmother Spider said with a smile. "But there is a danger. As with all things of value, this too has a price." She threw a glance at the Alphiri as she said this.

Thea felt the sting of tears in her eyes. "The danger is that the operation might be a success, but the patient might die," she said. "What you are saying is that if I offer this, then I give my own fire away."

"That is the way of it," Tawaha said. "If you give it, you give it as a gift. You give all. You may not hold back any. If you are very lucky, some might remain—perhaps enough. Or it might burn you in the backwash—there is peril here. Only you can make that choice."

Thea's eyes lingered on the dead Fire Element pigeon at her feet. Then she looked up at Tawaha, at Grandmother Spider, and finally at Tesla himself. All she could think of was that sad, sweet lullaby he had sung over the body of something he had loved. *I will pay the price of my folly*—he had said that, but she could see how much of a chasm it had left within him.

He was not asking. Would never ask. But he met

her eyes as she stared at him, squarely, without looking away.

"Yes," Thea said faintly, letting Tesla see her answer in her eyes, saying the word out loud for the benefit of the others. "Yes."

"Thea," Tesla said gently, stepping up to her and taking both her hands in his own, "are you certain? Your future still lies before you. Three of my gifts have returned to me—three I may have back. Is there need for this sacrifice?"

"Fire was your strongest, your most treasured. Your most beloved." Thea said. "You are its master; I have barely learned how to raise my eyes to look at it. You named me a new thing, not so long ago— perhaps I can cling to that, and you can have back the thing that made you who you are."

"It is Elemental magic," said Grandmother Spider. "You don't know what you might lose should you give up any of it. It may be that you could lose it all. Are you sure you wish to take this risk?"

"Thea, no." It was a whisper from the back. Thea thought it might have been Terry, or perhaps Cat, her reaction to this much the same as Thea's had been when Cat had been in this position, giving up the essence of herself.

Thea closed her mind to the whispered plea. "I am sure," she said.

"And I too must ask—because you have to answer three times," Tawaha said. "What you give can never be returned in the shape in which it was given. You give to fill a hole in another, but you may never be able to fill the hole you might leave in yourself. Are you certain you wish to proceed?"

Thea thought of the years in which she could find nothing in her father's face except disappointment and frustration, the first time she had woven two strands of light together, the destination that the powers that first woke in Cheveyo's country had led her to, the desperate act that had sealed one who was more like her than any other in her world into a living tomb.

The chance to set another Elemental free from a prison of his own making.

*We all pay the price of our folly.*

"Yes," Thea said.

Tesla, who had not let go of her hands, now lifted both to his lips, and then dropped them, stepping away. Thea was surprised to see that his eyes were filled with tears; she swallowed hard and turned to face Tawaha.

"What is it that I must do?" she said, and was surprised, under the circumstances, to see both him and Grandmother Spider smiling.

"You have given freely, and therefore it is in my power to do so also," Tawaha said. "Because you were willing to give the ember of your own gift, I do not have to take it from you. Do you remember, child, the day we first met?"

"In the First World," Thea said. "Beside the portal I had made."

Tawaha was nodding. "And do you recall what the last thing that you did in that world was, just before you stepped away through that portal back to this world, Cheveyo's world?"

Thea found herself smiling, too, as the memory returned. "I grabbed a ribbon of fire to weave," she said. "Your fire."

Tawaha nodded. "You did not know it yet, not then, but it is only because you have it in you to hold the Fire Element—because you are a Fire Elemental yourself—that you were able to hold that flame at all. You have carried it within yourself ever since you first touched it, and it is not your fire; it is mine. I loaned it, and now I can take it back without harming your own gift, the part of your power that is yours alone. The sun fire can serve as the spark to bring the other fire back to life."

"She does not carry it," Cheveyo said. He had not moved from his position by his hearth since this gathering had begun, but now he strode forward, leaning on his staff. "The morning she returned from the First World to my own hearth was the first and only time I have eaten breakfast cooked over a holy fire. She thrust your flame into my embers, Great One. It has long since burned away into ashes."

"Not all," Tawaha said tranquilly. "Enough remains. Hold out your hand to me, child."

Thea obeyed, offering her hand, flat and palm up, to Tawaha. The Sun God raised his own burnished hand and held it a span away from her own, close enough that she felt the heat blister her fingertips.

A spark crackled between her index finger and his, and then from every finger each to the other, until a fiery arc of white and gold light spanned their two hands, leaving a bright cradle of light into which Grandmother Spider gently laid the body of the Fire pigeon.

Electricity snapped and sparked in the air around Thea and Tawaha, and the bird was suspended in air and fire between them. It hung there for an instant, still motionless, and then it exploded in a flash of red-gold wings like a phoenix, its wingtips showering sparks as the wings beat powerfully to allow the bird to hover in place.

Tawaha broke the contact, clenching his hand into a fist. Thea staggered and nearly fell, glancing down at what she thought had to be blisters on her fingertips. She found none, even though she had literally held her hand in the sun's own corona. But she didn't have time to think about that, not just then. She looked up again, in time to notice the Fire pigeon fly like an arrow toward Tesla and land with grace and precision on his outstretched arm. Tesla was openly weeping, his face streaked with tears.

"Terry," Thea said in a low voice, without taking her eyes off Tesla and his pigeon, "finish it."

There was the sound of rapid typing, and the pigeon on Tesla's arm brightened into a shape of light almost impossible to look at without hurting one's eyes, and then it, too, was just a form of air and shadow like its fellows in the cage, glowing with an orange-yellow radiance. A final tap of a computer key, and the birdcage was open, the other three Elements free and clustering around Tesla in a cloud of multicolored light, bathing his face in a luminous brightness.

"We do not understand," the Alphiri Queen said into the rapt silence that followed.

Thea turned to look at her, and found the Queen staring straight back at her. Thea suddenly realized that the Queen's two escorts had not spoken in her wake, as was the Alphiri custom. They were standing beside the portal through which they had arrived, one on either side like an honor guard.

"This is not the kind of bargain we can make," the Queen said. "We sought . . . a legacy, something that might remain in memory of us when we pass away—as it is written that all must, in their time. We have done all that may be done within the rule of our law; we have bought all that could have been bought, and have offered payment for things that may not have been for sale—that is what we know how to do. We give fair price for what we consider to be fair service or fair trade. But we do not understand what you have just done. What was the bargain that you made? What did you choose? What was offered to you in return?"

"The things that cannot be measured or owned," Thea said. "A sense of losing a small part of self to become part of a bigger whole. None of us is alone, in the end; we are one, and it is not a loss to give when someone else receives."

The Queen narrowed her eyes and looked as though she was about to speak again, but Terry's computer was not yet done. Thea heard more keys tapping, and then something brightened to a fiery glow that rivaled Tawaha's before settling into a luminous aura that now surrounded Tesla. There was a light in his eyes that had not been there before, and he was actually smiling.

Kristin and Tess both had their hands half-covering their faces, and their eyes gleamed with astonished joy. Cat was crying openly. Ben was standing quite still, his eyes flickering from Thea to Tesla as though he was trying to commit it all to memory.

As for Humphrey May, he was gazing on Tesla with an air of resignation, and his thoughts were as plain as the expression on his face. Whatever his plans had originally been, what had happened here had derailed everything. He was now looking at an Elemental mage—now once again the only quad-Elemental in human history—and coming to terms with the fact that whatever his ideas had been on this score, they were now confetti in the wind.

Terry had been crouching with his laptop balanced on his knees; he laid it on the ground, got up, and took a few uncertain steps toward Thea.

"Are you all right?" he whispered.

In reply she lifted a hand; her fingers trembled. "I think I might fall down in a heap if I move an inch from where I'm standing."

He reached out and took her hand, squeezing it.

"What did you mean when you said that Tesla had named you a new thing?" he asked quietly.

"He named a new Element," Thea said. "One you're very familiar with. He called me a Cybermage."

They were given no further chance to talk, as the Alphiri Queen suddenly lifted her long skirts and walked toward Tesla, pausing briefly to rake Corey up and down with a cool glance.

"Er," Corey said. "Under the circumstances . . . I guess you won't be needing me any longer, for the time being, anyway. Give me a call if there's anything I can do for you in the future."

He flashed a look of frustration Thea's way, but was distracted by another feather popping into place just above his ear. He reached to pluck it with a growl.

"And I'm sure *we* will cross paths again," he said to Thea. His face darkening into a scowl, Corey blurred his shape and dropped onto all fours, turning his sharp coyote snout in what looked like a final defiant grin at Thea and at the other Elder Spirits, and trotted off across the broken scree that spilled at the foot of the mesa.

In the meantime, the Alphiri Queen moved to stand before Nikola Tesla.

Tesla offered her a small formal bow, meeting her gaze unflinchingly.

"We needed you," she said simply.

Her two companions said nothing to qualify that statement any further.

"Madam," Tesla said with old-world courtesy, "without the powers that I now hold, one of which you tried to withhold from me, I would have been of little use to you. In full possession of those powers, you could never have held me against my will—because I can mold the world to my wishes. The prison does not exist that could keep me where I do not wish to stay."

"That may be true," she said, "though we might have proved otherwise. But we have lost here. No matter, though."

Her head swiveled very slowly until her gaze, suddenly thoughtful and calculating, came to rest on Ben, Cat, Kristin, and Tess, who instinctively drew closer to one another, as though there was safety in that proximity. The Queen turned away from Tesla. Her two companions had left the portal, and once again fell into step beside her.

"We have found out," the Queen said, "many important things this day."

"We have lost a chance."

"But we have gained knowledge."

"We have learned that everyone has a price," the Queen said softly, looking at Cat.

"We just have to know what you treasure, and what you want."

The Queen let her hand brush over Kristin's face as the third Alphiri spoke.

"And we can find out."

The Queen paused, staring at each face as though committing them to memory, and then turned with slow and deliberate menace to where Thea stood a little way apart from the others. Terry, still holding Thea's hand, tightened his fingers.

"We know who has what we want," the Queen said.

"We know where it is."

"We know how to get it."

"We go now. We may have to start again, but we have done that many times before."

"We have time," said the first minion. "We have patience. We have resources we have yet to tap."

"We will return."

The Queen gazed at Thea's face, then glanced, with a small enigmatic smile, at Terry, and at the still clasped hands that linked the two.

A sudden black terror bloomed in Thea's mind.

*We know what you treasure, and what you want.*

The Queen had looked at every one of Thea's friends individually, as though each of them was prey, gazelles to a prowling lioness, to be stalked and slaughtered at a mere whim. But the look she had given Terry had been more that that, it had been a look that Thea herself had been meant to see, and understand.

*She*, Thea, was the new quarry. And the Alphiri, although they would obey the letter of the law and their Trade Codex, had shown how willing they were to ignore the spirit of that law. They would bend the law into a pretzel to make sure they were covered if challenged, but they would eventually find a way around every barrier that could be raised against them.

They had shown their hand too early this time, and had acted with more rash carelessness than prudent planning. From here on, they would lay their snares with more cunning and subtlety.

And it was entirely possible that nobody Thea cared about would ever be safe again.

## 16.

*You haven't felt Alphiri fury. Not yet. Not completely.*

Long after the Alphiri Queen and her escorts had stepped back through their portal and vanished from the plateau outside Cheveyo's house, these words of the Faele Queen pulsed in Thea's mind.

She had snatched her hand from Terry's even as the Alphiri Queen had walked away. She felt him flinch at the suddenness and force of it, but could not look at him, or any of them, as if the mere act of taking her own eyes off them would render them invisible to the Alphiri. She stumbled half-blindly around the ridge of red rock that rose at the back of Cheveyo's abode, and no footsteps followed her.

She felt, rather than saw, Tawaha taking his leave of the company—the day suddenly dipped into sunset around her, darkening into deeper shades

385

of twilight to the east. *Where you are and where light is, I will be with you.* Tawaha had promised her that, but now there seemed to be more at stake than just herself. Her mind raced with images of all the people she now needed Tawaha to watch over—her family, her friends, people like Lorenzo and Beltran de los Reyes, even random strangers off the street whose well-being she could not remotely be considered responsible for but whom she would find it difficult to simply abandon to a fate she knew to be uncomfortable or unpleasant at the hands of the Alphiri if the possibility of preventing that was dangled in front of her.

Even people who could be expected to be able to take care of themselves—Humphrey May and Nikola Tesla.

She sat on a nearby boulder and buried her face in her hands. She had been building up her world, slowly—from the inner circle of her family to the sphere of her friends at the Academy to the wider arena of people who were mentors or teachers and proud of what she was and she could yet become, but now it was crumbling around her again. What she had thought of as her strength was turning out to be her greatest vulnerability.

She suddenly understood the loneliness and isolation that she had often sensed in Nikola Tesla, who must have been faced with similar choices.

A skitter of pebbles and the soft sound of a footfall on red dust alerted Thea to the fact that she was no longer alone, but she waited for a moment before she wiped the tears from her cheeks and looked up.

Humphrey May stood above her, his hands in the pockets of his jeans.

"Your friend Cheveyo suggested we eat something," Humphrey said. "Are you hungry?"

Thea shook her head mutely.

Humphrey squatted down beside her, reaching out to lay a hand on her shoulder. "Thea, what did the Queen *say* to you? Did she threaten you? We can protect you—there are avenues—"

"They won't come for me," Thea said. "Not directly."

He looked a little startled, and then nodded slowly. "I understand," he murmured. "But we can deal with that. They can be constrained—the Polity Court has a long reach, and not even the Alphiri are beyond that."

"*You* just granted immunity to the Faele, for doing something on our behalf," Thea said. "There are too many things they could do. I used to think that I was scared of them, but I never knew what that really meant, not until now."

"I offered you a job at the FBM once," Humphrey said. His tone was light, but when Thea looked up at him, his face was completely serious. "That still stands, you know. And if you're part of the establishment, as it were, the Alphiri would think twice about harming you or the people close to you."

"Still trying to recruit a tame Elemental for the FBM?" another voice said, and Tesla stepped forward from behind the ridge of the mesa. They had not heard him coming—not surprisingly, since he could choose not to have enough of a physical presence for an audible footfall.

Humphrey uncoiled from his crouch beside Thea, and turned to face the new arrival. "That's hardly fair," he said.

Tesla raised an eyebrow. "Fair? When I was available and physically living in this world, your predecessors at the FBM tried very hard to put a leash on me. And it would have been pleasant, in a way, I will have to admit. The safety and security of it, the knowledge that I was behind a rampart and untouchable, the idea that I could have unlimited funds for what I needed for my work . . . so long as that work was done on your behalf, at your command. The ordinary, everyday magic of our kind—the kind practiced every day in our world, the one you are most closely charged with at the FBM—has been broken to saddle, and cultivated, and tamed."

"My father used to wrangle wild magic," Thea said. "When it escaped from its confines, and took over libraries."

"We had a lot more of that in my day," Tesla said. "Back then, we knew less about how things worked, but even so, we understood that there were rules, and that magic had to obey them." He paused. "All magic, except the Elemental. You have never been able to grasp that Elemental magic *cannot be* broken to your will. Not that, and stay what it is. Your trouble is that you understand magic but no longer completely believe in it. Enchantment shorn of a sense of wonder becomes empty words. And numbers. And bookkeeping."

"You were no stranger to bookkeeping when you lived among us, as you yourself point out," Humphrey snapped, losing his temper. "You, too, required money in order to exist. You might have commanded more power than any of us knew, but by all accounts you were appallingly bad at that bookkeeping you so despise. You were always letting money slip through your fingers, living off credit and beyond your means."

Tesla gazed at him with what was almost pity. "Yes, and I lived free," he said. "Ideas are cheap— I gave mine away for nothing, sometimes, when it seemed warranted. I often lent my power to endeavors that I found pleasing or worthy, and asked no return. But I never took money for anything that involved selling my soul."

Humphrey threw his hands in the air. "You're right, I don't *get* it." He looked down at Thea again. "Come eat something. Come back and talk to us. You shouldn't be alone right now."

"I agree," Tesla said unexpectedly. "But before you do, Thea, might I have a word . . . in private?"

Humphrey looked as though he was about to say something else, but then apparently thought better of it. He squared his shoulders and walked away without looking back.

"I cannot make up my mind about that man," Thea said in a low voice. She turned to Tesla. "Are you . . . all right now?"

He smiled and opened a hand; a ball of white lightning danced on his palm. "I am whole," he said. "And I have you to thank for that. Your friend Tawaha returned Fire to me—but Thea, when I rashly killed my own power, when my own fire died on that altar . . ." He smiled. "When I concocted this ill-conceived Kaschei plot so many decades ago, I had no idea that the most treasured, the most sacred, the most beloved part of what I chose to call my Kaschei's needle would one day be carried by a child who was yet to be born, and returned to me with so much grace. That was a brave and selfless choice that you made, back there."

"I gave you back what was yours," Thea said. "I saw you weep over it, when you thought it gone. If it was in my power to restore that . . ."

Tesla reached out a hand and laid it on her shoulder.

"You are an Elemental. We are too alike. You *do* understand," he said. "The Elemental power is vast, and with this new gift that you have, with so much of it spanning the globe in your day, your own powers can be even greater than I can now imagine. But you are still at the beginning of your journey, and I sense that there is much left for you to learn."

"But who is there to teach me?" Thea said. "Should I go with Humphrey May's people, after all?"

Tesla was shaking his head. "The choices you make are yours," he said, "but always remember what I have said about the FBM. If you do not wish to belong to anyone, then that is not the way to go."

"But other than them, who is there?" Thea asked again. "I seem to have run in front of the pack, and there's nobody out here but me . . . and maybe you." She paused. "What do you plan to do now? What do you want me to do with the cube?"

"There are . . . a number of things I have been discussing with Terry, among other people," Tesla said. "There is always the option of simply escaping into your cyberworld, and existing within your machines, for as long as they do."

"But that would not be any less of a prison than your cube ever was," Thea said. "You would be constrained by what the machines could do. You don't want to be like that hologram that our computer teacher left behind in the Nexus. Before Terry fixed that . . ."

"I helped out," Tesla said. "I could see the inner workings that were hard to see from the outside."

"Yes, but it still remains just a shadow," Thea said. "Something he left behind when he died. A bit of personality, maybe, and a limited ability to learn as an artificial intelligence, but Twitterpat himself is gone, and that thing will never be alive in the way that you are alive. I think you would find that there are many ways to raise prison bars around yourself."

"Even if I were to exist not in a single machine, as that other entity does, but in the space that Terry has described to me as cyberspace, which doesn't exist until you call upon it . . . Ah, yes, I begin to see your point." He frowned. "This is your world, not mine, this Cyber Element. It is you who must teach *me* in this regard, and there is much that I still do not understand."

"When you first made the Elemental cube, and you thought about what would come afterward, what were you planning to do?" Thea asked.

"I suppose it is inevitable that the future changes in unexpected ways," Tesla said. "But what I called my future has turned into your present; you know it better than I ever could, you know what is possible and what remains a dream. There were some things that I knew would happen, others I only hoped for—I dreamed of talking to the stars, once upon a time."

That drew an inadvertent smile from Thea, and Tesla lifted a questioning eyebrow.

"Oh, nothing," she said. "It's just that . . . talking to stars is not what you might have expected it to be."

"You speak as one who has done this," Tesla said.

Thea lifted her eyes to the darkening sky above her, where now a few of the stars were beginning to show their faces. "In a way," she said. "It seems a long time ago now. Back before I met the Trickster. Or Tawaha. Or knew anything about Elemental magic."

"Would you like to see them again?"

Grandmother Spider's approach had been soundless. She was suddenly there, beside them, with long, pale hair swept up in a kind of style that might have been familiar to Tesla on the women of his own time. He gave her a small bow.

"Would they come?" Thea asked.

Grandmother Spider glanced up in time to notice a shooting star fall across the sky. "Not here," she said. "But *that*—" She tilted her chin toward the falling star. "That tells me that they might well return. To the place where you first crossed their path. Do you want to come back to the First World, Thea?"

Thea glanced at Tesla. "Might I bring a companion?"

"It could be arranged," Grandmother Spider said. "You will have to carry him there, as you have already done through many portals. Do you still have your dream catcher?"

"That," Tesla said, with a faint smile, "is beginning to seem only right. I am getting comfortable with this manner of traveling. And if permitted, it would mean much to me to be able to see this marvel."

Grandmother Spider inclined her head by way of permission, and Thea fished out her little dream catcher from her pocket, spinning Tesla into it. When only she and Grandmother Spider stood in the shadow of the mesa, she realized that a hole had opened in the ground at her feet. She looked up, her face alight with memory.

"Through a *sipapu*, again?" she said.

"That is the gate into the First World," Grandmother Spider said. "All the other worlds that you have seen, or been in, or woven into your life, are like a deck of cards—you can shuffle them, and stack them, and go from one to another with the ease of stepping sideways and finding yourself in a shadow cast by a different sun. But the First World . . . is the First World. There is nothing beyond it, nothing before it. It is a beginning. There is only one way in."

"I made a portal there once," Thea said, and the words were a question.

"It is still there," Grandmother Spider said. "But it is a way *out*, not a way in. Not even you can step back into that world through such a portal. When you are ready, step into the *sipapu*."

Without any further hesitation, Thea raised her foot over what seemed to be an impossibly small opening in the ground—and stepped through it, onto a ledge under a different sky, velvet-black and full of huge, bright stars. Some streaked across the heavens like comets and trailed streams of light in their wake, which cast shadows edged in improbable shades of amber, pale blue, red-gold, or pure white. It was the First World she remembered, where she had first walked with Grandmother Spider and had first met Tawaha. And the Trickster.

The place where she had learned to be afraid of the Alphiri.

She fought a sense of panic at that last thought, and busied herself with restoring Tesla's presence, shutting her mind to all else except the presence of Tesla, and Grandmother Spider, and stars in the sky.

"I think I may have dreamed of this place," Tesla said, looking around him with fascinated curiosity.

"Many do," Grandmother Spider said. "You, of all others, might have done—you, who have held in your hands the Fire of the World and were not burned by it. Now, if you will give me a moment . . ."

Thea touched Tesla's elbow and motioned him back while Grandmother Spider lifted her face and her hands to the skies. Tesla watched with keen interest as first one of the stars overhead, then another, then a third and a fourth, seemed to leap out of the sky and come streaking down toward the three of them on the rocky ledge, bathing them in colored light.

Tesla lifted a hand and watched it cast different-colored shadows on the ground as the stars came closer.

"It is very much like the Elemental entities, the

ones that Terry created with his computer," he said. "It is energy. It is light. This is astonishing."

The four stars touched down on the ground, turning into four women.

One glowed with an inner light so rich and dark, she seemed to be glowing black, and yet underneath this shimmering darkness, there was a light that was bright and pure and almost unbearable. The one next to her had an amber glow, and long strands of red-gold hair seemed to dance about her face. The third one was a vision of bluish-green light as though glimpsed through deep water. And the last had a diamond-bright white light, with hair of spun starlight and eyes that were night sky flecked with stars.

Thea remembered that one.

It was mutual, because the white star smiled down at Thea in her turn.

"We meet again," she said, directly to Thea, and then, inclining her head to Tesla, continued, by way of introduction, "Maia, of the Pleiades, the Seven Sisters. And these are some of my sisters: Celaeno, Electra, Merope. Our other sisters—Alcyone, Taygeta, Asterope—were otherwise occupied this night. What news of the younger worlds?"

"Nikola Tesla, at your service," Tesla said, with one of his small formal bows. "A long time ago, I had dreamed of being able to speak to the stars, and I knew in my heart that there would be someone there who would hear. I never imagined that it could be . . . someone like you."

"In your world, it would not be," Maia said.

"Tesla, of the Fire," Celaeno said. "We have watched. We have seen. Your name is not unknown."

Tesla looked taken aback, even humbled. "I am honored," he said.

"You are not flesh, as the child is," Merope said. "You are essence, spirit."

"Like we are in this place," Maia said, nodding.

"This could be a world for you," Thea said slowly, turning to Tesla with a dawning sense of wonder. "It would be freedom—there would be no boundaries, and nobody could reach out here to harm you again. You can exist here . . . or out there . . . in a sense that none of us can imagine. You could be their companion, with whole worlds at your feet. And should you ever wish to contact us, there is always—"

"The cyberspace," Tesla finished, his own voice echoing the wonder in hers. "That . . . would be a high enchantment indeed."

"This is possible," Maia said. "You are not one of us, as we exist out there, but you are Fire, and you can burn brightly among us. You would never be alone. You would never be bound. And we would be glad and honored to have you in our ranks."

"You continue to be my path to liberty and salvation," Tesla said, turning to Thea. "This was but a dream to me, once; I would never have pursued it, not in this way, because I never knew it was possible. But if it *is* possible . . ." He looked at the four stars again. "The honor would be mine. Greater and deeper than I could ever express."

"Then come," Maia said, holding out one star-white hand. She shed light as she moved, sparks falling from her arm like water and fading into shadow before they reached the ground. "Come with us, and see your world in the palm of your hand, as you have never seen it before."

"I am in your debt," Tesla said to Grandmother Spider formally. And then, turning briefly back to Thea, "And in yours, Thea Winthrop. Eternally. You and I, I think, will need no artificial means to speak to each other. Even in your world, the younger world, you can call upon me and I will come."

He reached out and put both hands on her shoulders, drawing her closer to him, and kissed her on the forehead.

"You," he said, "are my legacy to the human race. I leave them in your care."

The four sisters began to dissolve into vortexes of light even as Tesla stepped up to them and said gravely, "I am ready." The four vortexes spun wider, then merged into a single sparkling whirlpool of light, swirled around Tesla until he was in the midst of it all as though he were standing in the eye of a hurricane. It was already almost too hard to see the shape of him through that veil. Then the whole thing lifted from the ground, hovered for a moment, shedding tiny stars into the night, and leaped into the sky, exploding high up like sparkling fireworks and merging into the whirling, shimmering sky above.

"Well," Grandmother Spider said, "that was new and strange. Many of the names those stars bear—at least the ones they introduce themselves to you by, they have very different identities for someone of a different polity or a different race—they come from your own mythologies, and it is you, the human kindred, who have named them thus and know them by the names of gods and nymphs whom you have created in your own dreams and imagination. If those creatures had ever been truly human, and living, that is lost in the dawn of time. But it has been some little while since a human soul was taken up into the fellowship of the stars."

"He was special," Thea said, staring up at the sky. Her eyes were full of tears again, but this time the tears were not born of pain, but rather of awe and joy.

"That he was," Grandmother Spider said. "The only quad-Element mage in human history, so I am told. But you, I think, have been named as holding three Elements in your own hand. That, too, is special. You have come a long way," she continued, smiling, "from the last time you stood here with me."

"Perhaps I stood still," Thea said, "and the world changed around me."

"Remember what Nikola Tesla told you, when he spoke to you of Elemental magic," Grandmother Spider said. "An Elemental mage changes the world every day, by being there. That is your task now."

Thea sighed. "Perhaps I had better return to the others," she said. "Cheveyo will want his peace and quiet back, we need to get back to school, and I guess

Humphrey May had better get that report of his in before too many other impossible things happen."

"Remember," Grandmother Spider said, "as Tesla said, so say I—you need only call and we will come to aid or counsel in what ways we are permitted. Nikola Tesla, Tawaha, and I are powerful allies, but we are allowed to do no more than advise in your world. Cheveyo told you once that if a battle is to come, then it is you who will choose your battle-fields—and in certain circumstances, we who watch over you may help, but not interfere. Your battles will still be your own to fight."

"The Trickster worked directly in our own world," Thea said.

"Yes, and you rightly brought him to us to take him to task for that. We are bound by the same rules," Grandmother Spider said.

"I'm afraid," Thea said. "When the Queen was right there in front of me, I felt pure panic, at those cold eyes, and the way she looked at me. And now, afterward, there's this flutter in my stomach every time I think about her. I'm on my guard now, and I will be careful, and there are things I need to do to protect those who need protection—but I am afraid."

"Remember those words," Grandmother Spider murmured. "The Alphiri are not done with you; they will come back. But the fear will never have compelling power over you, not if you remember that you are not controlled by it. Your portal, the one you raised, stands behind you; it will take you back to Cheveyo's house, as it did once before. Go, my granddaughter, with my blessing."

Thea cast a final look at the First World sky, where stars danced and shimmered, and raised a hand. Then she turned to face the portal she once built out of starlight and the music of the world's creation, and stepped through it.

She emerged right beside Cheveyo's front door, and was able to contemplate the others for a fraction of a second without them being aware of her. Ben sat cross-legged beside the hearth with Tess on one side of him and Kristin on the other, sharing a bowl of something with the two of them; Cat was gnawing on something she held grasped in greasy fingers; Terry sat with his knees drawn up into the circle of his arms, staring into the fire; and Humphrey May stood with his back to a large rock, hands thrust into his pockets and eyes raking the distant horizon.

It was Cheveyo who acknowledged Thea first,

without even lifting his eyes to her.

"You return, Catori," he said tranquilly. "You return alone."

Everyone exploded to their feet, Kristin overturning the bowl beside her with her foot and spilling its contents, Humphrey pushing off from his rock and turning around to stare at Thea, and then searching the shadows behind her.

"Thea! Where have you been?"

"We've been worried!"

"You just . . . disappeared," Terry said, his voice a little tight. "Is everything all right?

"What have you done with Tesla? Where is he?" Humphrey said, raking the shadows behind her with his eyes.

"I'm fine," Thea said, and lifted her eyes to the streak of stars against the Milky Way that spanned the sky above Cheveyo's hearth fire. "And everything is fine. As for that report that you're still mulling over, Mr. May, the answer to every question from here on . . . lies in the stars."

## 17.

IT TOOK BOTH TOO long and no time at all to explain
to everybody where Thea had been and where Tesla
had gone. It took no time, because before she had
gotten too far into the explanation, some of those
present—Cat and, of course, Cheveyo—were nodding with complete understanding and approval;
too long, because by the end of her account Humphrey May was still shaking his head in frustrated
incomprehension.

"There are some parts of this that I can figure
out," he said. "The Alphiri Queen, the Faele angle—
*that* they will understand, back in Washington. As
for the Tesla angle, I can explain the necessity for
the whole pigeon thing; that was already approved
at the highest levels. But the *Sun God*. Really. And
this star business. You have no idea how impossible
it is going to be to go back to a government institu-
tion and present a report so short on fact and so
overwhelmingly flooded with myth and fairy tale.
They're going to ask me what I've been drinking
if I tell them the half of it. It's going to take some

juggling. I'd better get back to the office. I've been away for far too long as it is." He glanced at his watch as he spoke, then looked up with an exasperated sigh as he realized that it had apparently stopped at twelve o'clock. "How *does* one get out of here?" he asked abruptly.

Thea lifted up the wrist with the keypad. "When do you want to be there? I can get you there within a specified time. Give or take a few minutes."

Humphrey's mouth thinned a little. "That thing," he muttered. "That's how you got into the FBM building without being detected, and snuck past every defense. When I gave it to you, Thea, I never expected you to use it selfishly, or against me."

"I never used it selfishly," Thea said. "And it was never against you. It was for Tesla. I was protecting him—and myself."

"You used it to break into a guarded facility, and you took an artifact from that facility that you were under no circumstances entitled to," Humphrey said. "You do realize that you actually broke the law, that we could actually prosecute for breaking and entering?"

"Except that you couldn't possibly prove anything, because there was no evidence," Thea said.

"And anyway . . ."

Tesla's cube, nothing more now than an interesting curiosity, was sitting in plain sight not too far from Thea; she strode over to it and lifted it up, turning it in her hands.

"A star," Thea said thoughtfully. "The symbol for that last Elemental face was a star. It's as though he knew." She held out the cube to Humphrey. "Here, you can take that back to them," she said. "I returned it to the person to whom it properly belonged, but Tesla doesn't have a use for it anymore. The FBM was merely the keeper of this thing. It took the five of us to even crack the thing because the Feds couldn't do it alone. So technically, I never stole it—it wasn't yours in the first place."

"You make the FBM sound like the Alphiri," Humphrey said sharply.

Thea winced. "No," she said. "But you do . . . seem a little high-handed."

"As if what you did was less so. Have you thought about what I offered?"

"A berth at the FBM? No. Tesla was right on that count; it wouldn't be for me."

"I'll have to take that keypad back," Humphrey

said. "We can't have you wandering into our offices whenever the whim takes you. There are some sensitive things that are kept protected for a . . ."

Thea was unfastening the strap around her wrist as he spoke, shaking her head slightly. "You can't keep me from a computer," she said, "and whenever I am at one, it's as though I still have this. It's a good idea, and it's very useful, but I can do without it. It'll take you back to the office. I can walk out of here on the Barefoot Road if need be."

"I have the laptop," Terry said quietly.

Thea could not help a quick grin. "Even out here," she said, "you can't keep me from a computer."

"Thea," Humphrey said, "I am not your enemy. Really, I am not."

Thea shook her head slowly. "No. You wouldn't wish me harm. But you are not my friend, either. Not quite in the way that matters." She looked at Humphrey, dangling the strap of the keypad from her fingers. "I've always *liked* you, Mr. May, and I respect you and what you can do. I have no doubt that our paths will cross again, whether I need you or you need me. But I don't know if I'll ever completely trust the Bureau again."

Humphrey sighed, looking down. "You say you

can take me back to the office . . . ? Say . . . this morning?"

Thea typed a line of text into the keypad and handed it to Humphrey. "Press ENTER and it will take you there," she said. "Good-bye, Mr. May."

"Thea, I . . ." He looked up, searched her eyes for an instant, and then tightened his fingers around the strap of the keypad and took it from her hand with rather more force than necessary. "You sure you can get home without this?" he asked brusquely. "I hardly want to leave you stranded."

She nodded.

"Well, then," he said. "I'll see you, I guess."

He hit the ENTER key and winked out.

Thea stood looking at the spot where he had been standing, unconsciously rubbing the wrist where the keypad had been, for long enough that Ben finally waved a hand before her face.

"Earth to Thea," he said. "Hello, we're still here. Are you sure you're okay? There's still stuff left from supper—you hungry?"

Thea shook her head, hugging her elbows with both hands, but turned back toward the fire.

"Er . . . how *do* you plan on getting us back?" Ben asked, hesitating. "I mean, school's still on break, so we have all the time in the world, but if you have a plan maybe you ought to be thinking about—"

"Where *did* you go?" Terry asked suddenly. "When you left me—when you ran away from the Queen after she said her piece just before she left . . . What's really wrong, Thea? Are you breaking up with me?"

Thea looked at him, startled. "Breaking *up* with you?"

"Oh?" Tess said, swiveling her head from one to the other. "So since when have you two been sneaking around?"

"Crashing the FBM must have been one hell of a first date," muttered Ben.

Terry flushed a little. "Well, the way you ran away, when the Alphiri Queen . . ."

"She as much as promised she'd be back," Thea said, a little desperately.

"You knew that," Terry said, frowning.

"Yes, but . . . not for me, not at me directly," Thea said, her own cheeks coloring. "She looked at all of you as though you were . . . pawns in a chess game. She looked at you . . ."

Terry began to nod slowly. "You think she will get at you through someone you care about," he said. "Hey, protect the rest, by all means, if you feel you need to, but as I recall Cat had Tesla himself promise her that he'd be standing up for her if anything should threaten her, and I think he'd manage to do that even from whatever other world he's gone to. Ben and Kristin can watch each other's backs, they've already had practice, back in New York. As for me and Tess, my uncle has no kids; all he's got is the two of us. He runs the FBM as a family business, and even if I had never laid a hand on the Nexus, I would have been groomed as the crown prince of that place in some capacity sooner or later. You don't have to worry about the Alphiri coming after me. I'm too well protected."

"How could you possibly be a crown prince of a place where you couldn't open your mouth without choking on something you said?" Thea said, but she let him take her hand, and she was smiling.

"Well, you fixed that," Terry said. "Cybermage."

"Tesla thought you were pretty good at Cybermagic yourself," Thea said. "And you proved it with what you did back there with Tesla's pigeons. You might or might not be shaping into another Elemental, but you're at the very least a journeyman Cybermage yourself."

Terry actually blushed. "Tesla said that?" he asked.

Not an Elemental, perhaps, but he would be a bright light in the new branch of magic, the perfect way into magic for a boy who could not speak its name out loud.

"You're right," Tess said. "We're probably safe from the Alphiri under the wing of the FBM—but are we safe from them?" She turned to Thea. "I don't think you realize it yet, Thea, but you haven't exactly made friends in the Bureau by what you did tonight. Humphrey wasn't happy."

"They won't damage their Elemental," Terry said.

"That's just it. She isn't *their* Elemental. And I don't think they'd give up on her any easier than the Alphiri would."

"But you can't be responsible for everyone else's well-being," Cat said to Thea. "Leaving the FBM out of it for now, the Queen looked at *you*. All of the rest of us, in the end, are expendable—it's *you* she really wants."

"You're the most vulnerable one of all of us," Tess said.

"Who's going to watch *your* back?" said Kristin. "It's well enough back at the school, where we can all keep an eye on one another, but . . ."

"I'll get you guys back to the school," Thea said. "But I'm not going back."

Terry's fingers tightened on hers, but he said nothing. Everyone else seemed to be struck dumb, too, because Thea could feel the weight of their eyes on her.

"You think Humphrey will spill it, back in Washington?" Tess said.

"If he doesn't, Luana will, or someone else will connect the dots. And once the media get ahold of it . . ." Ben's face fell into a black scowl.

"'Double Seventh at Last.' 'A New Elemental,'" Kristin said, sounding genuinely appalled. "I can just see the tabloids."

"At least it will give my mother something to stick into that wretched scrapbook she started for me when I was born," Thea said. "God knows there hasn't been much to put in it so far. But as for school, I'd better leave, before I am pushed. They won't take me back this time—not after the principal figures out what happened. And why should they? I don't belong there, not anymore, no more than I've ever really belonged anywhere at all."

The Last Ditch School for the Incurably Incompetent.

It had been so many things to Thea. At first just an odious place where she had once believed, if only for a brief while, her disappointed father was planning to wash his hands of her; then a sanctuary where she had found friends and space to grow; then a shelter from the rising dangers of her world, at a time when she had needed to stay safely concealed until she was strong enough to defend herself against them. But all of that was in the past. There were some things that simply could not be hidden anymore.

"What will you do?" Terry said, stepping closer without letting go of her hand.

She turned her head and lifted her chin to look at him, managing a smile. "Do? I have no idea. I'll have to talk about it with my folks; maybe they'll come up with something. I know they've been thinking about Amford ever since I kind of blossomed into something my father could pitch to them, but now . . ."

"Amford has precollege courses; you could finish high school with an accelerated program and then start college in the fall, or the following year," Ben said. "I know a cousin of mine did that."

"What," Kristin said succinctly, "could they possibly teach her at Amford?"

"Can you actually do Ars Magica now? In *our* world?" Cat asked, curious. "What if they handed you something to Transform?"

"So long as I had a computer . . ." Thea said, with a crooked grin.

"It isn't the teaching of something. Anything they've got on Elemental magic at Amford will probably be a restricted course anyway, and taught by someone who knows less about it than Thea does," Terry said. "It'll be about learning to survive as a mage in a world where you have the FBM peeved at you and just itching to have an opportunity to grab you for themselves—and this time probably without the kid gloves—and the Alphiri lurking in the wings, waiting for the next chance. But we'll miss you."

"You are always only a step away on the Barefoot Road," Cheveyo said unexpectedly, breaking into the conversation. "Your friends are always going to be with you, or within reach. These five will no doubt be watching out for you, back in your world, but do not forget that you also have me. Grandmother Spider. Tawaha. Your friend, the other Elemental wizard, Tesla, for whom you have done and risked so much."

Thea sighed, and allowed her head to rest for a moment on Terry's shoulder; then she looked around, meeting everyone's gaze—first Cheveyo's, then Cat's, Ben's, Kristin's, Tess's. Terry's.

"Sometimes," she said, "I get scared just thinking about the future."

"We'll be there if you need us," Terry said, speaking for all of them.

Thea managed a smile. "I'll need you," she said. "Come on, I'll take you guys back."

"Where are you going to go?" Cat asked.

Thea hadn't thought about it, not specifically, but all of a sudden she was aware of an unexpected Christmas tree scent of Douglas firs and red cedars; the soft carpet of fir needles underfoot, covering damp earth; white clouds caught like veils in the tall trees of the mountain country; the mellow green-gold light that was Tawaha's offering in the forests and clearings, and the garnet-tinged sunsets reflected off the snow from the distant peaks; waterfalls tumbling in a thunder of white spray, throwing out rainbows; hawks circling overhead with piercing cries while squirrels chittered in the trees and deer stepped gracefully through the woods.

The place where her mother spoke words of power to raise dough for bread, where her father sat in his old leather armchair on Sundays with a week's worth of the *Daily Magic Times* and the thick *Sunday Elixir* in untidy piles of newsprint around his feet, where her brothers squabbled and elbowed for the last slice of peach pie, where Aunt Zoë could hear the sunlight and see the wind.

"Home," she said. "I'm going home. And after that . . . whatever comes."

## Acknowledgments

Michelle Cope of Bryant Park Market Events/ID&A, LLC, and Joseph Kinney, Senior Project Engineer at the New Yorker Hotel Management Company, were both kind enough to respond to my requests for information by sending articles, photographs, and valuable insights into details that made my story stronger and better, and I am indebted to both of them.

Many friends helped me out by gathering information, sending photographs of places I was too far away from to explore myself, and giving me invaluable feedback about both story and its building blocks—too many to list, because I would be sure to omit some deserving name. To all of you out there, and you well know who you are, my grateful thanks.

To my usual staunch support crew—Jill, Ruth, a team of amazing copy editors at HarperCollins—you made this book what it is, as always. To my parents, who worried, and waited with increasingly impatient anticipation, and took up the slack of everything else that needed doing so that I'd have time to write, my boundless thanks. And then there's my husband, Deck, first reader and ruthless editor, who once again helped me mold my vision into a story.

And to you, the readers. Thank you for visiting Thea's world, and for being her friend.

# SO WHO WAS NIKOLA TESLA, REALLY?

## AUTHOR'S NOTE

The reader of the Worldweavers books would search in vain for Thea Winthrop, the FBM, or the Alphiri in *our* world—they are products of their own universe, and their existence doesn't spill over into ours.

But Nikola Tesla is real.

He was a Serbian-born inventor, physicist, and mechanical engineer, and has been almost universally acclaimed as the greatest electrical engineer in history. Born during a thunderstorm, sometime around midnight of July 10, 1856, he lived with lightning all the days of his life.

After an extended "apprenticeship" in Europe, where he worked for various telecommunications and electrical companies in Budapest and Paris,

Tesla arrived in the United States of America—armed with only a letter of recommendation for Thomas Edison and four cents in his pocket.

Even in our own magic-challenged world, he quickly earned the nickname New Wizard of the West. But Tesla, the greatest mind of his century, was not a practical man. He was in frequent financial trouble. He possessed an old-world sense of honor and the way "things were done," and would sign away the rights to the royalties for patents that would have supported him comfortably in his old age because of a sense of grace and obligation. The man who held hundreds of patents in his lifetime for motors, bladeless turbines, wireless transmission of energy, the logic gate technology that paved the way for modern computers—the man who practically invented the twentieth century as we knew it—would be almost unknown, his achievements glossed over or attributed to others.

It might have been Thomas Edison who invented the lightbulb, but it is Tesla's alternating current version of electricity, not Edison's direct current, that powers them today. If asked who invented the radio, most people would offer the name of Guglielmo Marconi—although a Supreme Court decision finally awarded that right to Nikola Tesla. Although there is a statue of Tesla at Niagara Falls, many people have no idea that it was Tesla, and Tesla's ideas and technology, that tamed that powerful resource into producing vast amounts of electrical energy.

Nikola Tesla did, dared, and achieved so much, and yet he died in poverty, alone, a tired and largely forgotten old man whose only friends were the pigeons of New York City.

Perhaps he really did have magic, in a world that could not understand or value it.

There are many books written about Tesla, and they paint a picture of a complex, fascinating, gifted human being. Some of these are listed below, if anyone should wish, after having met the fictional Tesla from *Cybermage*, to get to know the real man.

Lomas, Robert. *The Man Who Invented the Twentieth Century: Nikola Tesla, the Forgotten Genius of Electricity*. London: Headline Book Publishing Ltd, 2000. An accessible and simply written biography that might be a good place to start reading about Tesla.

Cheney, Margaret. *Tesla: Man Out of Time*. New York: Touchstone, 2001. One of the best and most accessible biographies of Nikola Tesla.

Seifer, Marc J. *Wizard: The Life and Times of Nikola Tesla—Biography of a Genius*. Secaucus, NJ: Citadel, 2001. Neither the first nor the last time he has been called a wizard.

Cheney, Margaret, and Robert Uth. *Tesla: Master of Lightning*. New York: Metrobooks, 2001. A coffee table book with lots of magnificent illustrations and photographs; may currently be difficult to obtain, but other similar books are no doubt out there and this one might still be available for those willing to invest a little time in the search for it.